# SURRENDER THE DAWN

# SURRENDER THE DAWN

AMANDA ASHLEY

*Surrender the Dawn*

Cover design by Cynthia Lucas

ISBN: 978-1-68068-237-3

This book is published on behalf of the author by the Ethan Ellenberg
Literary Agency.

You can reach the author at:
Email: darkwritr@aol.com
Website: www.amandaashley.net OR www.madelinebaker.net

# SURRENDER THE DAWN

Angelina Rossi has always been fascinated with vampires. She loves the movies, the TV shows, the books. After reading a love story between a woman and a vampire, she finds herself yearning for a love like that. What if vampires really do exist?

Determined to find out, Angie searches every Goth club in the city, ending up at a nightclub called Nick's Nightmare. The attraction between Angie and Declan Nicolae, the club's owner, is instant and undeniable.

Declan is an ancient vampire who, having once tasted Angie's blood, is determined to never let her go. For a time, romance blooms and all is well, until Samantha, Angie's best friend, becomes one of the Undead and Angie learns vampires do exist... and that the man she loves is one of them.

# DEDICATION

*To Tim Milosch*
*So he won't feel left out!*
*We love you ~*
*And the three beautiful girls*
*who share your life, too.*

# TABLE OF CONTENTS

# CHAPTER ONE

*A*nd so he bestowed on her the vampire's kiss, sweeping her into a world of love and a life that would never end.

With a heartfelt sigh, Angelina Rossi closed the book. If only she could find a love as lasting and fulfilling as the one portrayed in the novel. A love that was stronger, deeper, and more enduring than mere mortal attraction.

If only vampires truly existed. Not that she really wanted to meet one, but what if they *were* real? They had always fascinated her, ever since she saw her first *Dracula* movie at the tender age of eight. Instead of being frightened or rooting for the hero, she had been enchanted by the monster. She had even shed a tear when the hero drove a stake into the vampire's heart. To this day, in books, movies, or plays, she felt sympathy for the poor Undead creatures.

Setting the book aside, Angie padded to the front window, drew back the curtain, and peered out into the darkness. What if vampires were real? Was that really so far-fetched? After all, stories and legends of the Undead went back thousands of years and were cited in every nation and country on earth. If such creatures were only myth, why had the tales of their existence lasted so long? Bookstores and libraries had entire sections devoted to vampires and the supernatural. Why waste all that shelf space on something that never existed? People believed in witches. Why not vampires?

Even as the thought crossed her mind, she knew it wasn't a valid argument. After all, there were tons of books about Bigfoot and the Loch Ness monster and space aliens, too. There was no hard evidence to back up the existence of any of those creatures, either. Of course, lots of people said they had seen Bigfoot and Nessie. Some folks claimed to have pictures, although all the ones she had seen looked photoshopped. She had never heard of anyone who claimed to have seen a vampire. Then again, maybe those who saw one didn't live long enough to tell anyone.

A sobering thought.

Wishing real life was more like the romance novels she loved, Angie turned away from the window. And then she grinned. Maybe she should put an ad in the paper.

*Wanted: Tall, dark. handsome stranger who prefers the night. Objective...*

Angie frowned. She had no objective, just an over-active imagination. But she couldn't help wondering if tall, dark, handsome, creatures of the night did exist, and if so, were they as romantic as the ones she read about? Or scary, bloodsucking monsters like the ones portrayed in the movies?

With a shake of her head, Angie turned off the lights and went to bed. Maybe she needed to see a shrink, she mused as she pulled the covers up to her chin. After all, who in their right mind would *want* to come face-to-face with one of the children of the night?

In the morning, Angie carried a cup of coffee into her home office and settled down in front of her computer. She had been working as a freelance columnist for a local magazine for the last three years. It wasn't the best paying job in the world, but it was something she could do at home in her PJs, which was a big plus as far as she was concerned. Not only that, but her editor, Jennifer Martin, had given her *carte blanche* to pick and choose her own topics.

She worked steadily, taking a fifteen-minute break to stand and stretch every hour or so. As always when she was writing, the time flew by. She broke for lunch at one.

In the kitchen, while preparing a ham and cheese sandwich, she found herself thinking about vampires again. What if they *were* real, she mused while she ate. Did they really sleep in coffins? Were they truly dead to the world when the sun was up? Why would they be repelled by garlic? Or crosses? Or silver? What happened if they didn't like blood? Were they really immortal? If vampires didn't have a soul, and they weren't really alive, were they just animated corpses, like zombies? She shuddered. How disgusting would that be?

Maybe she needed to stop reading paranormal romances and start reading cozy mysteries instead.

And maybe not.

Back at her desk, she stared, unseeing at her computer screen. If someone wanted to find a vampire, where would they look?

Google, of course! She would go online as soon as she finished her work for the day.

Angie stood in front of the mirror in the bathroom, carefully applying her make-up. She had spent hours online looking for vampires, and while she hadn't found any links to the real thing, she had found numerous books and movies on the subject, as well as half a dozen web sites advertising

Goth clubs that claimed to be hangouts for creatures of the night. Curious to see what they were all about, she had jotted down the addresses of the five closest to home.

Hoping "creatures of the night" applied only to the Undead and not werewolves, zombies, demons, or trolls, Angie stepped into her heels, grabbed her handbag and keys, and left the house.

Drac's Den was the first tavern on her list. Angie shook her head when she stepped through the door. The walls were black, the floor tiled in bright red. No doubt so the blood wouldn't show, she thought with a grimace as she made her way toward the long, curved bar in the back.

The bartender, clad in a white shirt and long, black cape, leered at her as he took her order. It was all she could do not to laugh in his face when he flashed his obviously fake plastic fangs at her.

She carried her drink to a small table where she could people-watch. Men and women alike wore nothing but black. The men sported suits, some looking new while others looked like they had been bought from second-hand stores. The women all wore long dresses. Black lipstick and eye shadow made their faces look pale in the dim light. Most of them also had long, straight, black hair, real or fake.

With a shake of her head, Angie finished her drink and left the tavern. Maybe she would have better luck tomorrow night.

Angie went to a different nightclub every Saturday night for the next four weeks—Nick's Nightmare, the Devil's Tavern, Mel's Hell, and The Pit.

She was amazed to discover that so many people spent their weekends pretending to be creatures of the night. In her search for a genuine vampire, she had seen some truly bizarre things, like the man who had filed his teeth to sharp points, a woman who carried a flask rumored to be filled with real blood, and the man who led his girlfriend around on a slender gold chain. Angie had learned that some wanna-be vampires actually indulged in drinking from each other, which she found beyond gross.

At home that night, she tossed her handbag on the sofa, kicked off her shoes, and decided she had wasted enough time looking for the Undead. No more vampire haunts for her. The Pit had been the last stop. Goth clubs—and the people who frequented them—were just too weird.

Despite her good intentions, she found herself back at Nick's Nightmare the following Saturday night. Of all the places she had visited, this one seemed to be the most "normal." Sort of like Halloween every night, with men and women in bizarre costumes but behaving—mostly—like regular people with a peculiar penchant for the macabre. The décor was dark but not grim, the music low and sensual, the lighting subdued.

Angie had been sitting at the bar nursing a drink for about ten minutes when a man sat down next to her. He was of medium height and not bad looking, but the way he leered at her creeped her out.

"Hello, gorgeous," he drawled. "Can I buy you a drink?"

"No, thank you."

He rested one hand on her knee. "How about a dance?"

"No," she said, her voice frigid as she pushed his hand away. "Thank you."

"Come on, honey, don't play hard to get."

She was debating what to do next when a deep, male voice said, "Take a hike, Mulgrew."

The man stood and left without a word.

Angie glanced over her shoulder to see a tall, broad-shouldered man with dark hair and compelling green eyes looming over her. Like every other man in the place, he was dressed all in black, but on him, it looked fabulous. She recalled seeing him in a couple of the other nightclubs, always in the company of one pretty woman or another.

Tonight, he was alone.

He gestured at the stool beside her. "May I?"

"It's a free country."

"I've seen you in here before." He made a vague gesture with his hand, encompassing the room behind them. "You don't seem like the type to frequent places like this."

"Oh? Why is that?"

"Well, for starters, you're dressed all wrong."

Angie stared at her white slacks and navy-blue sweater and shrugged. "I left my Halloween costume at home."

His laugh was deep and sensual and the sound of it did funny things in the pit of her stomach. "The Goth crowd." His voice slid over her like silk over velvet. "They always look like they're in mourning, don't they?"

She lifted one brow. "So do you."

"*Touché*, my lady. I've seen you in some of the other nightclubs," he remarked. "Are you looking for something special?"

"Excuse me?"

Brow furrowed, he studied her a moment, and then he grinned. "Sorry."

Wondering what he was apologizing for, she said, "I've seen you in those other places, too. Were *you* looking for—how did you put it? Something special?"

"I was." His gaze moved over her.

The intensity of it made Angie's toes curl even as it sent a shaft of unexpected desire spiraling through her. She licked her lips, feeling as if she had suddenly strayed into unknown territory. "And now?" she asked, tremulously.

"I think maybe I've found it."

Suddenly frightened without knowing why, Angie grabbed her handbag, muttered, "It was nice meeting you. Good night," and practically ran out the door.

Back at home, safe inside her own house, with the front door double-locked behind her, she felt suddenly foolish. What on earth was wrong with her? Sure, it had been a long time since a handsome man flirted with her but that was no reason to behave like some silly schoolgirl.

With a sigh, she tossed her handbag on the sofa, kicked off her shoes and headed for her bedroom.

Muttering, "The next time some sexy guy makes a pass at you, try to act like a grown-up," she undressed and crawled into bed, only to lie there, wide-awake and restless, the memory of his deep, silky smooth voice echoing in her mind.

# CHAPTER TWO

Declan moved through the Nightmare, nodding to long-time patrons, like Jack Reynard, who had been a regular since the club opened five years ago. He paused to say a few words to Raj, who he'd known for more years than he liked to remember, before moving on. Strangers at the Nightmare were few and far between. Some folks wandered in and quickly took their leave. Others stayed for a drink and then left. Very few returned. Especially those like the woman tonight. The Nightmare, like Drac's Domain and several other nightclubs in the city, catered to a unique clientele. Most people instinctively sensed they didn't belong. Those who ignored that inner voice of warning sometimes lived to regret it.

He stepped behind the bar, frowned when he caught himself thinking about the woman again. She was a pretty thing, probably in her mid-twenties, with hair the color of ink and eyes the warm, clear blue of a summer sky. He couldn't help wondering why she'd been going from nightclub to nightclub. Was she looking for someone—or something—in particular? Or just looking for a momentary thrill?

He lifted a bottle from beneath the bar and poured himself a drink. What the hell difference did it make? It was just as well that he would probably never see her again.

Nevertheless, he found himself hoping she'd return next Saturday night.

Angie stood in front of the bathroom mirror, carefully applying her make-up, and chiding herself for being a complete idiot for even thinking of going back to Nick's Nightmare. But it didn't stop her from leaving the house.

When she reached the nightclub, she parked her car, then sat there, staring at the door with the odd silver runes drawn on it. What was she doing here? There were no real vampires in there. And if there was, meeting one not only seemed incredibly stupid but more than a little dangerous. But she had to see him again, the man with the compelling green eyes and silky soft voice. For a solid week, she had thought of little else. Whether she was writing, exercising, making the bed, or doing her laundry, her mind was inevitably drawn to him, and she didn't even know his name.

Angie blew out a sigh of exasperation as she tapped her fingers on the steering wheel. She really had to get out more, make some new friends. She rarely had a chance to see her best friend, Samantha, these days. And while she loved working at home, it didn't give her much of an opportunity to meet other people, and even less of a chance to meet eligible men. It had been six months since she'd had a date.

Six months! She blew out a sigh of disbelief. Had it really been that long? Maybe Samantha was right, Angie thought glumly. Maybe she was too picky. But she couldn't help it if she wanted an alpha male and not some guy who was going to fight her for her yoga mat. She wanted a man who was secure in his masculinity, one who would treat her like a lady in public and a desirable woman in the bedroom. A man … a man like the one she had met at Nick's Nightmare last week, she thought with a dreamy smile. Even though they had spent only a few minutes together, she had been instantly attracted to him. He had exuded raw masculine strength and confidence. Not to mention that he was tall, dark, and gorgeous. Of course, good looks didn't mean a thing. For all she knew, he could be a total jerk. But there was only one way to find out…

Deciding to walk on the wild side one more time, she turned off the engine, took a deep breath, and stepped out of the car.

Declan knew the moment she walked through the door. Coming out from behind the bar, he watched her stride toward him, hips swaying provocatively. Clad in a white sweater and a pair of black jeans that outlined every delectable curve, she looked like a daisy in a field of coal.

"I didn't think I'd see you in here again," he remarked.

"I didn't think so, either."

"What can I get you?"

"A strawberry daiquiri, please."

"Coming right up."

Taking a seat, Angie watched him walk behind the bar where he mixed her drink and poured a glass of red wine for himself. "I didn't know you worked here," she remarked when he returned.

"I don't. I own the place."

"Oh."

He handed her one of the glasses. "You married, or anything?"

"No. Are you?"

He shook his head. "Any chance I could take you out some night?"

Angie sipped her drink while she debated her answer. He was gorgeous, no doubt about it. He owned his own business. He seemed nice, but he looked to be in his mid-to-late thirties. A little too old for her. And still she hesitated.

He lifted one brow. "Anything I can say to improve the odds?"

Angie laughed softly. "Yes, but with one condition."

"You want to see my driver's license? My bank statement? A note from my mother?"

"No, but I do have a strict policy of knowing the names of the men I go out with."

"Declan Nicolae."

Angie frowned. "Irish and…?"

"Romanian."

"An odd combination," she murmured.

"Indeed, Miss…?"

"Angelina Rossi. Mostly Italian."

He held out his hand. "Nice to meet you, Miss Rossi."

She murmured, "Likewise, Mr. Nicolae," as his fingers closed around hers. His skin was cool, yet heat flooded her entire being, bringing a flush to her cheeks. Startled, she withdrew her hand. Had he felt it, too, that peculiar warmth?

"My time is pretty much my own," Declan said. "How about tomorrow night?"

Angie stared at him, still stunned by the heat that had passed between them. "What? Oh. That would be fine."

"Where would you like to go? Dining? Dancing? A movie?"

Definitely not dancing. If the mere touch of his hand had such a stunning effect on her, what would it be like to be in his arms? Some place with lots of people, she thought. "A movie sounds good."

"Pick you up at seven-thirty?"

She bit down on her lip, reluctant to give him her address.

"Or we could meet here at the club, if you'd rather."

Relieved, she murmured, "That sounds good. I'll see you tomorrow night. I need to get home to... to feed my cat."

Declan nodded. He knew she had felt the instant rush of attraction between them, a sensual heat he hadn't experienced in a long time. It had disconcerted her to the point where she was obviously having second thoughts about seeing him again. "Tomorrow night," he repeated.

Though he would be surprised if she showed up.

Angie couldn't stop thinking about the peculiar warmth that had engulfed her when she had shaken hands with Declan. Never in her life had she felt anything like that, a visceral connection beyond anything she had ever known or imagined. It had frightened her on some deep, primal level, even as it pricked her curiosity.

Declan Nicolae was a remarkably handsome man. Not in the pretty-boy, Hollywood fashion that was so popular now, but in a rough-hewn masculine way that was increasingly rare these days, as if he was a throw-back to an earlier generation when men cut a wide swath across the wilderness, conquered nations, built empires.

She thought about him on the drive home. And while she got ready for bed. He had an aura of sexual expertise that was intriguing even as it frightened her. She had little experience with men, and none with a man like Declan. Not to mention the fact that he was probably thirteen or fourteen years older—and wiser—than she was.

Tomorrow, she would call and make some excuse to cancel their date. Because as sure as the sun would rise in the east, Declan Nicolae was trouble with a capital T.

It wasn't until she crawled under the covers that she realized she didn't have his cell number. Maybe she could reach him at the nightclub. If not... maybe she would buy something new to wear tomorrow night, just in case she had to cancel their date in person.

When Angie woke in the morning, the first thought that crossed her mind was her upcoming date with the ultra-sexy Mr. Declan Nicolae. She called Nick's Nightmare, but no one answered the phone. Not surprising, she guessed, since they didn't open until seven that night. She thought about leaving a message but decided against it. It was a private call on a public phone, and she didn't want anyone else to hear it. She decided to try again later.

After breakfast, she sat at her computer, trying to come up with a human-interest story for the magazine that hadn't been done to death a dozen times before. And then it hit her. Why not a story about all the Goth clubs that had sprung up in the city in the last few years, and the people who frequented them? Maybe she could tie it to vampires, ask people if they believed in the Undead and if so, why, or why not? She could delve into the psychological appeal of the whole Goth culture and focus on why nightclubs like Nick's Nightmare and Drac's Domain were so popular.

Opening a new document, she began to write what she hoped would be her October column.

*What is it about vampires that so many people find intriguing? Why are so many men and women fascinated by the current Goth movement? What are they searching for? Is there more to the connection to the Goth lifestyle than a penchant for the color black? What is the mental, emotional and spiritual appeal of the Goth culture and nightclubs like Nick's Nightmare, Mel's Hell, The Pit, The Devil's Tavern, and Drac's Den?*

*What about those who actually believed themselves to be vampires and drink blood from their companions? Or those who shun the sunlight and prowl the deepening shadows of the night?*

*Vampire lore has been a part of mythology since the beginning of time. Every culture in the world has its own myths and beliefs, from the Strigoi of Romania to the Vrykolakas of Greece. Not all vampires drink blood. Some drain life and energy, some emotions. But it's the blood-drinkers who seem to generate the greatest fascination. Is it because they're presumed to live forever? Their ability to move at great speeds? To heal quickly? Or to defy age and gravity?*

Angie read it a second time, smiled with satisfaction, and emailed it to her editor, along with a short synopsis.

With that done, she answered her email, then pulled up the column she had written for next month's issue and went through the corrections Jennifer had suggested. Once the changes had been made, she sent it off to Jen.

When she finished, it was almost two. After dressing, Angie drove to the café around the corner for lunch. She ordered a turkey club, fries, and a soda, then pulled out her phone and tried Nick's Nightmare again.

Still no answer.

After lunch, she decided to stroll through the mall. A new store had opened at the far end. Angie couldn't help smiling when she saw the clothing displayed in the front window. Everything was black—dresses, nightgowns, thigh-high boots, lacy blouses and skin-tight leggings, gloves, hats, fishnet stockings, underwear, and wigs.

Suddenly curious to see how she'd look as a Goth, Angie ducked inside.

She was looking through a rack of long, black skirts when someone called her name. Glancing over her shoulder, Angie smiled when she saw her best friend, Samantha Lombardi, hurrying toward her. She must be on her lunch hour, Angie thought. Sam's boss insisted she wear a skirt and jacket at work and her hair up. Sam's preferred outfit was jeans and tee shirts, her long brown hair pulled back in a ponytail.

"Angie!" Samantha exclaimed, brown eyes wide. "What on earth are *you* doing in here? This is the last place I ever expected to see you."

"I could ask you the same thing. Don't tell me you're into all this."

"I've been into the Goth scene for over a year," Sam admitted with a sheepish grin.

"Seriously? You never mentioned it."

"I guess I'm sort of embarrassed by it all." Sam shrugged. "What about you?"

"Me? Oh, I'm, uh, thinking of writing a column about the vampire mythos and the whole Goth phenomenon."

Sam's brows lifted. "You sure it's not for some guy?"

"What guy? I haven't had a date in months." She could have had one tonight, Angie thought, if she hadn't chickened out. "Is that why *you're* into this? For a guy?"

Samantha nodded. "He's dreamy. Tall and blond and … honestly, Ian's the most gorgeous guy I've ever met."

"Well, that's great. When do I get to meet him?"

"So, are you thinking of buying that skirt?" Sam asked, changing the subject.

"No, I was just looking. The clothes in the window caught my attention, that's all. I was thinking I might snap a few photos for my column while I'm here."

"Vampires? Seriously?"

Angie shrugged. "I thought it would make a good column for the Halloween issue."

"Yeah, I guess it would at that."

"The idea was actually inspired by a book I read about a girl who fell in love with this sexy Undead guy." Angie pulled her phone from her pocket and took a picture of a mannequin dressed in full Goth mode. "Anyway, it gave me an idea for my October column for the magazine."

"Well, good luck with that. Listen, I'm on my lunch hour and I've got to get back to work."

"Kind of late for lunch, isn't it?"

Samantha shrugged. "I was lucky to get the time off. Grumpy's been up to his ears in writs, wills, and affidavits this past week."

Angie grinned. Grumpy was Samantha's nickname for her boss, a well-known, high-priced lawyer who expected her to be at his beck and call from seven-to-whenever and sometimes on weekends. "I can't believe you're still working for that tyrant."

Sam sighed dramatically. "Well, I was thinking of quitting, but he just gave me a twenty percent raise. He's working on this big murder case. You might have heard about it on the news."

"You don't mean the Hampton case?" The details of the gory murder had been splashed across the front pages of every newspaper and the lead story on the nightly news for weeks. Edward Hampton and his wife, Vanessa, a former

Miss America, had been found in their swimming pool, their throats slashed. Their only child, who stood to inherit several million dollars, was the lead suspect.

"That's the one," Sam said. "Grumpy's representing their son. Listen, I've got to get back. Let's do lunch one of these days."

"Sounds good."

With a wave of her hand, Samantha hurried out of the shop.

Angie stood there a moment, wondering what kind of monster would kill his own parents.

Then, shaking off her morbid thoughts, she pulled one of the skirts from the rack, found a lacy top, a sexy black bra and matching panties, added a pair of black fish net stockings, and carried everything into the dressing room.

Clad all in black, Angie stared at her reflection in the mirror, then shook her head. "You look like Morticia Addams," she muttered. Still, the outfit *was* flattering. And if she couldn't get in touch with Declan, she would have to go down to the nightclub and tell him she had changed her mind. After all, she told herself, it was the polite thing to do.

And tonight she would look like she belonged there.

# CHAPTER THREE

Declan grinned as he watched Angie sashay through the door. He'd been sure she wouldn't show up, and equally certain she wouldn't be wearing the sexiest Goth outfit he had ever seen if she did.

His grin faded when he got a good look at her expression as she approached him. She definitely wasn't happy to be there, so why was she?

"I tried to call you several times," she said, clutching her handbag to her chest. "But you didn't answer."

"So you came to break our date in person, is that it?" The blush that tinged her cheeks was all the answer he needed. "You could have saved yourself the trip," he said dryly. "I would have figured it out eventually."

"I'm sorry but…"

He waved her apology away. "I'm a big boy. I'll get over it."

Not knowing what else to say, Angie stared at him. He didn't seem very upset. She told herself that was a good thing, and yet it stung her pride just the same. He could have at least pretended to be a little disappointed.

"As long as you're here, you might as well have a drink," Declan suggested. "I hate to think of you coming all the way down here for nothing."

She glared at him. "I was trying to be polite, Mr. Nicolae. Something *you* apparently know nothing about."

He laughed softly. "You're right. I'm sorry, Miss Rossi. Please, sit down and have a drink on the house."

She hesitated a moment, then perched on the nearest stool.

Declan walked behind the bar. "What's your poison?"

"A Grasshopper." She hated the bugs, but she loved the minty taste of the cocktail.

"Coming right up."

Angie chewed on her thumbnail while she watched him mix her drink. Why did he have to be so devastatingly handsome and sexy? Looking at him—at those broad shoulders and hypnotic green eyes, she was suddenly sorry for breaking their date. She was tempted to tell him she had changed her mind, but her pride—and perhaps her good sense—got in the way.

"Here you go," he said as he placed her drink on a black cocktail napkin.

"Thank you."

"Change your mind, Angie."

His voice washed over her like warm, dark chocolate on a winter night. "I..."

"Come on," he coaxed with a beguiling smile. "It's a beautiful night. Let me spend part of it with a beautiful woman."

"And what would we do?" she asked, a quiver in her voice.

Declan squashed the answer that immediately came to mind. "We could go dancing under the stars. I know a nice place. Soft music. Dim lights. Decadent desserts."

"What kind of dessert?" she asked.

"Anything you want."

She knew what *he* wanted, she thought as she lifted her glass. She could see it smoldering in the depts of his eyes. Telling the voice of her conscience to shut up, she said, "All right. I'll follow you."

He grinned. Smart girl. She didn't trust him at all, that was for sure. "All right. Finish your drink while I tell Ian I'm leaving."

"Ian?"

"My second-in-command." He arched one brow. "Do you know him?"

Angie shook her head. "My best friend is dating a guy named Ian. Probably not the same one."

"Probably not," Declan agreed.

Angie finished her drink as she watched him stride to the other end of the bar. He spent a few moments there talking to a tall, good-looking guy with blond hair. She frowned. Sam's Ian was tall and blond. *Could* it be the same guy?

She put her glass aside when Declan came around the bar.

"Are you ready?" he asked.

"I guess so."

"Where are you parked?"

"Out front."

"Let's go."

She grabbed her purse and they left the nightclub.

He followed her to her car, waited while she unlocked the door to a late model Accord and slid behind the wheel, then closed the door for her.

Angie slid the key in the ignition, then watched, wide-eyed, as he climbed into a fire-engine red Maserati. Holy cow, the guy must be rich, she thought, as she followed him out of the parking lot. Rides like that cost over a hundred grand. She was definitely in the wrong business.

Traffic was light and she had no trouble keeping the Maserati in sight.

She felt a moment of trepidation when she followed him into a well-lit parking lot. She hadn't expected him to bring her to such a fancy restaurant, not the way she was dressed, she thought, as she pulled into the parking space beside his.

Declan opened her door for her. "What do you think?"

"It looks amazing, but I think I'm dressed all wrong."

He shrugged. "I'm sure they won't have a problem as long as we can pay the bill."

She grinned as they made their way along the flagstone path to the front entrance. This place was a far cry from Nick's Nightmare. The lighting out front was subdued. Lush greenery lined the walkway and bordered the street. Bright red flowers in ivory-colored urns stood on either side of the glass doors.

Amazing was an understatement, she thought, as they stepped inside. The only word she could think of to describe Castleton's was elegant—from the soft lighting and pale color choices to the round tables with their crisp white cloths, and the padded chairs covered in a rich pale blue velvet.

There were two dance floors—one inside and one outside.

As soon as they were seated, a waitress came to take their order. Angie had already eaten dinner, so she ordered apple pie ala mode and coffee. Declan ordered a glass of red wine.

"So," he said when the waitress left to turn in their order, "tell me about you."

"There isn't much to tell."

"I'm not asking for your social security number and driver's license," he said, with a faint smile.

"I'm an only child. I like reading and movies and going out to dinner, and I write a monthly column for a local magazine. *Pat's Potpourri*. Maybe you've heard of it?"

He had, but he had little interest in the latest fashions, movie stars, or cuisine. "Do you publish under your own name?"

"Yes."

"So what kind of stuff do you write?"

She shrugged. "Off-the-wall things, mostly. Do aliens exist? Is Bigfoot real? Fun facts about Nessie. That kind of thing."

"What are you working on now?"

"You'll laugh."

"Try me."

"All right. I'm doing a story about the popularity of the Goth movement and its relation to the whole vampire myth."

Declan stared at her. "Vampires? Are you sure you're not writing for *Science Fiction Digest?*"

"I know it seems like an odd topic in this day and age, but the whole Goth thing is really hot right now and that lends itself to the paranormal, which is the perfect subject for my next column, which is scheduled for October. Besides, it's fun to speculate about things that don't exist."

"If you say so." Damn, he thought, what were the odds? And then he grinned. If she was looking for the inside scoop on the Undead, she'd come to the right place. Unfortunately, his private life wasn't for public consumption.

He leaned back as the waitress brought their order. What would Angie say—what would she do—if she knew the truth about him?

She gestured at her plate. "Would you like a taste?"

"No, thanks."

After taking a bite, she said, "It's really good."

"I'm sure it is, but I'm not much for sweets." Unless they had inky-black hair and sky-blue eyes. "Tell me, Angie, do you believe in vampires?"

"Of course not. There's no such thing. Anymore than there are goblins or trolls."

"How do you know?"

Frowning, she swallowed a spoonful of ice cream. "Well, I don't *know*, but if there were monsters running around, don't you think it would be all over the nightly news?"

"I guess you're right." Desire unfurled within him as he watched her lick a bit of vanilla from her lips.

"I should hope so!"

"Still, myths are usually based on some degree of truth."

"Like the belief that Vlad the Impaler was a vampire?" she asked. "After all, they called him Dracul."

"Yes, but it doesn't mean vampire. It means devil, or dragon, in Romanian."

"How do you know?"

"My great-grandmother on my mother's side was born in Transylvania. I grew up on stories of Vlad the Impaler and his atrocities. He was born into a noble family. They called his father Dracul because he belonged to the Order of the Dragon. Dracula merely means son of Dracul."

"Really? Do you remember any of the other stories? I mean, maybe I could use one or two in my column."

"There are some truly gruesome ones. You can find them online in all their gory detail."

"Sure, but, hearing the stories the way your great-grandmother told them would be so much more interesting."

Declan shook his head, thinking he never should have started down this path. "If I think of anything else, I'll let you know. It's been a long time since my *străbunică* told me tales of Transylvania." Longer than Angie would believe, he mused with a wry grin. And it hadn't been his great-grandmother.

"Would you like to dance?" he asked when she pushed her plate aside.

"I ..." Excitement and apprehension fluttered in the pit of her stomach at the thought of being in his arms.

"I promise not to bite," he said. *This time.*

Telling herself she was over-reacting, Angie nodded. It was just a dance, for crying out loud.

Rising, he offered her his hand. "I promised you dancing under the stars," he murmured as he led her outside.

Angie swallowed hard as Declan's fingers closed around hers. She felt it again—that sudden rush of heat that spiraled through her and settled deep in the core of her being. It was both disconcerting and arousing at the same time.

Her eyes widened as she glanced around, thinking it looked like a fairyland. Twinkle lights outlined the edge of the dance floor. Lacy ferns and birds of paradise bloomed in white pots placed at intervals. Small, round, glass-topped tables were located in the corners. Overhead, the stars smiled down on them through a white latticework.

The orchestra was playing something soft and slow when Declan drew her into his arms. She was keenly aware of his nearness, of the way their bodies fit together, of the sudden tension between them. She had no trouble following his lead.

Declan knew asking Angie to dance had been a mistake the moment her body brushed his. The scent of her hair, her skin, the warmth of her hand in his fired his desire even as the intoxicating scent of her life's blood spiked his need. What was there about this woman that made her so hard to resist? In the course of his existence, he had known countless women—old, young, plain, and beautiful—none had aroused his hungers as quickly or as deeply. But even more surprising was the fact that he wanted to know everything about her — what she believed, what she thought, her ideas about life and love, her hopes and dreams for the future.

For countless seconds, he closed his eyes in an effort to resist the urge to sink his fangs into her warm, soft flesh and satisfy the awful hunger her nearness aroused.

Angie felt the change in him, though she had no idea what had caused it. When she looked up, his eyes were closed, as if he was in pain. But then the sensation passed, and he looked down at her, his heated gaze as tangible as a caress, making her heart skip a beat.

When the music ended, he escorted her back to their table.

"Your turn," Angie said, somewhat breathlessly. "Tell me about you."

He shrugged. "There's not a lot to tell. I'm single. I run a saloon." He smiled at her. "I enjoy dancing with beautiful women."

Angie blushed as his gaze caressed her again, the look in his eyes so intense it was almost as if he was actually running his fingertips across her cheek, down the length of her neck.

He ordered another round of drinks and they danced again. And again. She was Cinderella at the ball, he was the handsome prince, and for the first time in her life, she believed in fairy tales that ended with happily-ever-after.

She sighed as he rained feather-light kisses across her brow, her cheeks, along the side of her neck. She should protest, insist that he stop. He was a stranger, after all. But she couldn't form the words, couldn't think of anything but the unexpected wonder of his touch.

Declan swore under his breath. And then, unable to resist, he bent his head to her neck and bit her, ever so gently. A sip—two. And then three.

Lost in his thrall, she felt only the touch of his tongue against her flesh and a sudden rush of sensual heat.

They stayed until closing, then walked hand-in-hand to the parking lot.

"I had a wonderful time," Angie said as she unlocked her car and opened the door.

"As did I. It's late," he said. "Would you like me to drive you home?"

"Thank you, but I'll be fine. Besides you'd just have to find a way to come back here for your car."

"Okay, have it your way." He stood back as she slid behind the wheel, watched as she pulled out of the parking lot. She wasn't drunk, he knew that, but he had taken more from her than he'd intended, leaving her a little light-headed.

Feeling guilty, as well as responsible for her safety, he followed her home, careful not to let her see him. The last thing he wanted was for her to think he was stalking her. He stayed out of sight until she was safely inside.

Driving back to the Nightmare, he told himself he shouldn't see her again. Her interest in vampires intrigued him, but could also pose a danger, not only to him, but to those who frequented the nightclub. It would be better for all concerned if he ended whatever this was before it began.

But it was already too late. Her scent clung to his jacket, his hands. The sweetness of her blood lingered on his tongue. Right or wrong, he knew he had to see her again.

# CHAPTER FOUR

Feeling the need for someone to talk to, Angie called Samantha the next day and invited her to lunch. As luck would have it, Sam's boss had several cases in court that afternoon , which meant she was free until five. They met at Moretti's Spaghetti House at one-thirty where they split a large pepperoni pizza with olives and peppers.

"So, what's up?" Sam asked. "You sounded kind of funny on the phone."

"I met a guy."

"Well, it's about time."

"Yeah, yeah. We went out together last night."

"Great! Where'd you go?"

"Castleton's."

"Wow! How did you get in there on such short notice? I heard you had to make reservations at least three weeks in advance."

"Beats me," Angie said, sprinkling parmesan on a slice of pizza. "Maybe he knows the owner. All I can say is, it was beautiful."

"Lucky you. I've always wanted to go there. So, what's this new guy's name?"

"Declan Nicolae."

"Declan!" Sam exclaimed. "That's the name of Ian's boss."

"So it *was* him," Angie murmured. No wonder Sam was smitten.

"What?"

"I saw your boyfriend at Nick's Nightmare. At least I think it was him."

"Really? I've never been there. Ian's never taken me. He says he sees enough of the place when he's working. Are you going out with your guy again?"

"He's not *my* guy." Angie sipped her drink. "As for seeing him again, I don't know. There's something about him…"

"What do you mean?"

"He's kind of… I don't know. Scary."

"Scary?" Sam frowned at her. "In what way?"

"I'm not sure how to explain it. There's just something weird about him. I can't put my finger on it." Was it just because he worked in a Goth club that bothered her, or the fact that he seemed so at home with the bizarre clientele?

"Well, I've always said a girl should listen to her instincts."

"I know. The thing is, he's beyond gorgeous. Tall, black hair, shoulders a fullback would envy, and the most incredible green eyes. And to top it off, he drives a Maserati."

"Maybe you're over-reacting about the scary thing. You haven't dated for quite a while. Maybe it's just, I don't know, a case of nerves."

"I suppose that could be it. Anyway, it probably doesn't matter. He didn't say anything about wanting to see me again."

"You could call him."

"No way!"

"I could tell Ian you're interested and…"

"Don't you dare! I don't need a matchmaker!"

"Geez, calm down, Ange, I was only kidding. Oh, dang," Samantha exclaimed when her phone beeped. "I've got to go. Grumpy just texted me. He got out of court early and he's back in the office and needs me ASAP."

"All right. Catch ya later."

With a wave of her hand, Samantha hurried out the door.

Lost in thought, Angie nibbled on the last slice of pizza. Maybe Sam was right. Maybe she was just feeling a little gun-shy about dating someone new. It was understandable, considering her last two relationships had not ended well, to say the least.

Angie finished her soda, cleared the table, and headed for home. Like she'd told Sam, Declan hadn't said he wanted to see her again, so she was probably worrying for nothing.

Her phone buzzed just as she pulled into the driveway. She glanced at the screen, felt a moment of panic when she saw his name. She didn't remember giving him her number. How had he gotten it?

With some trepidation, she murmured, "Hello?"

"Hi. I was wondering what you're going for dinner tonight."

"I ... um ... haven't made any plans."

"I'd love to see you again."

"What did you have in mind?"

"Dinner and a movie?"

She drummed her fingers on the steering wheel. Should she, or shouldn't she?

"Angie?"

That voice. It sent a thrill of anticipation racing down her spine. "All right."

"Pick you up at seven? Show starts at eight-thirty."

She hesitated a moment before giving him her address.

"See you then," he said.

After murmuring, "goodbye," Angie stared at her phone, hoping she wasn't making a horrible mistake.

Angie dressed with care that night in a pair of white jeans and a navy-blue sweater. She debated putting her hair up but decided to leave it down. After applying her make-up, she tugged on a pair of white, high-heeled boots, took a last look in the mirror, and headed into the living room to wait.

Declan arrived promptly at seven, looking handsome as sin in black slacks and a dark-green shirt she thought was Armani.

He gave a low whistle when he saw her. "You look terrific. Are you ready?"

"Yes." He waited on the porch while she grabbed her keys and a small clutch bag. After locking the front door, she followed him down the stairs to his car, which was parked in the driveway with the motor running.

He opened the door for her, waited until she'd settled inside before closing it.

Angie watched him round the front of the Maserati, her heart pounding. She couldn't decide if she was so flustered because she was afraid to be alone with him or overly excited at the prospect.

He smiled at her as he slid behind the wheel. "I made reservations at Martinique's," he said, "but we can go somewhere else if you'd rather."

"No, that sounds wonderful." She had never been there, but they were supposed to have the best cuisine in town.

Declan glanced at her while waiting at a red light. Her pulse was racing, her cheeks flushed. A faint hint of fear clung to her skin. She was afraid of him, he thought, though she was trying hard not to show it.

The interior of Martinique's was luxurious, the colors bold, the lighting intimate. Once again, they were seated right away, making Angie think Declan must be well-known at two of the city's best restaurants.

A waitress brought their menus, water, and a basket of rolls still warm from the oven.

Angie frowned as she perused her choices. There were no prices listed on the menu.

Noting her expression, Declan said, "Order anything you like."

Taking him at his word, she decided on lobster, rice pilaf, and broccoli. Under the circumstances, she would have hesitated to order anything so expensive, but salved her conscience by reminding herself that any man who owned his own business and drove a Maserati could certainly afford it.

Declan asked for filet mignon, rare, and a bottle of wine. One of the perks of being a very old vampire was the ability to consume mortal food if he so desired. But it couldn't sustain his existence. Only human blood could do that, although he was able to survive on animal blood if nothing else was available.

"How did you get my phone number?" Angie asked after the waitress left to turn in their orders.

"From Ian. I mentioned your name and he wondered if you were the friend his girl was always talking about. I played a hunch and asked for your number and he gave it to me."

"*He* had my number?"

"His girlfriend did."

"Oh." She wasn't sure how she felt about Sam giving out her number, Angie thought as she buttered a roll. "Have you owned the Nightmare very long?"

"About five years."

"Whatever made you buy a Goth club?"

He shrugged. "It was too good a deal to pass up and I liked the atmosphere. The customers tend to be ... interesting."

"I'll bet. All those fake fangs and sexy women running around in those revealing Goth outfits. It's like every night is Halloween."

"I like Halloween," he said with a wink. "And I like the hours."

"You must be a night owl," she said, smiling. "Sleep all day and work all night."

"Something like that. What about you? Do you live your life by the clock?"

"Not really. I work at home, so I don't have to punch a time clock or anything. Of course, I have deadlines to meet, but I can write pretty much whenever I'm in the mood. Other than that, my time is my own and I prefer it that way. I like being able to set my own hours."

"It's good to be the boss," he said with a grin. "What about your parents? Do you see them often?"

"No. They divorced when I was nine. By the time I was twelve, they had both remarried. I never felt comfortable in either household. After I left home, I used to try to see my mom and dad once or twice a year, but they weren't any happier to see me than I was to see them. What about your parents?"

"They've been gone for some time," he said, and changed the subject.

Angie felt herself relaxing over dinner. Declan related humorous stories about some of his steady customers while they ate. One owned a Cadillac agency, one was a high-profile tech genius who had an affinity for snakes, another was a Hollywood mogul rumored to be quite a ladies' man. When Declan offered her a bite of his steak, she gave him a forkful of lobster in exchange. The food and the wine were excellent, as was the company, and the chocolate éclair she had for dessert.

"I'm so full!" she exclaimed as Declan handed her into the Maserati later than evening. "I'm not sure I'll ever need to eat again."

Declan grinned at her, his gaze lingering on the curve of her throat as he closed the door. The movie theater was only a few blocks away when he pulled over to the curb.

"What's wrong?" Angie asked, glancing around.

"How would you feel about going dancing instead?"

"I don't know. Why? I kind of had my heart set on the movie."

His gaze moved over her. "I'd rather hold you in my arms again." His voice, low and sensual, went through her like liquid fire. "Change your mind, Angie. We can see the movie another night."

"I…I…"

"Say yes," he coaxed as he closed the space between them and kissed her lightly.

"Yes," she murmured. "Oh, yes."

They went to Castleton's, where they had gone before. Since they had already eaten and the weather was warm, they chose the outdoor dance floor again.

The music was soft and romantic, the man tall and dark and ever so sexy. She rested her cheek against his chest as he guided her around the floor, wondering why she had ever been afraid of him. Being in Declan's arms again was like coming home, and how odd was that, since this was only their second date?

The songs blended one into another and time lost all meaning. There was only Declan holding her close, his voice whispering in her ear, the warmth of his tongue laving the side of her neck, followed by a sense of floating away on a red velvet cloud. It was a delightful sensation too quickly over, one she wished would last forever.

Angie hated to see the night end. There was something magical about being with Declan, she thought as he pulled into the driveway and then walked her to her door. "I had a wonderful time," she murmured.

"As did I." His gaze probed hers. "I'll call you tomorrow, okay?"

She nodded. "More than okay. Good night, Declan."

Declan brushed a kiss across her lips. "Sweet dreams, darlin'."

He waited until she stepped inside and closed the door before climbing into the Maserati. He had been dangerously close to taking more than a few sips tonight. How many times had he warned Ian to be careful? But, damn, she was so sweet.

Angie woke smiling. The more time she spent with Declan, the more she enjoyed his company. He was a wonderful dancer, entertaining company, and so darn sexy. If she wasn't careful, she was going to break her rule about no intimacy without a ring on her finger.

She grinned, thinking it was an old-fashioned rule. Maybe it was time to break it.

Sitting up, she wrapped her arms around her knees. Then, filled with a boundless surge of happiness and energy, she leaped out of bed, pulled on her jeans and a sweatshirt and pulled on a pair of sneakers. It was a beautiful day for walk. The sky was a bright, clear blue dotted with a few fluffy white clouds. She laughed at the antics of a preschooler splashing in a shallow plastic pool, waved to one of her neighbors. The world was a wonderful place, she thought. Life was good. And she was dangerously close to falling in love with a man she barely knew.

Her cell phone was buzzing when Angie returned home. "Declan, hi."

"Hi yourself. How are you this fine day?"

"Never better." She frowned when she heard him sigh. "You don't usually call me this early. Is something wrong?"

"Not a thing. I woke up thinking about you and decided to give you a call to see how you were doing."

"Like I said, never better. But I'm glad you called."

"Me, too. Do you have any plans for tonight?"

"Not at the moment."

"Good. I'll see if I can fix that. Have a good day, love."

Declan slid his cell phone into his back pocket, then drove his fist into the wall. The force of the blow cracked the plaster and sent chips of paint floating to the ground. Dammit!

Last night had been another close call. He needed to be sure he fed before spending any more time with Angie. His desire for her sweet kisses fired his yearning for her blood. It was a potent and dangerous combination.

After a late lunch, Angie plopped down in front of her computer, a cup of coffee at her elbow. She opened her vampire document and quickly read through what she'd previously written. After making a few corrections and additions, she began to write.

*There are many legends about how vampires are made. You might be in danger of becoming one of the Undead after you die if you were born with hair or teeth or a red birthmark, or if you were born with a caul over your head, or have the misfortune of being the illegitimate child of another illegitimate child.*

*If you're unlucky enough to die by your own hand, fail to be baptized, are killed by a vampire, or leave unfinished business behind, you may be reborn as one of the creatures of the night.*

*Of course, there are numerous books about vampires, some well-known. Others, like* The Vampire Cat, *written in 1918, are more obscure. Vampires are notoriously popular in movies and TV shows, from Dracula—easily the most famous bloodsucker of them all—to Blacula, Lestat, Barnabus Collins, Buffy's boyfriend, Angel, and my personal favorites, the sexy Salvatore brothers from The Vampire Diaries.*

Sitting back in her chair, Angie sighed as she thought about Damon and Stefan. Damon had always been her favorite. Samantha had preferred Stefan, but there had been something about Damon . . . although he had been far more cruel and blood thirsty. But in her opinion, far more sexy, as well. Probably because she'd always had a weakness for bad boys, which explained the failure of her last two relationships.

With a shake of her head, Angie saved her document and shut down her computer. It was past time for lunch and a beef dip sandwich from Tony's was calling her name.

Angie waited until six o'clock before calling Samantha, figuring she should be home from work by then.

"Hey, girlfriend," Sam said cheerfully. "How was your date?"

"Fine, but that's not why I'm calling."

"Is something wrong? You sound kind of upset."

"I am. How could you give my cell number to Ian without asking me first?"

There was a moment of silence before Sam said, "I thought it would be all right. I mean, you'd already gone out with the guy once."

"If I'd wanted Declan to have my number, I would have given it to him."

"I'm sorry, Ange. Honestly, I just didn't think you'd mind." Sam fell silent for the space of a heartbeat, then asked, "Friends again?"

"Of course," Angie murmured, and wondered why she had been so upset in the first place.

"So," Sam urged, "tell me all about him."

Ian punched Declan on the arm. "How'd things go with Samantha's friend?"

"None of your business."

"Hey, is that any way to talk to the guy who got her number for you on a moment's notice?"

Declan glared at him.

"What's wrong? Did she dump you?"

"No, although she probably should."

"Am I missing something?" Ian asked, frowning.

"It's getting harder and harder to keep my hands off her and my hunger in check. Last night..." Declan shook his head.

"Time to take your own advice, huh?"

"I'm afraid so."

Ian climbed onto the bar stool beside Declan's. "So, what happened?"

"We went out to dinner and then I took her dancing." Declan scrubbed his hand over his jaw. "I kissed her and then... let's just say it was a close call."

"Been there, done that," Ian said with a sympathetic grin. "Maybe we should double-date from now on, you know? That way we can keep an eye on each other."

"I don't need a babysitter so," Declan muttered irritably.

Then again, considering the way he felt about Angie, having a chaperone might not be a bad idea.

# CHAPTER FIVE

A ngie was deep into her research for her vampire column when the phone rang. A glance at the computer screen showed it was almost four-thirty. She couldn't believe she'd been working non-stop for the last three hours. But then, she had never imagined that vampires were such fascinating creatures, she thought, as she answered the phone.

Just hearing Declan's voice made her stomach flutter with excitement.

"How are you today?" he asked, in that warm, silky-smooth voice that made her toes curl with pleasure.

"Wonderful." She leaned back in her chair, feeling like a schoolgirl with her first big crush. "How are you?"

"I've been missing you all day. Can I see you tonight?"

She thought of playing hard to get, but quickly dismissed the idea because she missed him, too. "I'd like that."

"What time?"

Angie glanced at the computer's clock again. "Six?" That would give her plenty of time to shower and dress.

"I can't wait that long. How about five-thirty?"

"All right. What shall we do?"

"Whatever you want, sweetheart."

*Sweetheart.* The endearment made her smile.

"A carnival opened nearby this afternoon," he said. "Are you game?"

"Bring it on!"

❖    ❖    ❖

Declan arrived promptly at 5:30. Dressed in jeans and a long-sleeved black tee, Angie thought he looked like a part of the night.

The carnival was being held in a large vacant lot outside the city. It was the biggest one Angie had ever seen, with every ride and game imaginable.

"Have you had dinner?" Declan asked.

"No. I saved room for a corn dog and cotton candy."

Grinning, he took her hand and they threaded their way through the crowd toward the food vendors.

After a twenty-minute wait in line, Declan ordered two corn dogs, two sodas, and two bags of chips. It took another few minutes to find a place to sit.

"I love hot dogs," Angie said, smearing mustard on hers. "I know they're bad for you, but I just can't resist them at fairs and carnivals. They always seem to taste so much better here than at home."

"I think you're right," he agreed after taking a bite of his. "What would you like to do next?"

"The merry-go-round," Angie said after licking mustard off her lower lip. "And the Ferris wheel. And the giant slide."

After throwing away their cups and napkins, they headed for the rides. Declan willingly followed her from the tilt-a-whirl to the roller coaster, and from something called death drop to the bumper cars, but he insisted on going on the Ferris wheel several times.

They were at the top of the wheel on their fourth visit when Angie said, "I'm beginning to think this must be your favorite ride."

"It is tonight," he said with a wink.

"Oh? Why is that?"

"Because it's the only ride that's kind of quiet and private and lets me hold you close."

The look in his eyes, the husky tone of his voice, sent a thrill down her spine. His kiss was gentle, little more than the brush of his lips against hers, and yet she felt it right down to her toes. When she murmured, "More," he deepened the kiss, his tongue seeking hers as his arms drew her closer.

The noise fell away, the night seemed to close in around them, and there was nothing in all the world but Declan's arm around her, his mouth on hers.

"Hey, you two! Get a room."

Angie felt her cheeks heat when Declan let her go and she realized the ride was over and the operator was smirking as he waited for them to step out of the car.

Declan was laughing when they walked away.

Angie glared at him a moment, thinking she had never been more embarrassed. And then she laughed, too.

They decided to try their luck at the Fun Zone next—the ring toss, breaking balloons, the shooting gallery—he won them all. Refusing to be discouraged, she stopped in front of the next booth, determined to knock over the pyramid of old-fashioned milk bottles no matter how long it took. She let out a whoop and Declan applauded when, after five tries, she knocked over all the bottles and won a bright-pink elephant.

"Your turn." She stood back as he knocked the pyramid down with one throw. "Bet you can't do that again."

"Bet I can." And he did. Ten times in a row.

"Show off."

He grinned at her, his arms filled with stuffed animals. "Do you want any of these?"

"Just the cute little brown-and-white dog. It reminds me of a puppy I had when I was a girl."

Declan handed it to her. Fixing his gaze on the man in the booth, he said, "Give the rest of these as consolation prizes to the kids who don't win. Understand?"

The man nodded as he gathered up the nine stuffed toys and set them aside.

Their next stop was the Tunnel of Love. Angie shivered with anticipation as they settled into the boat. She leaned into Declan when he slipped his arm around her shoulders, his mouth seeking hers. Once again, it seemed as if the world faded away and there was just the two of them. He whispered her name as he nuzzled her neck and she felt again that sense of floating away on a crimson cloud.

As they neared the end of the ride, she looked at Declan. For a moment, she would have sworn that she saw a faint red glow in his eyes, but it was quickly gone and she grinned, realizing it was probably just the reflection of the light at the tunnel's exit

"Ready to go home?" Declan asked as he handed her out of the boat.

"No way. I'm not leaving until I get my cotton candy."

"I had a wonderful time," Angie said as Declan pulled up in front of her house and put the car in Park. "Thank you."

"Any time."

She hated to see the night end. She glanced out the window. It was late, but not that late. She could feel him watching her. Waiting for her to decide.

Taking a deep breath, she said, "Would you like to come in?"

"You know I would."

She tucked the pink elephant under her arm and slipped the stuffed puppy into her handbag when Declan cut the engine and got out of the car. He opened her door and then followed her up the porch steps.

Angie's hand trembled as she slid the key into the lock and turned the handle. She was acutely aware of the man behind her as she stepped inside and switched on the lights. There was a peculiar shift in the air as he followed her across the threshold, but it was gone so quickly she thought she must have imagined it. Shrugging it off, she dropped her handbag and the elephant on a side table.

Declan glanced around the room. "Nice place." The walls were pale gray, the carpet a darker shade. White wooden shutters covered the windows. A pair of overstuffed chairs upholstered in a quiet blue, gray and white plaid sat in front of a white brick fireplace. A high-backed sofa with the same print sat across from the chairs, a white, glass-topped coffee table in the middle.

Angie smiled her thanks, her nerves humming at his nearness. "Would you like something to drink?"

"Not right now."

"Well, have a seat."

"Why are you so nervous?"

"I don't know."

He knew. Her instincts were warning her that she had invited a dangerous creature into her home.

Declan sat on the sofa and gestured for her to join him.

After a moment's hesitation, she did so.

"Relax, Angie," he said quietly. "I'm not going to hurt you."

"I wouldn't have asked you in if I thought you would."

He smiled inwardly at her brave front. The scent of her fear filled his nostrils. It was exhilarating. Once, it would have been her undoing. He took a deep breath, reining in his desire even as he slipped his arm around her shoulders. "How's your magazine article coming along?"

His question caught her off-guard even as it took the focus off her fear, as he had intended.

"I'm really happy with it. You wouldn't believe the amount of information I found on Google. I was amazed that there were so many links to vampires and Goths and Transylvania," she said with a shake of her head. "I'm becoming a real expert on the subject. Did you know every country in the world has their own myths and stories, some dating back thousands of years?"

"It's been a popular subject ever since the first vampire novel was published."

"Right. *The Vampyre,* published in the nineteenth century."

"Eighteen-nineteen to be exact," Declan said. "At the time, people thought it had been written by the poet, Lord Byron, but it was actually published by his personal physician, Doctor John Polidori. And based on the life of Byron."

Angie grinned at him. "Looks like I'm not the only one doing vampire research."

Declan grunted softly. She had no idea.

"Have you read *Dracula*?" she asked.

"Of course. It was Stoker's book that really lit the fire under the genre, so to speak."

"I read it when I was in high school. And I think I've seen all the movies and TV shows, from *Nosferatu* to *Moonlight,* which was my all-time favorite and cancelled way too soon, in my opinion."

"Sounds like you're quite a fan of the Undead."

"You could say that, although I prefer the romantic vampires in the books I've read to the blood-thirsty monsters in the movies."

"Enough talk of vampires," Declan murmured as he caressed her cheek with his knuckles.

Angie closed her eyes, everything else forgotten as Declan claimed her lips with his. Lost in a sea of sensual pleasure, she moaned softly when she felt his tongue stroke the side of her neck and then she was once again floating, drifting toward oblivion on a warm, red cloud.

Cursing softly, Declan lifted her into his arms and carried her to bed. He removed her boots and then tucked her under the covers. Going into the kitchen, he filled a large glass with apple juice.

Back in the bedroom, he slid his arm behind her shoulders and held the glass to her lips. When he told her to drink it, she did so without protest, then slumped against him.

He held her until the color returned to her cheeks and her pulse was slow and steady. Reluctant to leave her, he murmured, "Forgive me, my sweet," as he brushed a kiss across her brow and then stalked out of the house, quietly cursing himself yet again for his lack of control as he drove to the nightclub. He hadn't taken enough to cause her any harm, but it was getting harder and harder to stop before he went too far.

# CHAPTER SIX

The next morning, Angie was at her desk, staring at the cute little stuffed dog Declan had won for her, when the phone rang. Still thinking of Declan, she picked it up without checking the caller I.D. "Hello?"

"Angie? Is that you?"

"Oh. Hi, Sam."

"You sound kinda funny, Ange. Like you're, oh, I don't know, like you're lost in another world."

"I am."

Samantha laughed. "Hot date last night?"

"We went to the carnival."

"Really? I never thought of fairs as being particularly romantic places."

"I guess it depends on whom you're with," Angie said with a sigh. "The Tunnel of Love is now my new favorite ride."

"I'm almost afraid to ask why," Sam muttered. "Should I call you back when you come down from Cloud Nine?"

"No, silly. What's up?"

"I talked to Ian late last night. How do you feel about double-dating?"

"With you and Ian? Sure. Why?"

"Well, I mentioned it to Ian and he said he was okay with it, too. So, ask Declan if tomorrow night is good for him, okay?"

"Sure. Sounds like fun."

"Great! Go back to Cloud Nine and I'll talk to you later."

Angie had just finished dinner when Declan called. She glanced outside as she picked up the phone. There was a storm coming. Dark clouds hovered low in the sky, and even as she said, "Hello," there was a drumroll of thunder followed by the patter of raindrops.

"What are you doing?" Declan asked.

"Watching the rain." It was coming down harder now. "What are you doing?"

"Wondering if you'd like to go for a walk."

"In the rain? You won't melt, will you?" she asked, a smile in her voice.

"That's the Wicked Witch of the West."

"Oh, right. Well, sure, sounds like fun. When will you be here?"

"I'm on the porch."

"How'd you know I'd say yes?" she asked, hurrying to the front door.

"I didn't know, but I hoped you would."

She grinned as she opened the door and saw him standing there, clad in nothing but a tee shirt, jeans, and a navy-blue windbreaker. "Come on in while I put on some boots and get a jacket."

He followed her inside, stood in the entryway, dripping water on the tile, while he waited for her.

Five minutes later, she was back wearing a pair of rain boots, a sweater, gloves, and a hooded jacket. "You're not really dressed for wet weather," she remarked as they left the house.

"I never get cold," he said, taking her hand.

"I love storms," Angie remarked as they strolled along the deserted sidewalk. The night smelled of damp grass and wet earth.

"Me, too. How was your day?"

"I had a phone call from Sam this afternoon. She wants to double-date tomorrow night. Is that okay with you?"

"Ian mentioned it to me. I'm in favor of anything that lets me spend more time with you. Just let me know what time to pick you up."

He knew just how to melt her heart, Angie thought, then gasped as he stopped beneath a tree and pulled her into his arms. She tilted her head back to give him easy access to her lips, closed her eyes as he covered her mouth with his. The storm raged around them, but it was nothing compared to the tempest aroused by Declan's ardent kisses.

She was breathless when he lifted his head. Murmuring his name, she cupped his face in her hands, went up on her tiptoes and brushed her lips across his. It was all the invitation he needed. Minutes ticked into eternity as he hugged her body against his while his tongue ravaged her mouth.

A bright burst of lightning, followed by a drumroll of thunder, sent them scurrying back to the house for shelter.

Angie was laughing as they ducked inside.

"Best walk I ever had," Declan said, his gaze caressing her. "I'd better let you go get dried off before you catch your death. I'll see you tomorrow night."

"All right."

He kissed her goodnight, a long, lingering kiss that had her humming softly as she went to take a shower.

Declan frowned at Ian. The kid had been a nervous wreck all night, fidgeting, dropping glasses, forgetting drink orders. "What's got your tail in a twist?" he asked, during a lull at the bar.

"You remember I said we should double-date?"

"Yeah?"

"Well, I was only kidding, but Samantha called me before I came to work. She said she talked it over with Angie this afternoon and now they want to get together tomorrow night if it's all right with you."

"Yeah, I know. Angie mentioned something about it earlier tonight. It's okay with me. Frank can cover for you."

"It's not okay! Apparently, Angie told Samantha about Castleton's and now Sam wants to go there."

"Ah. I'm beginning to see your dilemma."

"I thought you would. It was a great idea when I thought she just wanted to go out for drinks and dancing, or maybe a movie, but now? What am I gonna do in a restaurant? I can't just sit there while the rest of you are eating. What kind of excuse could I have for taking her out to dinner and not ordering anything? I'll just have to cancel, say I'm coming down with the flu or going out of town."

"Calm down. It'll be all right." Declan grinned inwardly. Ian had been a vampire less than a year. Since the kid had been deserted by his sire, Declan had taken him under his wing, so to speak. But the boy still had a lot to learn. "When we get to the restaurant, just order something. Doesn't matter what. Just leave the rest to me. A little vampire mind control will convince the girls you're eating and keep the waitress from remarking on your uneaten meal."

❧ ❧ ❧

Angie was working on her column the next morning when Sam called bubbling with excitement.

"I hear we're on for tonight! When I talked to Ian last night, I told him I wanted to go to Castleton's, if it's all right with you. It is, isn't it?"

"Sure, I'd love to go there again."

"Oh, good. Ian said Declan would take care of the reservations. What are you going to wear?"

"I don't know," Angie said. "Maybe I'll go out and buy something new."

"Maybe I will, too! I can't wait."

"Me, either. See you later." Dinner at Castleton's with Declan and her best friend, Angie mused as she ended the call. What could be better?

Angie worked for another hour, and then headed for her favorite dress shop, determined to look her best that night. She bought the first dress she tried on, an elegant yet simple black sheath with a provocative slit on one side.

Angie couldn't stop glancing at Declan as they drove to Castleton's. Clad in a pair of black slacks, a gray pinstripe shirt, and a black sport coat that emphasized his broad shoulders and dark good looks, he was positively mouth-watering.

"If you keep leering at me like that, we'll never make it to the restaurant."

She flushed when his gaze met hers. What was there about him that made her want to throw caution to the wind, leave her good sense behind, and succumb to the desire she read in his gorgeous green eyes?

Fortunately, they reached the restaurant before she abandoned all reason and suggested they skip dinner and go straight to the nearest motel instead.

He grinned as they pulled into the parking lot, making her wonder if he had somehow divined her thoughts. Thankfully, that was impossible.

Ian and Samantha were waiting inside. Ian looked quite handsome in tan slacks and a brown sports jacket.

Declan had made reservations and their table was ready.

"I see you bought a new dress," Angie said, admiring the blue silk that clung to Sam's figure as they walked into the dining room.

"So did you."

"Guilty."

At the table, Angie smiled inwardly as Ian took Samantha's hand in his. It was easy to see they were crazy about each other, she thought, as she opened her menu. In the past, Sam had dated a lot of men, but she had quickly grown bored with one and all. But Ian was different. Sam was nuts about him.

When the waitress came to take their order, Samantha and Angie both ordered the shrimp dinner. Declan ordered roast beef, rare. Ian glanced at the menu, looked uncertainly at Declan, and then back at the menu before deciding on sirloin steak. It was odd, Angie thought, almost as if he wasn't certain what to do. But that was ridiculous. Surely he'd been in a restaurant before.

Ian asked Sam about the Hampton case and the four of them discussed the grisly murder while waiting for dinner. The Hamptons' son had been taken in for questioning and warned not to leave town, but so far, no arrests had been made.

Declan listened quietly to the speculation around the table—was the son innocent or guilty? Was the murderer a resident, or some transient just passing through? Declan could have told them the Hampton's son had nothing to do with his parents' deaths. It had been a cleverly disguised vampire kill. Declan had his own ideas about who the guilty party was.

When he saw the waitress approaching with their dinners, he forgot about the murder and focused his attention on Angie, Samantha, and the waitress.

Angie felt an indescribable sensation when the waitress placed Ian's plate in front of him. For a moment, it was like she was seeing the world through a filter, but it quickly passed, and she soon forgot all about it.

Once dinner was over, they spent the rest of the evening dancing under the stars, taking time out from time to time to have a drink, or just sit and chat. Angie hated to see the night end.

"I had a wonderful time," she remarked on the drive home. "Ian seems very nice."

"Yes," Declan agreed.

"And Sam's crazy about him. A blind man could see that."

"He feels the same about her."

"I'm glad," she said, genuinely happy for her friend. "Do you think they'll get married?"

"I couldn't say. They haven't been dating long and Ian's still a young..." He broke off abruptly.

"A young what?"

"A young man," he replied smoothly.

Angie frowned at him. "He's not *that* young."

"No, I guess not," Declan agreed with a grin. "I guess I'm getting old. Everyone seems like a kid to me these days."

"How old are you, anyway?"

"Thirty-seven. You?"

"Twenty-four."

"Just a baby," he murmured as he pulled into her driveway and moved the gear shift to Park. "Can I see you tomorrow?"

"It's getting to be a habit."

"One I hope you like."

"You know I do."

"I'll call you when I get to the Nightmare and you can let me know what you'd like to do."

"What would *you* like to do?" She had to stop asking that, Angie thought as his gaze caressed her, once again leaving no doubt in her mind as to what he was thinking.

"Anything you want is fine with me."

"Okay. I'll think of something."

He walked her to the door, then drew her gently into his arms. "Angie. You're driving me crazy."

His fingertips grazed her lips, lighting fires of desire deep within her. "Am I?" she asked breathlessly.

He cupped her face in his palms and kissed her ever-so-gently. "I've never known anyone like you, anyone who…" His words trailed off.

She felt the tension in him as he kissed her again, deeper, longer, his tongue scorching hers.

He released her abruptly.

Angie looked at him askance.

"You're far too tempting." Brushing a kiss across her lips, he murmured, "Until tomorrow night," and left her standing there feeling as though she had missed something.

Angie met Samantha at their favorite buffet place for lunch the next afternoon.

"Thank goodness for a day off," Samantha said as they made their way along the food line. "That man is going to work me to death. So, what did you think of Ian?"

"He's very cute," Angie said as she debated between spaghetti alfredo and mac and cheese. "I have a feeling he's going to be around for a while."

"From now on if I have anything to say about it! He's perfect! Everything I ever dreamed of. I mean, honestly, he knows me better than I know myself. Sometimes I think he can read my mind."

"Really?" Funny, Angie mused, sometimes she had the same feeling about Declan.

"Really. And that guy you were with, wow, he's a bit of a hunk, too. I can't believe our guys both work at the same place."

"I know. It's quite a coincidence," Angie agreed as they made their way to a table by the window. Ian *was* cute, of that there was no doubt. But he fell far short of perfection as far as she was concerned. While Declan…just thinking about him made her feel warm all over.

"If Ian asks me to marry him, I'm definitely saying yes," Sam said, all dreamy-eyed.

"Kind of soon for that, isn't it? I mean, you've only been dating for a few months."

"I know." Samantha sighed dramatically. "I just hope I don't scare him off."

Angie laughed softly. They ate in silence for a time and then she said, "Did you notice anything funny during dinner last night?"

"I don't think so. Funny how?"

"I can't explain it. It happened right after our dinner arrived. It was kind of … of …" Angie shook her head. "It was the strangest feeling." She shrugged. "Maybe I imagined it."

"Probably just nerves from your first double date with a new guy, you know? I was a little worried myself."

"I guess you're right," Angie agreed dubiously.

"So, what are you doing the rest of the day?"

"I need to work on my column. Go to the store. I'm out of practically everything. Change the sheets on my bed. Nothing very exciting. How about you?"

Samantha groaned softly. "My mother and my older sister are coming to visit."

"Sucks to be you," Angie said with a grin. Sam's mother was horribly judgmental. Nothing Sam ever did was good enough. And her sister was just as bad, if not worse.

"Tell me about it."

After clearing their table, they hugged and said goodbye.

At home, Angie booted up her computer and opened her document. She frowned at the screen a moment, then began to write.

*Now that you know how people become vampires, it would be helpful to know how to destroy them. Fortunately, there are several ways—none very pleasant. You can lop off their heads. Set them on fire. Drive a wooden stake into their heart. Sunlight is also fatal.*

*Other beliefs are that vampires cannot cross running water or enter a home uninvited. They are able to shape-shift and are said to be able to travel faster than the human eye can follow. Silver is said to burn their skin. Some believe garlic will repel them. They do not photograph, cannot be seen in mirrors and cast no shadow. Some believe this is because vampires have no soul.*

*Animals avoid them.*

*Vampires must rest in their native soil during the day.*

*I must admit, the more I read, the more I am fascinated—and repelled—by these ancient, mythical creatures.*

*Some of my favorite vampire movies are…*

The buzzing of her cell phone immediately took her mind off vampires and jumped to Declan, who'd said he would call today. Her insides melted when she heard his voice.

"Are you busy?" he asked.

"Not too busy to talk to you. What are you doing?"

"Counting the hours until I can see you again."

He always knew just what to say, she thought.

"There's a new movie at the Roxy. The first show is in thirty minutes."

"I'll be ready in ten."

"I'll be there."

It didn't occur to Angie that she hadn't even asked what the movie was until she was changing clothes. And then she grinned, because she didn't really care as long as Declan was there beside her.

He was at her door ten minutes later, looking like a Fifties teen idol in blue jeans, a black jacket over a white tee shirt, and a pair of sunglasses.

He whistled when he saw her. "I always forget just how beautiful you are."

"Flatterer. What are we going to see?"

"I don't remember."

She laughed softly as she locked the front door and followed him down the porch steps. "Where's your car?" she asked when she didn't see the Maserati.

"I left that one home," he said as he opened the passenger door of a silver-gray Jaguar.

Angie slid into the seat, thinking she had never known anyone who owned one expensive car, let alone two. The engine purred to life when he slipped the key into the ignition. "I don't mean to be rude," she remarked, "but are you very rich?"

He laughed softly. "Richer than some, not so much as others."

That was hardly an answer, she thought, but decided not to pursue it. She wasn't a gold digger, after all. Just curious.

It was mid-afternoon and there were only a handful of people in the theater when they arrived.

Angie grinned as she looked around. "Gee, where do you want to sit?"

"Hard to decide," Declan said, removing his sunglasses. "How about the last row?"

"And why would we want to sit there?" she asked with feigned innocence.

His dark-green eyes burned into hers. "Why do you think?"

Angie felt a blush climb into her cheeks. "Gee, I haven't made out in a movie theater since I was a teenager."

"Then it's way past time you did it again." Taking her hand, he led her up the stairs to the last row. The seats in this theater had armrests that lifted up, thereby turning a single seat into a double.

A million butterflies took wing in the pit of Angie's stomach when Declan lifted the divider between them moments before the lights dimmed, enveloping them in a cocoon of darkness.

Everything around her faded away when he slipped his arm around her shoulders. Even in the dark, she could feel his gaze caressing her. A little thrill of anticipation sizzled through her and then he was kissing her, ever so slowly, ever so sweetly, his tongue dueling with hers in an age-old dance of seduction.

She had been kissed before, Angie thought, lost in a haze of pleasure. But never like this. His mouth was hot on hers, igniting a fire deep within her. She moaned low in her throat, wishing they were home, in her bed, grateful that they weren't, because at this moment, she knew she would have granted him anything he asked for. If there was a prize for most erotic kisses, she had no doubt he would win, hands down.

Occasionally, they took a time-out to catch their breath. Once, when Angie glanced at the action on the screen, she realized they were watching the latest Jurassic World movie. She loved Chris Pratt, but Declan was far more attractive. And he was here, his hooded gaze filled with yearning as he gathered her close once more, his arm rock-hard around her, his kisses growing more and more intense, until she thought the heat radiating from the two of them might set off the sprinklers or the fire alarm.

She hated to see the movie end, knew she would have happily sat through a double feature just to make-out with Declan a few minutes more.

She was feeling a little light-headed when they left the theater but attributed it his potent kisses.

"It's almost six," Declan said as he drove her home. "I need to go the Nightmare for a few hours."

"All right. Maybe next time we can watch the movie," she said with a grin.

He arched one brow. "Are you complaining?"

"What do you think?"

"I think I'd like to go back to the theater and do it all again." Pulling into the driveway, he put the car in Park and walked her to the door.

"Thanks for today," Angie said. "Will you call me tomorrow?"

"You know I will." He kissed her, long and slow. "Good night, darlin'."

Angie sighed as she watched him slide behind the wheel of the Jag. "Oh, lordy, I think I'm falling in love," she murmured, and waved as she watched him back out of the driveway, already counting the hours until she could be in his arms again.

# CHAPTER SEVEN

Declan frowned as he drove toward the Nightmare. Angie was falling in love with him. Though she had whispered the words, he'd had no trouble hearing them. He'd had no intention of caring for her, either. In the beginning, she had been just another pretty woman, someone to keep him company for a few days until the novelty wore off.

Only the novelty hadn't worn off.

He had lived too long, known too many women, to think they could have any kind of a long-lasting future together. But the more time he spent with her, the more he wanted to be with her. She was open and honest, while he was hiding who and what he was. Not that he had any choice. Still, withholding the truth left him feeling guilty, an emotion he rarely experienced these days.

Lost in thoughts of Angie, he pulled into the Nightmare's parking lot, killed the engine, and stepped out of the car. A faint scuffling noise behind him was his only warning. Spinning around, he ducked out of the way just in time to avoid the wooden stake aimed at his back.

Muttering an oath, he grabbed the hunter's arm, wrested the stake from his grasp, and drove it into the man's heart.

Wide-eyed with shock, the hunter stared at him while the light went out of his eyes and he sank to the ground.

*Shit!* Declan glanced around, but there was no one else lurking in the shadows. Pulling the stake from the man's chest, he tossed it into the bushes that bordered the parking lot. He'd burn it later. Slinging the body over his shoulder, he carried it to the vacant lot behind the Nightmare where a shovel waited.

After lowering the body to the ground, he quickly dug a hole. The acreage had come up for sale shortly after he bought the nightclub and he'd purchased the lot for just such an occasion. He had hired a company to plant a thick row of juniper trees on three sides to hide his actions from view. Fortunately, he hadn't had occasion to use it often.

When the grave was deep enough, Declan laid the body inside and filled in the hole. He stood there a moment, wondering how the hunter had arrived at the Nightmare since there were no other cars besides his Jag in the lot or on the street.

With a shrug, he put the shovel back where it belonged and entered the nightclub through the back door.

He would have to warn Ian and the others to be vigilant, he thought, as he turned on the lights. Where there was one hunter, there was bound to be another.

In the morning, Angie woke smiling and then she giggled. Since meeting Declan, she seemed to greet each new day with a smile. But she couldn't help it. She was totally, hopelessly, smitten and she had only known him a few days. How would she feel in a month? A year, if their relationship lasted that long?

She made do with cereal and toast for breakfast, then spent the morning working on her column.

She took a break in the early afternoon and went outside to get her mail—mostly ads, but also a book she had ordered from Amazon the day before. Tossing the mail on the kitchen table, she grabbed an apple and the paperback and headed for the backyard to soak up some sun and read for a while. By page two, she was lost in the latest romance by her favorite author.

She sighed when she reached the end of Chapter Three. Like it or not, it was time to get back to work.

Angie fixed a tuna sandwich for a late lunch, then padded into her office and fired up her computer, only to sit there staring at the blank screen, her thoughts again turning to Declan. She loved everything about the man. His beautiful green eyes, the sound of his voice, the gentlemanly way he treated her, the way his kisses made her feel all warm and gooey inside. Oh, she had it bad, she thought, but was it really love—or just a temporary infatuation with a tall, dark, handsome stranger? Only time would tell, she mused. But until then, she would enjoy every minute of his company.

After opening the document, Angie quickly read through the last two pages to refresh her memory. She paused when she reached the place where she'd left off, gathered her thoughts, and began to write.

*My favorite vampire movies are "Love at First Bite," with George Hamilton, "Dracula," starring Frank Langella (the sexiest vampire ever), and, of course, the "Twilight" saga. The first two movies in the series remain my favorites.*

*My favorite TV series, gone but not forgotten, are "Blood Ties", "Forever Knight", and "Moonlight", which was cancelled after only one season. Curse you, CBS, for taking the delicious Mick St. John away from thousands of loyal followers, and leaving us hanging and yearning for more.*

*As for books, there are far too many to mention.*

*So, I wish you all a very Happy Halloween filled with marsh-mallow ghosts and chocolate witches, but remind you to always WATCH YOUR NECK!*

Sitting back, Angie sipped the coffee she had brought with her. Had she covered everything? Did it need more? Less? Was it as good as she thought?

She read through the document again, corrected a couple of misspelled words, changed others, then hit Save and closed the file. She would do one last read through before sending it off to Jennifer.

It had been fun writing about the supernatural. Perhaps she could do a whole series of columns on the paranormal community—ghosts and werewolves, zombies and angels, elves and trolls. Or maybe a series about holiday myths and monsters. Or both.

A glance at her computer told her it was almost six. She had expected Declan to call by now, she thought with a frown. Had something come up at the club? She was tempted to call him, but quickly thrust the notion aside. She didn't want him to think she was checking up on him.

Of course, she could always drive over to the Nightmare. It was a public place, after all, but she discarded that idea, too. She drummed her fingertips on the desk top. She didn't feel like staying home and didn't feel comfortable calling Declan. What to do, what to do?

On a whim, she dashed into her room, took a quick shower, donned her Goth outfit and ran a comb through her hair. There were other nightclubs in town besides Nick's Nightmare. She'd go to The Pit for an hour or so, listen to the music, and people-watch. Maybe she could find some fresh material for her next column.

❧ ❧ ❧

The Pit seemed overly crowded for a week night. There were no vacant tables, but she spied two empty spots at the bar. Taking a seat, she ordered a Grasshopper from the cute guy behind the counter, then turned sideways so she could watch the room. The music was dark with a low, sensual beat, the lighting so subdued she could scarcely make out the couples on the dance floor. No surprise, since they were all wearing black.

"Can I buy you a drink?"

Angie looked up to find a tall, dark-haired man smiling at her. "No, thanks. I just ordered one."

His gaze moved over her. "Are you here with someone?"

"Well, no, but…"

"Mind if I sit down?"

Angie shrugged.

He took the seat beside hers, then waved the bartender over and ordered a glass of zinfandel. "So, pretty lady, do you come here often?"

"No."

"I didn't think so. I would have remembered you."

He was a rather handsome man, Angie thought, picking up the glass the bartender had set down in front of her. His eyes were brown, his complexion clear and pale. He looked vaguely familiar although she was certain she had never seen him before.

He smiled at her over the rim of his glass. It was a nice smile and yet it made her uncomfortable.

"Would you care to dance?" he asked, and something in his eyes compelled her to say yes.

Taking her hand, he led her onto the dance floor. "Are you new at this?" His voice was low and intimate.

Angie frowned at him. "No. I've danced before," she said, thinking it was a strange question.

His brow furrowed. And then he muttered, "Green as grass."

"Excuse me?"

"I said—"

"You've said enough."

Angie looked over her shoulder, surprised to find Declan standing behind her, his face dark with anger.

"Go find your own girl," the stranger drawled.

"This one's taken, Conor," Declan said, his voice as cold and hard as ice over steel.

"Ah, so that's the way it is."

"Exactly the way it is." Declan stared at his brother. He hadn't seen Conor in over a century, so what the hell had brought him here now? A death wish, perhaps?

"My mistake." Conor stepped away from Angie and sketched a slight, mocking bow in her direction. Then, whistling softly, he sauntered toward the bar.

"Are you all right?" Declan asked.

Angie blinked up at him. "Who was that?"

"Someone I knew a long time ago."

"Oh?" She waited for an explanation, but none was forthcoming. "What are you doing here?"

"I could ask you the same question."

"I got tired of sitting at home." She clamped her lips together, swallowing the words, *waiting for you to call.* "How did you know I was here?"

How, indeed? His gaze met hers. "It doesn't matter. As long as we're here, let's dance."

"That guy, Conor. You don't like him much, do you?" she asked after they'd been dancing for a few moments.

"Not much."

Deciding he wasn't going to tell her who the man was or how they knew each other, Angie rested her cheek on Declan's chest, content to be in his arms.

"I'm sorry I didn't get in touch with you earlier," he said. "Forgive me?"

"There's nothing to forgive." But his apology made her feel better, just the same.

Declan brushed a kiss across the top of her head. She'd had a close call tonight, he thought, although she would never know it. Conor was the epitome of what it meant to be a vampire, a merciless predator prone to killing those he preyed upon. And while Conor generally preferred innocent young women, he considered any mortal fair game.

It was after midnight when Declan drove Angie home. They had stayed at The Pit for a while, getting to know each other better over drinks, dancing cheek-to-cheek. He might have asked to stay the night, but he hadn't yet fed and after two close calls, he didn't trust himself to take just a little. Nor did he trust her to drive home alone now that Conor was in town.

Angie yawned behind her hand as he walked her to the door. "Thanks for bringing me home," she murmured. "But it wasn't necessary and now you have to go back for your car."

"Don't worry about it, love. Get some sleep. I'll call you tomorrow."

She sighed, her eyelids fluttering down as he took her in his arms and kissed her. For a night that had started so badly, she mused, it had ended wonderfully well.

# CHAPTER EIGHT

I an took a deep breath, counted to ten, and knocked on Samantha's apartment door. It was late and he knew it was dangerous to be here, even though he had fed a few hours ago. But sometimes, like now, he just needed to be with someone human, someone who cared if he lived or died. Sam made the hell his life had become worth living.

To his relief, she smiled when she saw him. "Hi."

"Hey. Are you sure it's not too late for me to be here?" Ian asked.

"Not at all. I don't have to work tomorrow, you know. Don't just stand there. Come on in."

"I won't stay long, I promise," Ian said, glancing around her apartment. "I just needed to see you tonight."

"Oh, why?" Her brow furrowed. "Is something wrong?"

"No, I just meant I really wanted to see you."

"Well, whatever the reason, I'm glad you're here." Taking a seat on the small, floral sofa, Samantha patted the cushion beside her, a silent invitation. "How was your day?"

"Not very exciting, I'm afraid. I slept through most of it." All of it, actually, but he didn't tell her that. Taking the place she indicated, he stretched his legs out in front of him.

"I'd hate to work the hours that you do." She shook her head. "I don't how you do it. Day for night. Night for day."

"Yeah. It's not easy at first, but you get used to it after a while." He slipped his arm around her shoulders and took a deep breath. She smelled so good. Warm and feminine and human. It was an intoxicating mix. "Nice place you've got here," he remarked, trying not to notice the pulse throbbing in the hollow of her throat or the sweet symphony of her heart beat.

"I like it, but I'd love to have a house someday, you know, with a big back yard and maybe a dog, and a couple of fruit trees. Maybe a small pool."

"I used to dream about having a place like that."

"What happened? Why did you stop?"

He shrugged. "You know how it is, things happen, times change." He caught her gaze with his. "I'm crazy about you, Samantha. You know that, don't you? When I'm awake, you're all I can think about."

"Well, I'm nuts about you, too. believe me. These last few months have been wonderful." She cupped his face in her palms, leaned forward, and kissed him. "I've never known anyone quite like you."

"I can believe that," he muttered.

"What?"

"Never mind." Holding her close, he claimed her lips with his while his hand slid up and down her back. All his senses came to life as he deepened the kiss, his tongue teasing hers. He listened to the beat of her heart getting faster and faster as passion flared between them. The scent of her blood sparked his hunger, the press of her breasts, warm and soft against his chest, enflamed his desire. It was a potent combination. He told himself he hadn't intended to drink from her when he stopped by, but he knew it was a lie. Murmuring that he loved her, he bit her as gently as he could, but one taste wasn't enough. Just one more, he thought. Maybe two...

Alarm bells sounded in the back of Samantha's mind as she realized that what she'd thought was just a love bite was much more than that.

Ian was drinking her blood.

With a muffled cry, she reared back—and let out a scream when she saw the hint of red in his eyes, the blood on his lips. And teeth. Only they weren't teeth, but fangs.

When she screamed again, Ian panicked and vanished from the room.

Sobbing with fear, Samantha reached for her phone.

# CHAPTER NINE

Angie buried her head under her pillow in an effort to block the annoying buzz of her cell phone. It stopped momentarily, only to start again. This time it didn't stop.

Throwing the covers aside, Angie answered with an annoyed, "What?"

"Ange?"

The frightened tone in Samantha's voice was like a splash of ice water in Angie's face. "Sam, what's wrong? Where are you? Are you all right?"

"Far from it. Can you come over right away?"

"Sure. I'll be there as soon as I get dressed."

Angie glanced at the clock on the night table. It was after one a.m. What on earth could have happened to upset Sam so badly at this time of the morning, she wondered as she pulled on a pair of jeans and a sweatshirt over her Pjs, tied her hair back in a pony-tail, grabbed her purse and her keys, and ran out of the house.

Samantha answered the door in a shorty nightgown and robe, her eyes red and swollen and frightened. "Oh, Angie!" she wailed.

Angie took Sam by the hand and led her to the sofa. Drawing her down beside her, Angie murmured meaning-less words of comfort as she patted her friend's back. A good five minutes passed before Sam's tears slowed and trickled to a stop.

Pulling a Kleenex from her pocket, Angie wiped Sam's eyes. "What has you so upset? So...so frightened?"

"Ian..." A fresh spate of tears spilled down Samantha's cheeks. "Ian is a...he's..."

"He's what?" Possibilities paraded through Angie's mind. Ian is dead? Sick? A pervert? Breaking up with her? Married?

"He's a vampire!"

Angie stared at Sam, speechless. For a moment, she thought it was some kind of bizarre joke that had to do with the column she was writing, but the fear lurking in Sam's eyes was all too real. "Sam, you know there's no such thing. Maybe you've just been spending too much time in Goth mode and you're starting to believe the fantasy."

"I'm not imagining anything!" Samantha was trembling from head to foot, her face pale, her eyes wide and afraid.

"All right," Angie said, keeping her voice low and steady. "Why do you think it's true?"

"Because he bit me a little while ago! And I saw his fangs!"

"I'm sure they were fake."

"They weren't! I know they weren't. I saw blood on them. *My* blood. I'm so afraid!"

"Maybe it was just a gag. Some of those fake fangs are sharp. I'm sure he just nicked your skin by mistake."

"No! I could feel him drinking from me!" Sam exclaimed, and burst into tears again. "And his eyes...his eyes were red!"

Stunned by this revelation, Angie stared at Samantha. What if it *was* true? But that was impossible. There was no such thing.

"It could have been contacts," Angie said, trying to keep her voice calm and rational in the light of Sam's remarks. "Or a trick of the light."

"It wasn't! Why won't you believe me? I know what I saw, what I felt! What am I going to do? He's a vampire. I know he is! You'd know it, too, if you'd seen him!"

Mind whirling, Angie poured Samantha a glass of wine, hoping it would calm her down.

"Thanks," Samantha said, sniffling. She sipped it slowly. Gradually, she seemed to relax a little.

"Maybe you should try to get some sleep?" Angie suggested when Sam's eyelids began to droop.

"Will you stay here with me tonight?" Samantha asked. "I don't want to be alone."

"Sure." Angie followed Sam to her room and tucked her into bed. "I'll see you in the morning."

Once Samantha was asleep, Angie returned to the living room and sank down on the sofa. Maybe Sam had just had a horrible nightmare and when she woke up in the morning, they would both have a good laugh over it.

Needing someone to talk to, Angie called Declan. Had it been anyone else, she would have hesitated to call so late, but the Nightmare stayed open until two. His phone rang several times before he answered.

"Hey, Angie, what are you doing up so late? Is something wrong?"

"You'll think I'm crazy, or Samantha is, but she's convinced that Ian is a vampire." After a long silence, Angie said, "Declan? Are you still there? Did you hear what I said?"

"Yeah."

"I tried to tell her there's no such thing, but she's terrified."

"Are you with her now?"

"Yes. She's asleep. I'm going to spend the night here."

"Do you want me to come over?"

"No, but thanks for offering. Declan..."

"Yeah?"

"You don't think she's right, do you?"

"Hey, you're the one who's doing all the research," he said. "I guess that makes you the expert."

"Right. I'm sorry to bother you at work. I hope I didn't catch you in the middle of anything."

"You didn't. I was just closing up. Give me a call if you need me."

Declan drummed his fingers on the bar top. How many times had he warned Ian of the danger of succumbing to the hunger, warned him that the longer he dated a woman, the harder it would be to hide what he was? He scrubbed his hand over his jaw. Dammit! How could he blame the boy for what had happened when he was fighting the same damn temptation with Angie?

It was early afternoon when Samantha, still wearing her nightgown, shuffled into the living room and slumped down on the sofa beside Angie.

"Are you feeling any better?" Angie asked.

"Not really. But thanks for staying." She fiddled with the hem of her nightgown. "You don't think I'm crazy, do you?"

"Of course not."

"I've been lying in bed telling myself I must have imagined the whole thing, but I just can't shake it off. It wasn't a dream. It really happened. I know it did."

"Maybe it was one of those horrible nightmares that stay with you long after you wake up," Angie suggested. "One that was so vivid you thought it was real. I've had dreams like that."

"Maybe," Samantha agreed, but she didn't sound convinced. "Do you really think a dream could have affected me like that?" She lifted a hand to her neck, then brushed her hair aside. "Do you see any bite marks?"

After a careful look, Angie said, "There's nothing there."

"Maybe it *was* just a nightmare. I mean, if he'd bit me, wouldn't there be a mark of some kind? There's always a tell-tale sign in the movies."

"That's true," Angie agreed, hoping to further reassure Sam that she had imagined the whole thing. She was about to suggest they go out for lunch or order a pizza when her phone buzzed. Smiling, she picked it up and said, "Hi, Declan."

"How's Samantha doing?"

"Feeling a little better, I think."

"I'm glad to hear it. Have you two had lunch?"

"No, I was just thinking about ordering a pizza."

"How about if I pick one up and bring it over?"

"That would be great," she said, and gave him Sam's address.

"Pepperoni okay?" he asked.

"My favorite. See you soon."

"You've been seeing a lot of him, haven't you?" Samantha remarked when the call ended.

"Yeah. He's bringing lunch."

"Oh. I am kind of hungry."

"Why don't you get dressed while I set the table?"

"All right."

Angie blew out a sigh as she watched Samantha shuffle out of the room. *Vampires, indeed.* With a shake of her head, she went into the kitchen. After setting the table, she took a look in the refrigerator where she found a Caesar salad kit and several cans of soda. Good enough for the spur of the moment, she thought.

The doorbell rang twenty minutes later. Angie was about to answer it when Sam called, "I'll get it."

Samantha smiled faintly when she saw Declan in the hallway holding two pizza boxes. "It was nice of you to do this," she said.

"Happy to help," he replied with a wink.

"Well, don't just stand there, come on in. Angie's in the kitchen."

Angie smiled at Declan when he came through the door. "Thanks for bringing lunch," she said as he set the boxes on the countertop. "The cupboard is bare and I don't think Samantha is up to going out."

"No problem."

"Sit down and be comfortable," she invited, gesturing at the table in the corner.

Angie and Sam spent the next few minutes mixing the salad and filling glasses with ice and soda before they joined Declan at the table.

For a moment, no one spoke, and then Samantha said, "Did Angie tell you about... about last night?"

"Yes." Declan's gaze captured and held hers. "It was nothing more than a bad dream, just as Angie said. Do you understand, Samantha? It was only a bad dream. There are no such things as vampires."

"No such thing," Sam murmured. And then she blinked. And smiled. "I feel silly for making such a fuss."

"Dreams can be frightening sometimes," Declan said. "I know I've had more than my share of nightmares."

Angie glanced from Declan to Sam, feeling, once again, that she had missed something.

# CHAPTER TEN

Angie grinned as Declan opened the car door for her. "I was hoping you'd bring this one." Declan had left Samantha's place soon after lunch, but not before he and Angie had arranged to meet at her place later that afternoon.

"Like it, do you?" he asked as he opened the passenger door of the Maserati.

"What's not to like? It's gorgeous! What year is it?"

"Two thousand sixteen. Do you want to drive?"

"Really? You mean it?"

"Go for it." He handed her the key. After settling in the passenger seat, he reached for a pair of sunglasses.

Heart racing, Angie slid behind the wheel, inserted the key in the ignition, and felt a thrill of excitement as the engine purred to life. She glanced over her shoulder and from side to side before backing carefully out of the driveway. Riding in the car had been fun, driving it was exhilarating. She could feel the power beneath the hood just waiting to be unleashed. She had read somewhere that the engine could go zero to sixty in less than five seconds and she believed it.

"So, where are we going?" Declan asked.

"Someplace far away where we can have dessert," she said with a grin.

"Go as far as you want, love. I've got all day." He smiled at her. "And all night."

The thought of driving for hours was tempting, but she was all too aware that this car cost many times more than her Honda. She finally decided on Johnston's because they served the best pie in twenty miles.

Declan laughed when she chose a parking place in the back lot well away from all the other cars. "I'm insured, you know," he said as they walked around to the front of the restaurant.

Angie shrugged. "Better safe than sorry. I couldn't afford to buy the steering wheel on a car like that."

He shook his head, amused and enchanted at the same time.

It was a little too early for dinner, so the crowd was light. The hostess showed them to a table by the window, but Declan asked for a booth in the back. "So," he asked when they were seated, "what's it going to be?"

"Lemon meringue pie. Or maybe some of that," she said when a waitress passed by carrying a slice of twelve-layer chocolate fudge cake.

"Why don't you order the pie," he suggested, removing his sunglasses. "I'll get the cake and we'll share?"

"Now why didn't I think of that?"

"How's Samantha doing?" Declan asked after giving their order to the waitress.

"She seemed fine when I left. Your talk really did the trick. It's almost like she doesn't even remember how scared she was."

He didn't miss the note of suspicion in her voice.

"And, of course, I made sure we didn't talk about it," Angie added quickly. "No sense reminding her."

"Very wise." He glanced up when the waitress arrived with their order.

"Decadent chocolate cake," the woman murmured, a come hither look in her eyes as she smiled at Declan. "And pie for the lady." She sent him one last, sultry look before she left the table, hips swaying provocatively.

"I think she likes you," Angie said dryly.

"What makes you say that?"

"Well, for one thing, it looks like she gave you about half of the cake. And this…" Angie gestured at her own plate, "is the smallest slice of pie I've ever had."

"What can I say?" he asked with a teasing grin. "Some women find me utterly irresistible. What about you?"

Stifling a grin of her own, she said, "What about me?"

"Do you think I'm irresistible?"

"I find you completely resistible," she replied, faking a yawn behind her hand. "Maybe you'd rather take the waitress home?"

"No room in the car." Declan took a bite of cake. He rarely ate sweets, but he would have eaten ten slices just to spend time with Angie. "Do you want a bite?"

"You know I do." The pie was good but the cake looked amazing, layers and layers of chocolate with fudge frosting in-between.

He lifted a forkful and fed it to her.

Angie closed her eyes as she swallowed. "Wow, it tastes even better than it looks."

"Do you want to trade?"

"Would you mind very much?"

"No." He slid his plate across the table and took hers in return.

She savored every bite.

It was all Declan could do not to lean across the table and lick the chocolate from her lips. Watching her, he couldn't help wondering if he would be able to arouse that same expression of utter delight when he made love to her.

Because he meant to have her. Sooner or later.

"After pizza and that enormous pierce of cake, I don't think I'll be needing dinner tonight," Angie remarked as he drove her home. "And maybe not tomorrow night, either."

"Or the night after," he teased.

"I guess I made a pig of myself, but I'm not sorry. Although I probably will be when I get on the scale tomorrow."

Declan laughed.

"It's not funny. Men never seem to worry about gaining weight, do they?"

Declan shrugged. "I don't."

She stuck her tongue out at him. It was a childish thing to do and she immediately regretted it. But he only laughed.

"Do you really want to go home?" he asked.

"Not really, why?"

"I thought we could go for a drive. I know a great place to watch the sun set."

"All right."

Three blocks later, he turned left onto the freeway.

"So, where, exactly, are we going?"

"Up in the hills."

"Oh?" Suddenly filled with trepidation, Angie slid a sideways glance at him. He was handsome. He was polite. He was sexy. But what did she really know about him? Nothing. She told herself she was over-reacting, but fear congealed in her belly. She thought about the Hampton case. The son's alibi had been confirmed by several people and he was no longer a suspect, which meant there was still a killer loose in the city...

Declan swore under his breath as the scent of Angie's unease filled the air. "We can go somewhere else if you'd rather. There's a tavern with a live country band off the next exit if you feel like dancing."

"Let's do that."

A green neon sign announced they had arrived at the Wild Mustang Bar and Grill. Music and raucous laughter drifted out of the building as Declan pulled into the parking lot and tossed his sunglasses on the dash board.

Angie glanced at him. She never would have guessed he'd even know where to find a country bar, it seemed so out of character for him.

Once inside, he surprised her still more when he pulled her onto the dance floor where several other couples were line dancing.

Soon, she was having such a good time, all of her nameless fears were forgotten. They danced and drank imported beer and danced some more until the wee hours of the morning.

Angie was half-asleep when Declan pulled into the driveway and switched off the engine. Handing her out of the car, he walked her to the door. "Do you need me to carry you inside?" he asked with a grin.

She blinked up at him through heavy-lidded eyes. "Would you?"

It was as good as an invitation.

She handed him her key, sighed as he lifted her effortlessly into his arms, opened the door, and carried her across the threshold, just like a knight of the realm in a fairy tale, she thought with a sigh.

He nudged the door shut with his heel, then paused at the arch that led to the hall. "Which way?"

"First door on the right."

It was a large, square room with pale pink walls and white trim. A bookcase was crammed with books, a flowered spread covered the bed, white shutters covered the window.

He lowered her gently to her feet. "Anything else I can do for you, my lady fair?"

"No, thank you, Sir Knight. It was fun."

"For me, too, " Declan murmured, thinking his life had been sorely lacking in fun until he met Angie. He brushed a kiss across her lips. "Good night, love."

"Night."

He left the room and closed the door behind him. Lingering in the hallway, he listened to her undress and brush her teeth, heard the rustle of sheets as she climbed into bed, the soft sound of her breathing as she quickly fell asleep.

She never stirred when he returned to her room and brushed the hair away from her neck. Then, hating himself for the need that drove him, he bit her ever so gently, his eyes closing with pleasure as he sipped the warmth of her life's blood—careful to take only a small taste.

Leaving her house, he locked the front door with a wave of his hand, then, whistling softly, he slid behind the wheel of the Maserati and headed for his lair.

# CHAPTER ELEVEN

Ian hated hunting, hated skulking through the deep shadows of the night searching for prey like some depraved monster out of an old black-and-white horror movie. But he loved the blood—the salty metallic taste of it on his tongue, the warmth of it sliding smoothly down his throat. He reveled in the tantalizing smell of it. The color, the texture.

He quickened his pace when he caught the scent of prey, caught the woman unawares when she paused to look in a store window. Ian glanced around. Seeing there was no one else nearby, he wrapped her in his arms, his mind overpowering hers, weakening her resistance until she stood pliant in his embrace. He bent his head to her throat and drank, knowing that anyone passing by would think he was merely kissing her neck.

Only the memory of Declan's wrath—and his recent, frightening encounter with Samantha—kept him from taking too much.

With a sigh of resignation, he ran his tongue over the two tiny puncture wounds to seal them. By tomorrow, they would be gone.

A word sent the woman on her way, the whole experience wiped from her memory.

Whistling softly, he pulled out his cell phone and checked the time, then called Samantha to see if she was home. Thanks to Declan, Sam believed what happened the last time they had been together had been a dream.

And he had two hours to kill before he had to be at the Nightmare

# CHAPTER TWELVE

A ngie woke with a smile on her lips, silently chiding herself for her foolish fears about Declan the night before.

Swinging her legs over the edge of the mattress, she padded into the bathroom to wash her face then scuffed into the kitchen. She was famished, but no doubt that was to be expected. She hadn't had dinner last night, although she had pigged out on pizza at Sam's, devoured an enormous slice of the best chocolate fudge cake on the planet at Johnston's, and put away several bottles of beer at the Wild Mustang Bar and Grill.

After a big breakfast, she shuffled into her office to read her email. First up was a note from Jennifer saying she loved the column Angie had written for October and asking if she had thought of maybe doing a series on the paranormal. Angie grinned. She had, indeed.

There was a fan letter from a lady who had read Angie's last column and said it was her best one yet, and another from a reader who wanted a photo and an autograph, and one from a wanna-be writer asking for advice on how to get started.

After answering her reader mail, she deleted the spam and her old mail, then showered and dressed. She had neglected cleaning the house all week. It was past time to

dust and vacuum and do the laundry. But she didn't mind.
It would help pass the time until she saw Declan again.

Declan rarely fed in the same city where he kept his lair,
but tonight he'd made an exception when a lovely young
woman crossed his path. He took what little he needed and
sent her on her way. He was about to head for the Nightmare
when the wind kicked up, carrying with it the scent of fresh
blood. And vampire.

Conor.

It took only a moment to follow the scents to a large
house located in the hills above the city. He got there just
as Conor threw the body of a middle-aged woman into
the swimming pool. Declan was about to go in after her
when he realized it was too late. A bright crimson stain
spread across the surface of the water as the body sank to
the bottom.

"So, we meet again, brother mine," Conor drawled.

For a moment, their gazes met and held across the
length of the pool.

Hands clenched, Declan growled, "What the hell are
you doing in my town?"

"I should think that would be obvious," Conor replied,
glancing at the red tint spreading across the water. And
then he shrugged. "Actually, I got bored with Italy, but I
can see you're not bored," he said with a wolfish grin. "You
always did have good taste in women."

"Touch her and I'll destroy you."

Conor snorted. "You'll try."

"I want you to stop killing in my territory. In fact, I want
you to get the hell out of here."

"Yeah? I want a lot of things, too," his brother retorted. "Like that pretty little female." And with a cavalier wave of his hand, he vanished from sight

Declan muttered an oath as he sent a last glance at the dead woman. Dammit! Sooner or later, the police or, worse, some hunter, would figure out that there was a rogue vampire behind the killings in the city.

And when that happened, the proverbial shit would hit the fan.

Angie grinned as she listened to Sam go on and on about how terrific Ian was, how funny, how sweet, and wondered if that was how she sounded when she talked about Declan. They had been on the phone for almost an hour when Samantha suggested they get together for another double date.

"Sure, sounds like fun. What day did you have in … Sam, hold on a minute." Angie turned up the volume on the TV show she'd been watching when a reporter broke in with breaking news.

"Hey, Angie, are you still there?"

"There's been another murder," she said. "Some guy on the news just mentioned that this latest killing is eerily similar to the Hampton murder."

"What? Who? When?"

"They think it happened earlier tonight. The husband came home from work and found the body in the swimming pool when he let the dog out. They haven't released the name of the victim yet."

"Sounds like there's a serial killer loose in the city," Samantha said. "Geez, I hope Grumpy doesn't catch this case, too. I've already got more work that I can handle.

Listen, I'll talk to you tomorrow. I'm going to go make sure all my doors and windows are closed and locked."

"I think we're safe," Angie said, hoping to lighten the mood. "Neither one of us has a pool."

Still, after saying goodbye, she followed Sam's example and wandered through the house, making sure everything was closed and locked and the drapes drawn. She was surprised when she glanced at the clock. It was almost eight. Declan usually called before now...

The thought had no soon crossed her mind than her phone rang. Smiling, she picked it up. "Hi, Declan."

"Are you busy?"

"Not really."

"Okay if I come over?"

Her gaze darted around the room. Thank goodness she had cleaned the house earlier. "Sure."

"Have you had dinner?"

"Not yet. I kind of forgot about it."

"Would you like to go out?"

"Okay, but no place fancy. I don't feel like getting dressed up."

"Works for me. I'm in jeans and a tee shirt."

"Perfect. I'll be ready when you get here."

Angie took a last look in the mirror when the doorbell rang. She had changed into her favorite skinny jeans and a casual shirt. She ran a hand over her hair, freshened her lipstick and ran to answer the door. "Hi!"

He whistled softly. "Hi, yourself. I thought we weren't dressing up?"

"This old thing?"

He grinned as he drew her into his arms. "You'd look good in a burlap bag."

"So would you." He looked as gorgeous as always in what she'd come to think of as his uniform—jeans and a black leather jacket worn over a tee shirt. This one was the same shade of green as his eyes.

"Where would you like to go?" he asked, still holding her close.

"How do you feel about Italian?"

"Moretti's okay with you?"

"It's the best," she said, smiling.

Angie ordered spaghetti alfredo, Declan opted for meatloaf with Italian sausage, and a bottle of the house wine.

Angie sighed as she took the last bite of a breadstick still warm from the oven. "So, I guess you slept the day away," she remarked.

"Pretty much."

"I don't know how you keep those hours."

He shrugged. "You get used to it."

"I guess."

The waitress arrived with their dinner a short time later. Angie was about to comment on the wine when Declan's cell phone rang.

Angie watched his face harden as he listened to the call. It definitely wasn't good news.

"I'll be there in five minutes," he said tersely and slid the phone into his jacket pocket. "Angie, I've got to go. Stay and enjoy your dinner. Have dessert. I'll call you later." He reached into his pocket and withdrew a hundred dollar bill. "This will cover dinner and a cab to get you home."

Before she could ask what was going on, he was striding out of the restaurant.

Angie stared after him. She had never seen him look so angry. Or so frightening.

Declan knelt beside Samantha. She lay on her back on the bed in Ian's apartment, her face deathly pale, her heartbeat barely audible. Ian stood beside the bed looking almost as pale. Declan didn't have to ask what had happened. The evidence was right before his eyes. Sam was naked beneath the sheet. Ian had pulled on his briefs. They had been making love when the hunger had overcome Ian's desire. He had bitten Samantha, got lost in the ecstasy of feeding, and hadn't stopped in time.

"What do you want to do?" Declan asked.

"Do?"

"You've got two choices. You can either turn her or let her die."

Ian stared at him, brown eyes wide with horror. "I...but...I...can't *you* do something?"

"This isn't my problem," Declan said flatly. "It's yours. Now you have to live with the consequences."

"I can't be her sire! I wouldn't know how."

"You've got about two minutes to make up your mind."

"Can't you do it?" Ian asked, a note of desperation in his voice.

"Samantha's not my responsibility," Declan said. Though if Ian refused to do what had to be done, he would turn Angie's best friend rather than watch her die. "She's yours."

"I can't let her go like this! I love her!"

"All right. Calm down. I'll walk you through it."

Angie glanced at her phone yet again. She had taken a cab home hours ago. What was taking Declan so long to call? She'd been so worried, she had called him a few minutes ago, but her call had gone straight to voice mail so she'd left a message. What on earth could have happened to make him leave the restaurant like that?

At midnight, she took a quick shower, changed into her PJs, and curled up the sofa, her phone beside her.

But he didn't call.

Ian looked up at Declan. "Is she going to be okay?"

Declan nodded. "You did just fine. She'll sleep through the rest of the night and all day tomorrow. When she wakes up tomorrow night, she'll be confused, maybe frightened. And hungry as hell. She'll need to feed right away."

Ian grunted softly. "When I take her hunting, will you go with us?"

"Sure, if that's what you want."

Ian shifted from one foot to the other. "I never meant for this to happen. I thought I had everything under control."

"It gets easier as you get older. You were lucky this time."

"Lucky?" Ian snorted. "She's going to hate me now," he muttered. "First woman I've ever really loved and I've ruined her life." He looked up at Declan, his eyes haunted. "Did I make the right decision? Should I have let her die?"

"That's always a hard call. Some people take to being turned like a duck to water. Some are miserable for the rest of their existence."

"How was it for you?"

"It took me a long time to accept it," Declan said with a shrug. "My brother embraced it wholeheartedly."

Ian's brows shot up. "Brother?"

"Yeah. We were turned at the same time by a vampire and his mate."

"That's ... hell, I don't know what that is. Where's your brother now?"

"Here, in the city somewhere. He's the one behind the recent murders."

Ian stared at him.

"I can sense his presence now and then, but I can't track him. There's no blood link between us."

"Are you close?"

"We were. Until Conor took it into his head to make our mother one of us. He didn't discuss it with me. He didn't bother to ask her if it was what she wanted. He just decided to do it. The hell of it is, he didn't know what the devil he was doing and she died in my arms. I've never forgiven him for that. And I never will. He went rogue soon after that, killing indiscriminately." Declan paused, his hands clenching until the knuckles went white. "He has to be stopped and I'm the only one who can do it."

"I don't know what to say."

"You don't have to say anything. It happened centuries ago." Declan blew out a sigh. "I'm going home. Call me when she wakes up."

"I will. Thanks for everything. Declan?"

"Yeah?"

"Would you be human again, if you could?"

"No. I'll talk to you tomorrow night."

# CHAPTER THIRTEEN

Conor prowled the dark streets of his brother's territory. It gave him a sense of power, knowing that even though he and Declan were brothers, Declan couldn't track him because they had been turned by two different vampires. Hard to believe it had been so many centuries ago. Declan had taken the transition hard. He supposed he couldn't blame his brother for that, seeing as how Declan had lost his wife and four children during the vampires' attack on their village. He had raged against what they had become for over a year, refusing to feed until the pain grew so agonizing that he could no longer fight it.

Conor snorted with the memory. Once the shock of what had happened faded, he'd found himself wishing he had been turned sooner. He loved the strength, the supernatural power, the sense of being indomitable. And the blood...the warm, sweet, coppery taste of it on his tongue, sliding down his throat, the stark terror in the eyes of his victims, the thrill of the hunt, the unbelievable sensation of taking another life, feeling his prey grow weak, weaker, as he drained the life out of them.

He had never understood his older brother's horror, his reluctance to revel in the unequaled power that was now theirs. Nothing was beyond them. Mortality no longer held them fast in its embrace. The laws of mankind no longer applied to them.

He had hoped they would travel the world together. And they had, for a time. Until they returned home to visit their parents, only to learn that their father had been killed the year before by invaders and their mother was sick in bed with a fever.

In that instance, Conor had known he wasn't ready to lose his mother. As much as he loved being a vampire, a small part of his identity remained bound to her, reminding him that he had once been human. He hadn't asked for his brother's advice or approval, hadn't discussed his plan to save her. He had been so certain that turning their mother was the right thing to do, so certain he could do it. In his zeal to save her life, he had taken too much, and then, at the thought of facing Declan, he had panicked.

Declan had arrived moments before her last breath. She had died in his brother's arms, taking Conor's last tie to humanity with her.

After one look at the outrage in his brother's eyes, Conor had fled for his life.

The two of them had played a game of cat-and-mouse for a few centuries, with Conor always managing to elude his brother at the last minute. And then, for reasons unknown, Declan had stopped pursuing him.

Fool that he was, Conor missed the game, missed that brief contact with his only remaining kin. Worse, he had grown bored with his existence.

And so he had tracked his brother down, even though he knew that, given the chance, Declan would destroy him without a qualm.

# CHAPTER FOURTEEN

Angie's thoughts were troubled as she cooked up a late breakfast. Had she said or done something to make Declan leave the restaurant so abruptly last night? She didn't think so. Everything had been fine until he got that phone call. It must have been bad news. There was no other explanation. And then she frowned. Or was there? Maybe it had been a call from an old girlfriend.

Or a wife.

She shook the thought aside. She had asked about his marital state early on. Of course, he might have been lying when he said he was single. Lots of men betrayed their marriage vows these days. Still, he could have at least called to tell her what happened or to apologize for leaving like that, or at least to let her know he was all right. Then again, they had only been seeing each other a short time. He didn't owe her any explanations. But a logical reason for his abrupt departure or an apology would have been nice.

Feeling frustrated, Angie called Sam, but there was no answer.

With a sigh of exasperation, she went into her office and booted up her computer, only to sit there staring at the blank screen, too upset to write.

Declan rose earlier than usual, his first thought for Angie. He had meant to call her last night, but it had been well past midnight when he finally left Ian's. Rolling onto his side, he grabbed his phone. "Hey, Angie," he said when she picked up. "It's me."

"Hi." She felt a rush of relief when she heard his voice. "Are you all right?"

"I'm fine." He paused. Then, hating to lie to her, he said, "I'm sorry about last night. There was some trouble at the Nightmare and by the time it was over, it was too late to call."

"What kind of trouble?"

"Some guy pulled a gun and tried to hold us up," he said, making it up as he went along. "By the time the cops came and questioned everyone and hauled the guy away, it was well after midnight."

"Was anyone hurt?"

"No."

"Next time, call me, okay? I don't care what time it is."

"Will do. I didn't mean to worry you. Listen, I've got some business to take care of at the Nightmare this evening. I'm not sure how long it will take, but I'll get in touch with you when I'm finished."

"All right. Bye for now." Angie smiled as the call ended, glad that all her worries had been for nothing.

As an old vampire, Declan was able to rise long before the sun went down. Being able to endure the light of day had happened gradually over the last century. At first, he'd been hesitant to leave his lair when the sun was shining. Now he took it for granted, grateful that he no longer had to come up with reasons to avoid daytime commitments. Being able to consume human food was another advantage of having existed for such a long time. Never had he appreciated it more than now, when he no longer had to make excuses for why he couldn't attend a dinner or meet Angie for lunch. It didn't matter that the food had little taste, or that he had no real appetite or desire for it. It was enough that he could share a meal with Angie.

Given a choice, he would rather spend the evening with her instead of introducing a new vampire to the ways of the Undead, but leaving that task to Ian was out of the question. Fledgling vampires were remarkably unstable and sometimes hard to control. Most of the time, Ian seemed to be handling it better than most. At least until last night. But leaving Ian to guide Sam was like the blind leading the blind. They were both going to fall into a ditch.

Declan had often wondered who sired Ian, but the boy didn't know anything except that the one who'd turned him had been a female who appeared to be in her late forties. For reasons unknown, the vampire had turned him and fled.

Declan had found Ian roaming the city a few days after he'd been turned, half-mad with hunger and with no idea of what had happened to him. Although Declan wasn't Ian's sire, the boy was in his territory and he'd felt responsible for him.

Declan materialized in Ian's lair a few minutes after sunset. Ian and Samantha were lying side-by-side in bed, still at rest.

Ian woke first, with a start. He glanced around the bedroom, his eyes wild, until he realized where he was.

Declan remembered what that was like. On waking from the dark sleep as a new vampire, he had often forgotten what and where he was.

"Hey," Ian said when he saw Declan. "Thanks for coming."

"I said I would."

"I know, but..." Ian shrugged, then glanced at Samantha. She bolted upright with an incoherent cry, her eyes filled with fear and confusion, her whole body tense until she saw Ian.

"Hey, honey, how ya doing?" he asked.

"Oh, Ian," Samantha murmured. "I had the most dreadful nightmare." She frowned when she noticed Declan standing by the door. Brow furrowed, she whispered, "What's he doing here?" before she doubled over, her hands clutching her stomach.

Overcome with guilt, Ian could only stare at her.

"Ian! What's wrong with me?"

He looked up at Declan.

"Just tell her," he said flatly.

Ian took a deep breath, then slipped his arm around Samantha's shoulders. "I don't know exactly how to tell you this, honey, but I'm not like any of the other guys you've dated."

"I know." She tried to smile at him and failed. "That's why I love you."

Ian glanced at Declan again, then cleared his throat. "I had a life-altering experience a few months back. It changed me, made me different from other people."

She stared at him blankly. "What are you talking about?"

"I know I should have told you sooner, but... well... I was afraid of losing you. The thing is... Dammit, Sam, I'm a vampire."

"Ian, just stop it! If you're trying to break up with me, just say so. You don't have to invent some bizarre story."

"It's true! Last night while we were making love, I...I bit you."

"I remember that," Samantha said, frowning.

"Yeah, well." Ian paused, took a deep breath, and blurted the rest. "The thing is, I couldn't stop drinking from you and I took too much and you almost died and I called Declan for help and he said if I didn't turn you, you'd die and I couldn't let that happen, so..." He took another deep breath. "I turned you into a vampire. That awful pain you're feeling means you need to feed," he finished lamely.

For a moment, Samantha stared at him in stunned disbelief. She started to push him away, and then she lunged at him and buried her fangs in his throat.

Ian let out a shriek.

In a blur of movement, Declan grabbed Samantha, pulled her off the boy, and wrapped his arms around her chest, holding her body tight to his. "Stop it, Sam."

She looked up at him, her eyes blood-red and confused, her fangs dripping with the kid's blood.

"Calm down," Declan said, his voice low and soothing, the force of his gaze overpowering her urge to resist. "There's nothing to be afraid of."

"What's wrong with me?" she asked woodenly.

"Ian told you. You're a vampire now. You'll sleep by day and hunt by night. Ian and I will take you out and show you how to find prey and how to feed. Do you understand?"

Samantha stared at him for a moment, her eyes filled with confusion and denial. And then his words registered and she began to cry, great gulping sobs that shook her whole body.

Declan stroked her hair. "Hush, now," he murmured. "It's not as bad as you think."

Samantha stared at Ian as tears trailed down her cheeks. "How could you do such a thing to me?" she wailed softly. "I thought you loved me."

Still sitting on the mattress, Ian said, "I do love you, Sam. You have to believe that."

"So you turned me into a monster?"

"You're not a monster," Declan said, releasing his hold on her. "You're still Samantha." It was mostly true.

"What will I tell my parents? My boss? I'll have to quit my job! How will I pay my bills? Where will I live...?" She cried out, her hands clenching as pain ripped through her. "Someone make it stop!"

"Ian, let's go," Declan said. "You can tell Sam everything she needs to know later. Right now, she's in no condition to hear it. And she needs to feed. It will calm her down."

It was almost eleven by the time Declan took his leave from Ian and Sam. She was still dazed, still in denial, even after feeding, but he was reasonably sure she would be all right once she accepted what had happened to her. At least he hoped so, for her sake. And for Ian's.

Sliding behind the wheel of the Jag, he called Angie.

"Hi," she said cheerfully. "Did you get your business taken care of?"

"For now. Is it too late to come over?"

"I'm game if you are."

Declan smothered a laugh. She had no idea how true that was. "I'll be there ten minutes."

Angie called Samantha again while waiting for Declan, but there was still no answer. Something was wrong, she thought as she dropped her cell phone on the table beside the sofa. She had never known Sam to ignore a call or a text message. Maybe she had lost her phone. Or the battery was dead. Or…

Angie shook off the morbid thoughts that tumbled through her mind. No doubt there was a simple, logical explanation.

But she couldn't stop worrying.

Declan had no sooner crossed the threshold and said hello when Angie voiced her concern. "I've called Sam a dozen times since yesterday and left half a dozen text messages and she still hasn't answered. I just know something's wrong. Can you call Ian and see if he knows anything?"

Damn! He should have seen this coming. Thinking fast, he said, "She's with him. They decided to go away together for a few days. No phones, no TV, just the two of them."

Angie stared at him. "She wouldn't do that without telling me. And what about her job? Her boss is in the middle of that high-profile murder case. There's no way he would let her take a vacation now."

"She was fired but she didn't want to tell you. Ian thought a few days away might cheer her up." Damn, he hated lying to Angie, but what else could he do? He could hardly tell her the truth. Seeing the disbelief in her eyes, he spoke to her mind, wiping away her doubts.

"Well, in a way I'm glad Grumpy fired her," Angie said. "Even though the money was good, he was a real slave-driver. I hope she has a good time with Ian. Do you think they'll get married?"

"It wouldn't surprise me," Declan muttered. "They have a lot in common."

After leaving Angie's place, Declan drove to the Nightmare, only to sit in his car, his thoughts turned inward. He hadn't thought of Mihaela more than three or four times in over a century, but Angie's remark about marriage stirred old memories. He rarely let himself think of his past. Once he'd accepted what he was, he had shut the door on that part of his life. Remembering was too painful and served no purpose. But tonight the floodgates were open.

Mihaela had lived in the town where he'd been born—a nameless little village high in the hills of Transylvania. They had grown up together—Conor, Declan and Mihaela. As they grew older, what he felt for Mihaela had grown deeper, stronger. Conor, too, had fallen in love with her. It had caused a breach between himself and Conor as they both vied for her affection.

One night, Conor had demanded that they fight for her. Whoever won would claim the prize. Declan had refused but day after day Conor insisted. In the end, they agreed to meet in the hills after dark.

It had been a bloody battle, but before either could claim the victory, Mihaela arrived and put an end to the fight, declaring her love for Declan. He had married Mihaela six months later. There had been bad blood between himself and his brother ever since.

In their poor village, there were few occasions for merriment other than marriages and births. They had wed in the morning one fine day in spring. Conor had not attended the wedding. The celebration had lasted far into the wee hours of the night, with most of the villagers in attendance. It had been the happiest day of his life.

They hadn't had much in the way of material possessions, but life had been good and they had been desperately in love. She had blessed him with three fine sons and a daughter. The years passed by swiftly, years filled with sacrifice and struggle that drew the two of them closer together.

He had been dancing with Mihaela on the night of their oldest son's wedding when the vampires came. Only two of them, but they had slaughtered the guests like wolves hunting lambs. The men of the village had fought bravely, but their knives and scythes were puny weapons against razor sharp fangs and elongated nails that resembled claws. Mihaela and the women had grabbed their children and run for the hills, but the carnage had been devastating.

He and Conor had fought as long as they were able. He had always wondered why the vampires had chosen to turn them rather than kill them, like the others. There had been times soon after he'd been turned when he'd thought death would have been preferable. A handful of villagers had survived the slaughter, their mother among them. His wife and children had all been slain.

A year after they'd been turned, Conor had tried, unsuccessfully, to transform their mother. Declan would never forget holding her in his arms, watching the flicker of life fade from her eyes while Conor ran away. He had held her until her body grew cold and then he buried her beside his father and his family. Standing at her graveside, he had vowed to destroy his brother if it was the last thing he ever did. That had been almost eight centuries ago. For a time, he had spent every waking hour searching for Conor. He had found him from time to time, but Conor had always managed to elude him. Gradually, his lust for his brother's blood had cooled.

But now Conor was here, in the city, stirring old memories, reviving old hurts. Perhaps the time had finally come to avenge his mother's death.

# CHAPTER FIFTEEN

After breakfast, Angie sat in front of her computer and opened her email. The first was from her editor, Jennifer, saying she loved the vampire column and had approved it for the October issue of the magazine. Most of the other email was spam, which she quickly deleted.

Sitting back in her chair, Angie sipped her coffee and thought about Samantha. Why had Grumpy fired her so soon after giving her a raise? It just didn't make sense. And neither did Samantha going off with Ian without saying a word about it. It just wasn't like her. They had always shared everything—hopes and dreams, tears and laughter, good news and bad.

It just wasn't like Sam to keep a secret from her.

Shaking off her troubled thoughts, Angie opened a new document, then sat staring at the blank screen. Writing about vampires had been fun, even educational. Of course, Halloween was really the only holiday where writing about supernatural creatures seemed appropriate. Wasn't it?

Curious, she switched over to Google and looked up Christmas monsters. To her surprise, there were several, like Gryla, who kidnapped misbehaving children and cooked them in a stew. And Krampus, half-goat, half-demon, with shaggy fur, horns, fangs, and a long, black tongue. He had become a very popular character in recent years. There had even been a movie about him—aptly named "Krampus"—a few years ago. But it was Perchta, also known as Berchta or Bertha, who sparked Angie's interest.

She sat at the computer doing research and making notes until her neck started to ache and her stomach growled.

Saving her work, she stood and stretched her back and shoulders before stuffing a load of clothes in the washer. When that was done, she went in search of something to fix for lunch.

It was after three when she finished cleaning the kitchen. Deciding to take a break from writing, she tossed her clothes in the dryer, then curled up on the sofa in front of the TV and watched a couple of recent episodes of *Blue Bloods* on Netflix. She loved Tom Selleck, but her favorite character was Danny Reagan, played by Donnie Wahlberg. She was halfway through the third episode when she fell asleep.

The incessant buzzing of her cell phone dragged Angie out of the dream she'd been having about Declan—a wonderfully romantic dream she hated to see end. She frowned at the unfamiliar number, but something compelled her to answer it anyway. "Hello?"

"Angie!"

"Sam. Hi. How are—?"

"Are you alone?"

"Yes, but—"

"Can I come over?"

"Of course. Is something wrong? Sam? Sam, are you still there?" Angie stared at her phone, wondering what the devil was going on, when the doorbell rang.

Darkness had fallen while she slept and she flicked on the outside light. To her surprise, she found Samantha standing on the porch, eyes swollen, hair disheveled. Angie frowned as her gaze swept the curb. There was no sign of Sam's Prius. How had she gotten here so fast?

"Angie," Sam murmured, and burst into tears—tears that looked faintly red in the porch light.

"Sam, what's wrong? Is it Ian?"

"Is it okay if I come in?"

Angie hesitated a moment. What an odd question, she thought. Sam had been here a hundred times and had never asked permission before. Warning bells sounded in her head. Something was wrong. Sam looked the same, yet different somehow. Not quite herself. Was she sick? On drugs?

"Ange?"

Unable to think of a logical reason to say no, Angie said, "Well, sure." She took a step back and felt a peculiar tremor in the air as her friend crossed the threshold. She had felt that same thing before, Angie thought absently, but there was no time to wonder about it now. "Can I get you anything? A coke? Coffee? Aspirin?"

"No."

Angie gestured at the sofa. "Why don't you sit down and tell me what's wrong? I thought you'd gone away with Ian."

Samantha didn't move, just stood there staring at her, nostrils flaring. "You smell so good."

Angie frowned, thinking it was an odd thing for Sam to notice when she seemed so upset. "How was your trip?"

"My trip?"

"With Ian. Where did you go?"

"Go?" Samantha blinked at her, then licked her lips.

A shiver of alarm skated down Angie's spine. Something was definitely wrong. She wondered again if Sam was on drugs.

"You're my friend, aren't you?" Sam took a step forward. "You'd do anything for me, wouldn't you?"

"Well, almost anything, you know that," Angie said, taking a wary step backward.

"I won't hurt you."

Angie backed up another step, only to come up short as she bumped into the arm of the couch. "Sam, what's going on?"

"You wouldn't believe me if I told you." Samantha licked her lips again as her eyes again took on that faintly red glow. "Or maybe you would."

The world seemed to stand still for stretched seconds and then the front door flew open and Declan was suddenly standing beside Samantha, his hand gripping her arm.

"Let me go!" Sam shrieked. "I'm so hungry!"

Angie glanced from Declan to Sam and back again. "What's wrong with her?" she asked, refusing to believe the evidence of her own eyes.

"I need to get her out of here," he said curtly. "We can talk about it later."

"Let me go!" Samantha wailed. "The scent of her blood is driving me crazy. Ian won't let me drink as much as I want. But Angie will. She's my friend."

Angie went cold all over as she stared at her best friend. Sam's eyes were definitely red now. She was panting as if she had just finished a marathon, her lips drawn back in a feral snarl to reveal her ... fangs.

Angie looked at Declan. "Is she ... she can't be ... there's no such thing."

"I need to get her out of here," he said again. "I'll explain everything later."

Angie watched, numb with shock, as Declan wrestled a wild-eyed Samantha out of the house. What on earth was going on?

Taking a deep breath, she closed the door, turned the lock, slid the deadbolt in place.

And burst into tears. Was it possible? Could it be, that her best friend in the world was now a vampire?

Declan muttered a vile oath when he hauled Samantha into Ian's lair and found the boy sitting on the sofa, his head cradled in his hands. Dried blood matted his hair and stained his shirt collar. He glanced up, relief clearly written on his face when he saw Samantha.

"What the hell happened?" Declan growled. "She was out of control." He had used his preternatural powers to restrain Sam, who now stood placid beside him, her expression blank.

"She bit me and when I tried to push her away, she grabbed the fireplace poker and bashed me over the head. Knocked me out cold. When I came to, she was gone. I knew where she was, but…" He spread his hands in a gesture of defeat. "I was about to go after her when I sensed where she was and that you were already there, so…" He shrugged. "I knew Sam was in good hands and that you'd be able to explain things to Angie a lot better than I could." Ian took a deep breath. "Does Angie know about me now? And you?"

"Right now, she doesn't know anything. But after all the research she's done, it won't take her long to put two and two together and get vampire. But at the moment, that's the least of our worries."

"Yeah." Ian looked at Samantha, his expression worried. She had been completely out of control, that was for damn sure. And even though he was her sire, he was still a fledgling, not fully in control of his own hunger. He quietly cursed the vampire who had turned him and abandoned him. The first couple of days after he'd been turned had been hell. He'd been like a wild animal, lusting for blood, not caring who he hurt, wanting only to satisfy the awful hunger that had plagued his every waking moment. And then Declan, a master vampire, had found him and taught him everything he needed to know. Declan had been endlessly patient and forgiving and for that, Ian was eternally in his debt.

Taking a deep breath, Ian said, "What are we going to do about Sam?"

Declan shook his head. "Damned if I know." If it had been anyone but Angie's best friend, he would have destroyed Samantha then and there. Some people didn't react well to being turned and he was afraid Sam was one of them. Unless he was mistaken, she would have to be carefully watched to keep her under control. Tugging her by the hand, he took her into the bedroom and compelled her to rest until the following night.

"What'll I do when she wakes up?"

Declan glanced over his shoulder to see Ian standing in the doorway.

"Call me if you need me. Right now I have to get in touch with Angie. Tonight, you go find yourself a pair of sturdy gloves to protect your hands, then find a thick silver chain and bind Sam to the bed frame. That'll keep her from attacking you again, or running off until we decide what to do."

Ian nodded. Crossing to the bed, he brushed a lock of hair behind Sam's ear. "I'm sorry, sweetheart," he murmured, his voice thick with regret. "So damn sorry."

Declan sat in his car outside Angie's house, cell phone in hand, wondering what the hell he could say, how he could explain about Samantha without revealing the truth about himself.

Through the shutters at the front window, he could see her pacing the living room floor, her brow furrowed, her cheeks damp with tears.

Dammit! Conor was in the city. There were two new hunters sniffing around the Nightmare. Sam was running amuck. Ian was on shaky ground. What the hell else could go wrong?

Taking a deep breath, he called Angie. He closed his eyes when he heard her voice.

"Declan, what's going on?"

"Sam's been infected with a rare virus that has compromised her immune system and made her temporarily irrational. I've sent her to a facility where she'll be cared for. Ian's gone with her."

Angie was silent a moment before saying, "I don't believe you. She had fangs. And her eyes were red. And she wanted my blood. That doesn't sound like a virus to me."

"No?" Dammit, he'd been afraid she wouldn't believe him. "What does it sound like?"

"Like … like she's a vampire."

*Vampire.* The word hung between them like an ax ready to fall.

"It's true, isn't it?" Angie asked, her voice thick with unshed tears.

Declan swore under his breath. Should he confirm her suspicions? Or go inside and wipe everything that had happened earlier tonight from her mind? He could make her forget all of it. Make her forget she ever knew Samantha and Ian. It was the easiest solution and the best one for everyone concerned.

But was it the right one?

"Declan?"

"I need to see you. I'll be there in a few minutes."

Sitting on the sofa, Angie pulled a fuzzy throw over her legs and stared at the wall, her thoughts in turmoil. She didn't believe in vampires, yet she had no doubt that Sam had been turned. She'd seen the evidence with her own eyes. Asking for an invitation to come into the house even though she had been here a hundred times before. The hellish red glow in her eyes. The fangs. Wanting blood. Thank the Lord Declan had arrived when he had.

Declan. She went cold all over as a new, unwelcome thought surged to the front of her mind.

How had Declan known where to find Sam?

# Chapter Sixteen

Apprehension skittered down Angie's spine when the doorbell rang. She hesitated a moment before she opened the door to let Declan in. "What's going on?" she asked as she padded back into the living room.

"Sit down and I'll try to explain."

Angie took a seat in the chair and not on the sofa, a move that wasn't lost on Declan. She obviously meant to keep some distance between them. Tension radiated from her like heat from a forest fire. "Well?"

He decided on the truth. "As you suspected, Samantha was turned by a vampire."

Even though she had known it was true, hearing it put into words made it all the more real. And somehow more terrible. "Why did you tell me she'd gone away with Ian? How did you know what happened to her? How did you even know she was here?"

All good questions, he mused. "Ian told me."

"Ian?"

"He's the vampire who transformed her."

"So Samantha was right about him," Angie muttered, and then she frowned. "You knew he was a vampire and yet you hired him? Why would you do that?"

Damn. "He was good for business. A few of my regulars get a kick out of letting a real vampire feed on them."

"That's sick and disgusting!"

"Maybe so. But he's a nice kid."

"Nice! Nice! He turned my best friend into a blood-thirsty monster! Why didn't you warn Sam before it was too late?"

"I thought Ian had things under control."

"Well, you were wrong, weren't you? And now my friend is paying the price. What's going to happen to her?"

Another good question, he thought ruefully. "Ian will look after her."

"Right," she snapped. "He's done a hell of a fine job so far."

"Angie, listen..."

"No." Tears welled in her eyes. "I've lost my best friend and it's all your fault."

"She'll be all right, once she adjusts to what's happened," he said, and hoped it was true—although after tonight, he wasn't so sure. "It just takes time."

"How do you know?"

She had finally asked the question he didn't want to answer. He paced the floor in front of the sofa, hands clenched at his sides. Should he tell her the truth about this, too? He had no doubt what her reaction would be, especially now when she had seen her best friend at her worst, when Sam was angry and confused and half-crazy with thirst. When she blamed him for what had happened to Samantha. And why shouldn't she? Hell, maybe he *was* to blame.

Angie watched his every move, her eyes narrowed, cheeks damp with tears.

Dammit, he loved her as he had never loved anyone else. And because of that, he owed her the truth, no matter the consequences. And perhaps it was for the best. Tempting as she was, he feared it was only a matter of time before he made the same mistake as Ian and had to make the same life-altering decision. "Because I'm one of them."

She fought back a wave of hysterical laughter. Be careful what you wish for, she thought. She had wanted to find a vampire and now one stood before her.

Refusing to believe it, she said, "It can't be true! I've seen you during the day. I watched you eat." Yet even as she shook her head in denial, Angie knew it was true. Lifting a hand to her neck, she stared at him. "Did you … have you ever …?"

"Yes."

She recalled the nights when her memories seemed fragmented, the times she'd felt light-headed and he had insisted she have something to drink, to rest. It was because he'd taken her blood. Still reluctant to believe, she said, "But there were no marks."

He shrugged. "There are ways to make them disappear."

A fresh wave of tears spilled down her cheeks. "Go away. I never want to see you again."

He nodded, hands clenched at his sides to keep from reaching for her, from going down on his knees to beg her forgiveness. "If you ever need me …"

"I won't. Please, just go."

He longed to take her in his arms one last time, taste her sweet lips, tell her he loved her, would always love her.

Instead, he turned and headed for the door.

Angie stared after him, her heart filled with pain and anger and confusion. How could she have fallen in love with a vampire? He seemed so normal and yet … she remembered telling Sam there was something off about him.

Samantha. A vampire. It was incredible. Impossible. And yet it was all too true. How could Declan have been so

115

uncaring as to let her friend date a vampire? He must have known something like this could happen...

The thought sent an icy chill down her spine.

It could have happened to her.

Feeling suddenly helpless and vulnerable, Angie hurried from room to room, locking the doors and windows, closing the shutters. She needed a sharp stake. Some holy water. Garlic...

Returning to the living room, she collapsed on the sofa and cried until there were no tears left. She had lost her best friend and the man she loved all in one night and it was more than she could bear.

Declan stalked the night like the angel of death. For the first time in centuries, he hated what he was. He raged at fate for letting him find Angie, only to lose her. He never should have let himself fall in love with her. He had known from the beginning that it wouldn't end well, but he hadn't been able to stay away. Her sweet spirit had filled him with a kind of peace he hadn't known since he was turned. With Angie, he hadn't felt like a monster. He had taken her out to dinner and the movies, held her in his arms when they danced, and pretended he was just like any other man. Of all the lies he had told himself through the centuries, that one had been the biggest of them all.

As he prowled the dark streets, his rage grew, fueling his hunger. He preyed on the first lone woman he saw. Her blood was fresh and warm and it infuriated him because it wasn't as sweet or as satisfying as Angie's. Angie. It was only the thought of her, of how horrified she would be if she could see him now, that cooled the rage inside him and spared the woman's life. After releasing his prey from his thrall, he sent her on her way.

Hands shoved deep in his pockets, he glided through the night, a part of it, a part of the darkness itself.

The scuff of a boot heel was his only warning.

Declan pivoted to face the threat, which turned out to be a hunter who must have weighed a good three hundred pounds. Declan reacted instinctively, blocking the hunter's thrust with his forearm so that the silver-bladed dagger meant for his heart plunged into his left shoulder instead. At the same time, his free hand curled around the man's throat, choking the life out of him.

After releasing his hold on the hunter, Declan yanked the knife from his shoulder and tossed it aside, then stood there, cursing in Romanian, as pain from the silver lanced through him, spreading like acid from his shoulder outward.

When the pain eased, he transported himself to the Nightmare.

It was late and the Nightmare was in full swing when he arrived. Ian stood behind the bar. His eyes grew wide when he saw the bloody wound in Declan's shoulder. "What the hell happened to you?"

"Hunter."

Ian grunted softly. "Samantha's still resting."

Declan nodded, though at the moment, he didn't give a damn. For one, uncharacteristic moment, he was tempted to destroy Ian and the girl and be done with it. But Samantha was—or had been—Angie's best friend.

Angie. He closed his eyes, the pain in his heart worse than the throbbing ache in his shoulder.

"Hey, you okay?" Ian asked.

"Fine."

"What happened?"

"I told you. A hunter attacked me."

"No." Ian shook his head, his expression thoughtful. "It's more than that."

"I told Angie the truth. We're through."

"Shit, man, I'm sorry."

"Yeah, me, too." He had let himself care for a mortal woman. It was a mistake he would not make again.

Yet an hour later, he was standing outside Angie's house, simply to be near her.

Angie lay in bed, the covers pulled up to her chin, as she tried to come to grips with all that had happened in the last few hours. But it was impossible. It was like a bad dream from which she couldn't awake. She knew Declan had told her the truth but she couldn't wrap her mind around it, couldn't visualize the man she loved as some kind of blood-thirsty monster—like Samantha.

Sam. She would never forget the savage look on her friend's face, her eyes as red as a fiery hell, her lips drawn back in a snarl, revealing her fangs, all sign of humanity gone.

Angie shuddered at the image, wishing she could forget it, but it had been seared into her memory. She saw it every time she closed her eyes.

Guilt ripped through Declan's soul as he sensed Angie's torment. Calling on his preternatural power, he spoke to her mind, easing the pain, dulling the violent images of Samantha when she had been out of control. He had considered erasing the memory of all of it from Angie's mind, but on second thought, he had decided against it. For better or worse, she needed to know the truth so she could protect herself. From Samantha and Ian.

And himself.

He listened to her intermittent tears subside, heard her breathing become slow and regular as she drifted off to sleep.

Unable to help himself, he slipped into her dreams, desperate to hold her close one last time.

Angie woke slowly, tears filling her eyes as she remembered her dreams. Declan had wandered through them, his smile melting her heart, his kisses arousing her, making her yearn for more as he caressed her ever so gently. His voice, filled with yearning, had made her weep. Why had he lied to her about what he was? Let her fall in love with him? In a way, she wished he had never told her the truth. Being with him had made her so happy…

Thinking of Declan reminded her of Sam. Pounding her fist on the pillow, Angie sobbed, "Damn you, Declan Nicolae, I'll hate you until the day I die!" even though she feared, deep in her heart, that she still loved him. Would always love him.

The day yawned before her. She had no appetite for breakfast, no interest in reading or writing or anything else. Curled up on the sofa, a pillow clutched to her chest, she stared at the wall and cried herself to sleep.

When she woke up an hour later, Declan was slouched in the chair across from her. She felt her cheeks grow warm as she remembered her dreams.

Sitting up, holding the pillow between them like a shield, she asked, "What are you doing here?"

"I don't know. You've got me tied in knots."

"Declan, please, leave me alone."

"Angie, I'm sorry for what's happened to Samantha. I'm sorry I didn't tell you the truth about... about what I am. But I never wanted to hurt you or cause you pain. You have to believe that if you believe nothing else."

He meant every word, of that she had no doubt. But it didn't change the fact that he was a vampire. He had taken her blood without her consent, as if she would ever have given it! Because of him, Sam was now what he was... How could she ever forgive him for that?

"I should have warned her," he said quietly. "You're right about that."

Her brows rushed together. "Are you... are you reading my mind?"

*Shit.* "I guess that particular ability wasn't mentioned in all that research you did."

"I guess not."

"I really am sorry for everything," he said quietly. "I hope someday you'll find it in your heart to understand and forgive me." Rising, he brushed a kiss across her brow.

And vanished from the room.

Angie blinked at the empty space where he'd stood. She told herself she was glad he was gone, that she never wanted to see him again, and wondered when she had started lying to herself.

Samantha glared at Declan over the head of the young man she held in her arms. "Why can't I take it all?"

"Because I said so."

"You're not the boss of me," she retorted, her eyes blazing with defiance.

"No, he's not," Ian said. "But I am. And I'm telling you that killing is forbidden. If you're still thirsty after you feed the first time, you can find other prey and feed again until you're satisfied. But you *can't* kill them."

"And if I do?"

"If you do," Declan said harshly, "I'll destroy you."

"Are you threatening me?" she exclaimed.

"It's not a threat. We already have one rogue vampire in the city. We sure as hell don't need another."

"Oh, all right." Releasing the man from her thrall, Sam sent him on his way.

Declan's gaze trapped hers. "I meant what I said, Samantha. There are no second chances. Not for Ian. And not for you."

"I believe you," she whispered as the force of his power twisted through her.

"See that you do."

"I want to see Angie."

Ian shook his head. "I don't think that's a good idea."

"I need to apologize for scaring her to death. She is … was … my best friend."

Ian glanced at Declan, one brow raised.

"Maybe in a few days," Declan said. "When you're more in control."

A week passed. Two. For Angie, the days seemed surreal. She ate and slept, she wrote on her Christmas monsters column, she rearranged the furniture in the living room and changed it back again, but no matter the task, she felt empty inside, as if a vital part of her had gone missing. Still, it was the writing that saved her. Lost in researching ancient myths and beliefs, she could, for at least a little while, forget the real world and the unrelenting ache in her heart.

But late at night, in bed, she wondered what Declan was doing, how Sam was getting along. There had been three more murders in the city, all similar to the first one. Police had no suspects. No clues, no evidence, other than half a dozen bodies drained of blood.

Angie had no doubt a vampire was to blame. But which one? Declan? Ian? Sam? All three? Or was there another bloodsucker preying on the town's citizens? Now that she knew vampires existed, she often wondered how many of the patrons at the local Goth clubs weren't merely pretending, how many of the fangs she had thought were fake had been real.

She rarely went out at night, found herself reluctant to leave the house even during the day. Sure, vampires were supposed to be active only after sundown, but maybe that was a myth, too. She had seen Declan on several occasions when the sun as up. If he could be out and about during the daylight hours, maybe the others could, too. How was she to know?

The buzzing of the phone startled Angie out of her thoughts. She felt an unwanted thrill when she saw it was Declan calling. She debated letting it go to voice mail but curiosity—and an undeniable yearning to hear his voice again—got the better of her. "Hello."

"Hi."

The sound of his voice washed over her like sunlight after a long, cold winter. "What do you want?"

"A favor."

"Excuse me?" The man had all the nerve in the world, she thought bitterly. She hadn't heard from him in weeks and now he wanted a favor! Never mind that she'd told herself she never wanted to see him again. It wasn't true and she knew it. Desperate to see him and ashamed to admit it, she knew she would agree to whatever he asked.

"Samantha would like to see you. We're on your front porch."

"Are you out of your mind?"

"It will be good for her."

"But will it be good for me?"

"She wants to apologize. And she needs to feel like she still has a friend."

Angie felt a burst of hysterical laughter coming on. My best friend is a vampire. Wasn't there a movie by that name years ago? Something about a new vampire trying to be a good one and not kill people? She seemed to remember seeing it on TV late one night.

"Angie, listen to me. She's a lot better now than she was the last time you saw her."

She grunted, thinking her friend could hardly be worse. "I don't know."

"I won't let her hurt you."

She mulled it over for a moment, sorely tempted to agree, not because she wanted to see Sam, but because she missed Declan more than she had ever thought possible. *I miss you, too.* His silky-smooth voice whispered in the back of her mind. "Well..."

"If she does anything that frightens you, all you have to do is say her name and revoke her invitation to your house and she'll be forced to leave."

She didn't remember reading anything about that, Angie thought absently, but it was good to know. "Would it work on you, too?"

He hesitated a moment. "Yes."

"All right."

"Thank you."

Hoping she wasn't making a dreadful, perhaps fatal, mistake, Angie took a deep breath and unlocked the front door.

"Hi, Angie," Samantha said, careful not to get too close.

"How are you, Sam? Really?"

"Better than I was."

"Come in and sit down."

In the living room, Samantha took the chair. Declan sat at one end of the sofa and Angie took the other. The tension in the room was palpable.

Samantha cleared her throat and clasped her hands in her lap. "I wanted to tell you how sorry I am for what happened the other night. I was out of control and I...I never would have forgiven myself if I'd hurt you. You're my best friend. Can you ever forgive me?"

Angie bit down on her lower lip. She and Sam had been best friend for years. They had laughed together, cried together, consoled each other. But that Samantha no longer existed. Still, for old times' sake, she said, "Yes. I forgive you."

"Is there any chance we can still be friends? Any chance at all?"

"I don't know."

Shoulders sagging, Sam murmured, "I understand. I guess I can't blame you."

"Maybe, in time," Angie said. "I don't know if I'm ready to hang out again, but if you ever just want to talk… call me."

A smile spread over her friend's face and for that brief moment, Sam looked like her old self, happy and carefree.

"Samantha," Declan said. "Go wait for me on the porch."

"All right. Thanks for seeing me, Angie. It means a lot."

"Keep in touch."

"I will." Bounding to her feet, Samantha left the house.

"You have my thanks, too," Declan said. "It makes the transition a little easier when you have people behind you, grounding you, reminding you of who you are."

"That makes, sense, I guess. Will she…will she be like you, in time?"

"What do you mean?"

"You always seemed so normal. You ate dinner with me. We went to the movies during the day. I never once suspected what you are."

"I've been a vampire a good long while. We grow stronger, more resilient with age. It's only been in the last few decades that I've been able to consume more than blood, and walk in the daylight."

"How long have you been a vampire?"

His gaze searched hers. "Do you really want to know?"

"I think so," she said. Though now she wasn't sure at all.

"Eight hundred years, give or take a decade or two."
Eight hundred and twenty-three, to be exact.

Eight. Hundred. Years. It was inconceivable.

Noting Angie's suddenly pale cheeks, Declan said,
"You're not going to faint on me, are you?"

"I don't think so." Although she did feel suddenly light-
headed when she thought of all the amazing things he must
have witnessed during that time—the changes in everyday
life, in clothing and transportation, in science and medicine, music and movies and countless other inventions too
numerous to mention.

"Angie?"

She looked up at him, her mind reeling. Surely there
was no one else on earth like him.

"Would it be okay if I came by tomorrow night?"

Angie bit down on her lower lip. She should say no. He
was like a creature from another world, powerful, invincible,
perhaps even immortal. But how could she deny the love in
his eyes, the pleading note in his voice, the yearning of her
own heart? Unable to refuse him, she nodded. And felt as if
the weight of the world had been lifted from her shoulders.

His smile was devastating. "Would it be okay if I kissed
you goodnight?"

"Yes, please," she murmured, her eyelids fluttering down
as his mouth closed over hers. It was, she thought, like coming home after a long absence and as he deepened the kiss,
she vowed then and there to never let him go again.

# CHAPTER SEVENTEEN

Conor had just mesmerized his prey when he caught the scent of vampire coming toward him. And not just any vampire, but his brother. He lifted his head as he realized Declan wasn't alone but in the company of two other nightwalkers.

Curious, he sent his prey away. Shoved his hands in his pockets. And waited.

Declan came to an abrupt halt when he saw Conor standing on the street corner. Ian and Samantha stopped a short distance behind him.

For a long moment, Declan stared at his brother.

"So, brother mine, we meet yet again," Conor drawled.

"I thought I told you to get out of my territory."

"Did you?" Conor sneered. "Guess I forgot."

"What do you want?"

"That pretty little female of yours would do for a start."

"Didn't we already have this conversation?"

Conor's gaze ran over Samantha, who was standing behind Ian. "This one's not bad. I'll take her instead."

"Like hell!" Ian snarled. "She's mine!"

Conor snorted. "You young pup. I could destroy you in a heartbeat."

Ian swallowed hard, but held his ground.

"Well, this has been fun," Conor remarked. "But I haven't fed yet and I smell something sweet coming this way."

Before Declan could say or do anything, Conor was gone.

"He's tons of fun," Samantha muttered.

"He used to be," Declan said. *About eight hundred years ago.* Now, his brother was a menace to mankind. One that had to be stopped.

Angie was almost giddy with anticipation at the thought of seeing Declan again. She found herself smiling whenever she thought about him—whether doing a little housework, making lunch, or shopping at the market. Nothing bothered her. Not the traffic, not standing in line behind a woman with a mountain of groceries. Everything was wonderful because Declan was coming over. Vampire or not, she couldn't wait to see him again.

She flew across the floor when the doorbell rang and flung it open. "Declan, I'm so…" The words died in her throat when she saw the man standing on the porch. She frowned, thinking he looked vaguely familiar, and then she remembered where she'd seen him before. It had been at The Pit. He had asked her to dance. "You! What are you doing here?"

He lifted one shoulder in a negligent shrug. "I just wanted to see you again. May I come in?"

"I don't think so. I don't even know who you are."

"I'm Declan's little brother."

Angie frowned as she noted the similarity. And then she took a step back. Was he a vampire, too? What were the odds? And yet, as Declan's brother, he had to be, or he would have surely passed away centuries ago.

She was trying to decide what to do when a voice behind her said, "Get the hell out of here."

Startled, Angie glanced over her shoulder to find Declan standing behind her, his eyes dark with rage. "What... how?"

Reaching around her, he slammed the door in his brother's face. "Don't *ever* invite that man inside. Do you understand? No matter what he says."

"Is he really your brother?" she asked, returning to the living room.

"Unfortunately."

"You don't like each other very much, do you?"

"No."

"Is he dangerous?"

"He can be."

Angie settled onto the sofa. It was obvious he didn't want to talk about his relationship with Conor, which was too bad, because she couldn't help wondering what had caused the rift between them. "Sam seems better."

"Yeah. I think she'll be fine now."

"I hope so, although I don't think I'll ever feel at ease in her company again."

"Give it time." He gestured toward the sofa. "Do you mind?"

Smiling, she shook her head, felt her heart skip a beat as he took the place beside her. No other man had ever affected her like this. A smile, the sound of his voice, and her insides melted like butter left too long in the sun.

Declan slipped his arm around her shoulders, his gaze searching hers. "Are we going to be okay?"

"I hope so."

"It won't be easy for either one of us."

"I know." She worried her lower lip between her teeth. "Declan, I don't think… I mean, I'm not ready to …"

He watched her cheeks grow rosy with embarrassment. "I know what you're trying to say, sweetheart. Nothing more than hugs and kisses."

Her gaze searched his. "Are you all right with that?"

"If I have to be."

"I'm sorry, it's just that …"

"Hey, I understand."

"Thank you."

He caressed her cheek with his knuckles, slid his fingertips across her lower lip. "So, kisses are okay?"

Murmuring, "Definitely," she closed her eyes, felt a thrill of anticipation as his mouth covered hers. Warmth spread through her from head to heel as his tongue teased hers. She moaned softly as his hand stroked her back, slid up and down her thigh, brushed the curve of her breast.

Somehow, they were lying side-by-side on the sofa, his body pressed intimately to hers.

He lifted his head, his gaze burning into hers, her name a groan on his lips.

"What's wrong?" She hated the tremor in her voice caused by a sudden shiver of alarm, although she had no idea what had caused it.

Declan sat up, bringing her with him, and blew out a heavy sigh. "Before this goes any farther, there are a few things you should know."

His words, the look on his face, quickly smothered her desire. Hands clenched in her lap, she said, "Tell me."

"Vampires tend to be very passionate creatures."

Did he think he had to tell her that *now*, when she could still taste his kisses?

"Desire is closely tied to our need for blood. It's hard not to taste you when you're in my arms, when I can hear your every breath, the sound of your beating heart."

She stared at him, eyes wide. "You can hear that?"

"And smell the blood flowing warm and sweet in your veins."

That was just plain creepy, she thought, suppressing a shiver. "So when you...you drink from someone, do you seduce them, too?" Merciful heavens, he was hundreds of years old. How many women had he fed on? Made love to?

"No, love," he said with an indulgent smile. "There's a big difference between satisfying my hunger and holding you in my arms."

"Oh. Did you want to...to bite me just now when you were kissing me?"

"More than you can imagine."

She couldn't imagine it at all—and didn't want to.

"If I ever get carried away, if I ever frighten you, just say, 'Declan, I revoke your invitation' and I'll be gone. Hopefully, it will never come to that."

"Yes," she murmured. *Hopefully.*

He stroked her cheek tenderly. "I've never felt this way about another woman." Seeing her dubious expression, he said, "You don't believe me?"

"I'd like to, but...I mean, there's nothing special about me. Surely, in eight hundred years you've known a lot of women, and I mean that in the Biblical sense."

His easy laughter washed over her, doing funny things in the pit of her stomach. "Like I said, we're very passionate. But there's a world of difference between satisfying one's lust and genuine affection."

"Is that what you feel for me? Affection?"

"I'm afraid it's a bit deeper than that."

"Afraid?"

"I'm a vampire."

"Yes," she said dryly. "I know."

"It's been centuries since I was a married man. Unlike most marriages in those days, ours was a love match. On the night of our oldest son's wedding, vampires attacked our village. That's when Conor and I were turned. My wife and children were killed. The only survivors were my mother and a handful of others who managed to escape the carnage."

"I'm so sorry," she murmured, though she had no idea how what had happened in his distant past affected her.

"It was a long time ago." Since losing Mihaela all those centuries ago, he had carefully guarded his heart, unwilling to suffer the heartache of losing another woman he cared for. For lose Angie he would, whether to accident or illness or old age. "Like I said, I'm a vampire." He paused. "And you're not." He watched comprehension dawn in her eyes.

As if she could forget. Declan had already lived over eight hundred years. He might survive eight hundred more. If she was lucky, she might live to be a hundred. "You're afraid to fall in love again, aren't you? Afraid of losing someone you care for."

He nodded. "But I don't want to let you go."

"Well, we could just be friends with benefits." Unable to believe she'd said such a thing out loud, Angie clapped her hand over her mouth, felt herself blush from head to foot.

Declan stared at her a moment, then burst out laughing. "Don't worry, darlin'," he said. "I know you didn't mean it."

She took a deep breath and let it out in a long, slow sigh. "But what if I did?"

"Are you serious?"

"Yes. But … I still want take it slow, you know? I mean, we …"

"I understand. I'm a patient man. We'll take it nice and easy. When you say stop, I'll stop. Okay?"

"Okay."

He slipped his arm around her shoulders again. "So, what do you say we take up where we left off?"

# CHAPTER EIGHTEEN

Samantha licked her lips as she sent her prey—a handsome young man with curly blond hair—on his way. She would have loved to drain him dry, but that was forbidden. On some deep inner level, she knew the thought should have horrified her. Human or vampire, killing was wrong. And yet... it was hard to fight the temptation to take it all. Only Declan's very real threat to destroy her if she took a life, and Ian's constant presence, kept her from doing so. Since she couldn't kill, she had to drink from several people to satisfy her thirst. She had to admit, there were perks to drinking from more than one. After all, variety was said to be the spice of life and she was quickly learning that not all blood tasted the same, although she couldn't define the difference or what caused it. But it was there.

She glanced at Ian, who had just released the young man's wife from his thrall, and smiled as the woman hurried after her husband. "Shall we go home?" Her appetite for blood had been satisfied, but there was another need, even more personal and intimate.

"Sure, honey." He wrapped his arm around her waist and whisked the two of them to the lair she now shared with him.

When they were sitting side by side on the sofa, Ian kissed her cheek. "I'm proud of you," he said. "You're doing really well." He was lying to her and to himself, he thought ruefully. He had no doubt that without Declan's threat hanging over Sam's head, she would kill those she preyed on without a qualm.

"Thanks. But…"

"But?"

"I feel bad for leaving my job without any explanation. And I miss working. And my parents and my sister—they must wonder what's happened to me."

"You can call them, Sam. And when you've got your hunger fully under control, you can visit them."

"You'll go with me, won't you?"

He nodded. As if he'd let her go anywhere alone.

She tapped her finger against her cheek. Thinking out loud, she said, "Maybe Declan could give me a job at his nightclub? There's got to be more to my life than just hunting prey for an hour or two a night. Besides, I can use the money. I have some saved up, but it won't last forever. And Ian?"

"Yeah?"

"I need to go to my place and pick up my things and move out before this month's rent is due."

"Okay. How's tomorrow night? I have to be at work in thirty minutes."

"You won't forget to ask Declan about letting me work there?"

"I won't forget. And you're right. Having a job helps pass the time." He grinned at her. "Plus there are a few people who frequent the place who are more than willing to give you a sip or two."

"A job?" Declan lifted one brow. "Sam wants to work here?"

"She's used to being busy, you know? She can't go back to her old employer. And she needs the money. What do you say? Besides, I can keep an eye on her that way."

"Speaking of keeping an eye on her, do you think it was a good idea to leave her home alone?"

"Well, I sort of warded the house so she can't leave."

"I guess you're not as dumb as you look," Declan said with a grin.

"Yeah, well, I don't know if Sam believed you when you said you'd destroy her if she killed anybody, but I sure as hell did. So, what about that job?"

"I guess we can use her. Tell her she can start whenever she wants."

In his mist form, Conor floated near the ceiling in a dark corner of the Nightmare, virtually undetectable to human and vampire alike. His brother had found a sweet deal for himself, he thought bitterly. A Goth bar was the perfect hangout for vampires. He noted a few of the Undead lingering at the bar drinking red wine laced with blood. Others huddled in booths with mortals who got a kick out of feeding nightwalkers. Yessir, a sweet deal.

One he wouldn't mind having for himself. But it wouldn't be easy to take. Though he and his brother had been turned at the same time, his sire had been a fledgling while Declan's had been an ancient master vampire. It made all the difference in the world, as part of a sire's power was transferred to his fledgling and then grew stronger with age. No matter how long he and Declan lived, Declan would always be the more powerful. It was just one more reason why he hated—and envied—his brother.

# CHAPTER NINETEEN

Angie sat back in her chair as she read over what she'd written for her Christmas monsters column …

*Perchta's roots go back to the Middle Ages. She is a unique Christmas monster, sometimes known as angelic and sometimes as demonic, but she is always portrayed as a domestic goddess—either beautiful with snow-white skin, or as an ugly, old crone with a hooked nose and ragged clothing. Perchta was one of the characters in the movie, Krampus, and was portrayed as a demonic angel doll.*

*She often carries a broom—for cleaning or flying, and because of that is believed to be a witch—and not a good one, like Glinda, but more like the Wicked Witch of the West on steroids.*

*One outstanding feature is that she has one overly-large foot— said to be from spending so much time using the pedals in front of a spinning wheel. Perchta is also rumored to be able to shape-shift into a goose. Legend has it that she was the inspiration for Mother Goose, though there is nothing the least bit sweet or motherly about her.*

*Perchta, also known as La Befana, Baboushka, Frau Faste, Berhta-Baba, and by many other names, is a stickler for cleanliness and politeness. She rewards good children and servants by giving them silver coins. Disobedient boys and girls are disemboweled and their innards stuffed with garbage. Not a pretty picture!*

*She also commands the Straggele—horned beasts who help her punish naughty children.*

Pushing away from the desk, Angie stood and stretched her back and shoulders. It was past time for lunch.

In the kitchen, she slapped a sandwich together, grabbed a can of soda, and ambled out to the small gazebo in the back yard.

Nibbling on her sandwich, she wondered what Declan was doing. Though she rarely saw him or heard from him during the day, she had seen him when the sun was up, which would seem to indicate that he didn't have to sleep in his coffin during the daylight hours. If that was true, she wondered why she didn't hear from him more often in the daytime.

*Did* he sleep in a coffin? If so, where did he keep it? Did she really want to know? Did he look dead when he was inside of it? Did she sleep with the lid open or closed?

Angie thrust the gruesome image from her mind and turned her thoughts to Samantha. How was she getting along? She missed chatting on the phone and going to lunch with her best friend. How awful, to be turned into a vampire against your will. Would Sam ever get used to it? Did she like what she'd become? Did Ian? Or Declan, for that matter?

Angie tried to imagine herself in Sam's place but just couldn't do it. Hunting people for nourishment and being hunted in return. Resting in a crypt. Denied the sunlight. Drinking blood...Angie shuddered. How did anyone ever get used to that? How had Declan?

She finished her sandwich and soda, watered a few plants, and returned to the house.

She was in the middle of more research when Declan called. After a quick hello, he said, "Would you like to meet me at the Nightmare later?"

"Well, sure, I guess. Why?"

"Ian and Sam are coming by. I hired Sam. She's going to stay after closing tonight so Ian can show her the ropes. I thought you might like to see her again."

"Sam's working at the Nightmare?" Angie shook her head.

"It was Ian's idea."

"Can I ask you something?"

"Anything, love, any time."

"Do you like being a vampire? Was it hard to get used to?"

Her question was met with silence. When he finally answered, she had the feeling he was choosing his words carefully.

"It was damned hard, at first. I missed all the usual things fledglings miss—food and drink, sunshine, my family. The life I had once taken for granted. But after a while you either adjust or go crazy."

"Did you ever . . . have you ever killed anyone?"

"Yes," he said, his voice curt.

"Very many?"

She heard him take a deep breath. "I guess that depends on your interpretation of 'many'."

"I'm sorry. I shouldn't have asked. It's none of my business, really."

"But you need to know. In the beginning, when Conor and I were first made, we didn't know what to do. Our sires had abandoned us. You can't imagine how excruciating the hunger was those first few nights. There are no words to describe it. Back then, we didn't know you could satisfy the craving without killing those you fed on. There was only an insatiable thirst that couldn't be denied."

Angie listened, wide-eyed, unable to imagine what he was describing.

"Once we discovered that we didn't have to kill, I never took another life except to preserve my own, whereas Conor...Conor delighted in the hunt, in the shedding of blood. He still does." Declan paused. He wasn't being entirely truthful with her. He debated for a moment whether to tell her about the hunters he had killed over the years. He regretted none of them. It had been their life or his.

In the end, he decided against it.

"Would you like to be human again?" Angie asked.

"Honestly? No. I barely remember what it was like. What brought all this up?"

"I was just thinking about Sam and wondering how she was doing, how she would feel years from now."

"She's a strong woman. I think she'll be okay."

"I hope so,' Angie said fervently, and then frowned as a new thought popped into her mind. "Does Sam have to sleep in a coffin now?" she asked, fervently hoping that was another myth.

"Some of the old ones do. But it isn't necessary. We don't have to rest in caskets or sleep on our native. All we need is a safe lair."

"Oh." Summoning her nerve, she asked, "Do you? Sleep in one?"

"No." He had, centuries ago, but he saw no need to tell her that. "Any more questions, love?"

"Not at the moment. What time should I meet you?"

"Eight?"

"All right. See you then." There was more to being a vampire than she had ever imagined, Angie thought as she put her phone down. How frightening, to be turned and have no one to tell you how to survive your new existence. It intrigued her that two men who were brothers had responded so differently. Sam was lucky, if you could call it that, to have Ian and Declan to help her make the transition.

Wanting to fit in, Angie dressed in her black skirt, blouse and boots, grabbed her bag and a black, fringed jacket and headed for Nick's Nightmare at seven forty-five.

Now that she knew not all of the nightclub's customers were merely playing at being vampires, she felt a wave of trepidation as she stepped out of the car. Was she crazy for agreeing to meet Declan here? She wasn't a vampire. She didn't want to be one—or feed one. But Samantha was expecting her. And so was Declan.

Squaring her shoulders, Angie took a deep breath and pushed the door open.

She kept her gaze fixed on the bar as she walked toward it, and didn't relax until she saw Declan seated at the end. He smiled when he saw her and all of her fears evaporated.

"How's my little Goth queen?" he asked as he stood and took her in his arms.

Angie made a face at him. "Very funny," she muttered, looking around. "Where's Sam?"

"They're on their way. Can I get you a drink?"

"Not right now."

Declan resumed his seat and Angie perched on the stool beside his.

"So, how's business?" she asked.

"Booming, as you can see."

"Is it like this every night?" Most of the tables were occupied, the dance floor was crowded. Music with a slow, sensual beat drifted over the sound system.

"No. Like most nightclubs, weekends are the busiest. Would you care to dance?"

"Love to." Any excuse to be near him, she thought as he drew her into his arms. She felt a little thrill of excitement every time his body brushed against hers.

Holding Angie so close made Declan glad he'd fed before he arrived at the club. Just being near her fired his desire and aroused his hunger, but she was in no danger tonight. Her body was soft and warm against his as they swayed back and forth. The scent of her perfume teased his nostrils as he rained kisses on her brow, her cheeks, the curve of her throat. He heard the uptick in her heartbeat as he caressed her. She wanted him, he thought, almost as much as he wanted her. It was only a matter of time.

Ian and Samantha arrived and slid into a booth in the back just as the song ended.

Taking Angie by the hand, Declan led her around the dance floor to where they waited.

Angie smiled tentatively at Sam as she slid into the booth. Sam looked the same, but not. Her skin seemed a trifle paler, her hair looked thicker, more lustrous, but the biggest change was the faint aura of preternatural power that clung to her. It was the same power Angie sensed in Ian and Declan, though not nearly as strong.

Samantha met Angie's smile with one equally uncertain. "I'm glad you came. I've missed you."

"I've missed you, too. How are you feeling, Sam, really?"

"Wonderful!"

"Oh. Well, that's good. I'm ..." Angie paused. She had been about to say *I'm happy for you*, but nothing could be further from the truth.

"It's not near as bad as you might think," Samantha said cheerfully. "Ian and Declan have been a big help to me. And

I've never felt better or stronger or more alive in my whole life."

*Alive.* The word seemed to echo in Angie's mind—*alive, alive, alive.* But Sam wasn't alive, not really. And neither was Declan. It was a sobering thought. And yet, somehow, with Declan, it didn't seem to matter. Was it just because she had never known him when he was human? Truthfully, she couldn't imagine him as anything but what he was.

Ian beamed at Sam, but Declan was watching Angie's face. She was making a valiant effort to hide her discomfort and disbelief as she tried to reconcile the new Samantha with the old one—and failing miserably. But that was to be expected. Becoming a vampire wasn't like changing the color of your hair. There were deep emotional changes to be reckoned with, a whole new reality to every aspect of your life. New powers. New, stronger, emotions that had to be curbed, a different way of thinking about the world around you. None of it was easy. And it was all alien and beyond the comprehension of mere mortals.

A waitress came to take their drink orders. Declan ordered the house special—red wine mixed with a little blood—for himself, Ian, and Sam. Angie asked for a glass of chardonnay.

An uneasy silence fell over the table.

"So, Angie," Sam said brightly, "how's your column going? What are you working on now?"

Angie groaned inwardly, wishing she was writing about anything but monsters. "I'm almost finished with the Christmas one and then I'll start doing research for New Year's."

"What's it about?"

"I've been doing a series on holidays," she said, and prayed Sam wouldn't ask any more questions.

"Like how and why we celebrate them?"

"In a way." Angie sent a silent plea to Declan. *Help me.*

"Enough chit-chat," Declan said, taking Angie by the hand. "I want to dance with my woman."

She smiled her gratitude as he led her away from the table. "Thank you."

"You looked a little ill at ease back there," he remarked as he drew her close. "I guess I can't blame you for not wanting to talk about monsters."

"I didn't mean you."

He chuckled. "I know."

Angie glanced at the table where Samantha and Ian sat with their heads close together. "Sam's so different, I don't know how to handle it." She laughed self-consciously. "I guess I'm just not any good at making small talk with vampires."

"You don't seem to have any trouble talking to me."

"It's hardly the same thing. To me, you've always been the way you are now."

He grunted softly. "And I've had a long time to adjust."

"Exactly. You don't think I hurt Sam's feelings, do you?"

"No. She's just as uncomfortable as you are. The thing is, the two of you will have to decide if you want to work at sustaining your friendship or let it go."

That was the real question, wasn't it? Angie thought glumly. Did she have the courage to remain friends with a fledgling vampire who might not be in complete control of herself? It wasn't a decision to be made lightly. The wrong choice could be fatal.

Then again, so could dating a vampire.

Declan grinned inwardly as he read Angie's thoughts. She was in no danger from him. He could control his hunger.

He wasn't so sure about his desire.

Angie felt a wave of relief as they bid goodnight to Samantha and Ian. The last hour had been strained, to say the least, with everyone making small talk and trying to pretend it was just an ordinary double date.

"I've known Sam for years, but I'm not sure our friendship is going to survive this," Angie remarked with a sigh. "This is the first time I've been relaxed all evening. I know Sam was trying hard to be her old self tonight, but..." Angie shook her head, remembering how many times Sam's gaze had drifted to her throat. "I'm never going to feel safe around her again unless you or Ian are with us."

"I'd like to tell you there's nothing to worry about, but that would be a lie. No matter how rational she sounds, or how under control she seems to be, you can't trust her right now. It takes at least a year for new vampires to develop any kind of self-control, sometimes longer. Ian's almost there, but he's still got a few months to go." And even then, Declan thought, thinking of his brother, there were no guarantees.

Declan pulled into the driveway a few minutes later and switched off the engine.

"How will you get back to the Nightmare?" Angie asked.

"Don't worry about me. I'll be there before you take your shoes off."

"So that whole 'vampires can travel faster than the human eye can follow thing' is true?"

"Yep."

"And shape-shifting?"

"Also true."

"Wow. Is that something you do a lot?"

"Not really much call for it these days."

"But there was, in the past?"

"Sadly, yes."

"Did you turn into other people?"

"No. Wolves, mostly."

Angie's brows shot up to her hairline. "Wolves? Seriously?"

"Wolves and vampires have a lot in common. We're often hunted. We're both predators. We both defend our own."

Angie nodded slowly, thinking she still had a lot to learn, and a lot to think about. She wondered what he looked like as a wolf, what it felt like.

Declan walked her to the door, then took her in his arms. "I'm in love with you, Angie. You know that, don't you?"

She stared at him, speechless. She had known he liked her, that he desired her. But love?

"You can't be surprised," he said with a faint smile.

"But... I am. I mean, I don't know what to say."

"You don't have to say anything. I just wanted you to know how I feel before things go any further between us." He kissed her again, his lips moving slowly and sweetly over hers. "Sweet dreams, darlin'. Be sure to lock up when you go inside."

Angie stared after him as he jogged down the walkway toward the street, turned and waved, and disappeared from sight.

Inside, she locked the door, then headed for her room to get ready for bed. Declan loved her, she mused as she changed into her nightgown and slid under the covers.

She *really* had a lot to think about now.

# CHAPTER TWENTY

At the Nightmare, Declan locked up for the night and turned off the lights. Siting at the bar, he sipped a glass of wine, his thoughts, as always, turning to Angie. He loved her with every fiber of his being. He knew she was falling for him. In all the years since his wife had died, he had never felt this way about another woman. Angie was strong and brave and sweet and kind. But was she brave enough to spend the rest of her life with him? Was he strong enough, honorable enough, to let her go?

He had nothing to offer a woman—no home except the Nightmare and a small stone house that he used as a secondary lair. It had no modern conveniences, the only furniture a small leather couch, a chair, and a double bed. If Angie agreed to marry him, she would never have children. That, alone, was a big price to pay. Had she thought of that? She would age and he would not. How could he watch her grow old, feeble, helpless? If she would agree to let him turn her ten or fifteen years down the road, that would solve one problem.

Declan downed the last of his drink and started for the stairs that led to his lair on the second floor when the world exploded around him. Flames spread across the ceiling, crackled down the wall behind the bar, and licked at his clothing before the sprinklers came on.

Willing himself outside, eyes and throat stinging from the smoke, he reached for his phone to call 911.

He caught a familiar scent moments before his brother materialized out of the shadows. With a wild cry, Conor buried his fangs in his throat.

"Angie. Angie."

She woke with a start, screamed before she recognized the man staggering across the bedroom floor toward her. "Declan!" She switched on the bedside light, let out a gasp when she saw his face. He looked deathly pale. His eyes were red and swollen, his left cheek was badly burned, his left arm was scorched. Dark-red blood gleamed wetly on his shirt collar and leaked from a ghastly wound in the side of his neck. His hair was damp and sprinkled with ashes, his clothing tattered. "What…what happened?"

"My brother." Head hanging, he dropped to his knees.

Angie tossed the covers aside and knelt beside him. "What can I do?"

"I need blood."

She bit down on her lower lip. He wasn't asking, merely stating a fact. She took a deep breath, let it out in a long, slow sigh of resignation before she turned her head to the side and said, "Take what you need."

"You don't have to do this."

"I think maybe I do." His face was so pale, the skin across his cheekbones drawn tight, his flesh burned and blistered.

"Don't let me take too much," he rasped. "Tell me to stop after a minute to two. If I don't, order me out of the house. Do you understand?"

Heart pounding with trepidation, she nodded.

"Remember what I said. Only a few minutes. I'm in a lot of pain right now and it's going to be hard for me to let you go."

"I understand."

Muttering, "I hope so," he reached for her arm and sank his fangs into the large vein in her wrist.

Angie winced, then closed her eyes as she counted off the seconds. One minute. Two. Three. "Declan, stop."

He growled at her, but he didn't let go.

"Declan! Stop! Please." She was about to rescind his invitation when he lifted his head. He looked a little better, but not much.

He didn't meet her gaze as he ran his tongue over the tiny puncture wounds in her wrist, then licked the blood from his lips. "Thank you."

"Are you going to be all right?" she asked, trying not to let her horror show in her expression even as she watched the tiny wounds in her wrist vanish before her eyes.

"Eventually. Burns take a long time to heal."

"Would you like to clean up a little?"

"Yeah, thanks."

She stood and offered him her hand. He stared at it a moment before letting her help him to his feet. "There are clean towels in the cupboard and a new toothbrush in the medicine cabinet."

Nodding, he staggered into the bathroom and closed the door.

Declan stood in the middle of the shower, his eyes closed, his forehead resting on the tile as hot water sprayed over his back and shoulders. The burn on his cheek throbbed relentlessly, as did the vicious bite on his neck. Damn Conor to hell. They been locked in a violent struggle—might be fighting still—but at the sound of approaching sirens, Conor had dissolved into mist and fled the scene. Declan had barely managed to transport himself to Angie's before his strength gave out.

He stood under the blessedly hot water for a good twenty minutes before he turned off the faucet and reached for a towel.

Angie was sitting cross-legged on the end of the bed when Declan emerged from the bathroom, a towel wrapped around his lean hips. "You said your brother did this. But...why?"

A muscle twitched in his jaw. "Because he hates me even more than I hate him."

She patted the mattress, inviting him to sit beside her. "Do you want to talk about it?"

"No."

"Is there anything I can do?"

"No, love. You've done more than you know."

Her cheeks pinked when she glanced at the towel covering him. "You can stay here tonight, if you like. And I can go out tomorrow and buy you something to wear."

He nodded. His clothes and all his personal effects had gone up in smoke, along with the second floor of the Nightmare. Had he been at rest upstairs, he'd likely be nothing but ashes now. Reaching for her hand, he kissed her palm. "I don't know how I'll repay you for this."

"No need. I made up the bed in the guestroom while you were in the shower."

Declan took the hint. Rising, he brushed a kiss across her forehead. "Again, thanks for everything."

Trying not to imagine him lying naked in the bedroom down the hall, she murmured, "Good night, Declan."

"Good night, darlin'."

Declan lay naked on the bed, a single sheet covering him from the waist down. Angie's blood had eased the worst of the pain, but his face and his arm still throbbed relentlessly from the burns. Dammit, there was nothing that hurt worse or was more feared by vampires than fire, although silver on preternatural skin was a close second.

Hands clenched at his sides, he stared up at the ceiling. Conor had gone too far this time. And in so doing, he had signed his own death warrant. Declan couldn't take a chance on his brother coming after him while he was at Angie's, or worse, catching Angie helpless and alone. Conor had to be stopped. He should have destroyed his brother long before this. Even now, he wasn't sure why he hadn't done it years ago.

Eyes closed, he sank into the dark sleep of oblivion.

Conor prowled the grounds around the woman's house. Angie. She was a pretty thing. Warm, alive, and apparently not afraid of vampires. If he destroyed Declan, he could claim the woman for his own.

It was something to think about.

Angie woke late after a restless night. It had been hard to relax, knowing Declan was in the spare bedroom clad in nothing at all.

Throwing the covers aside, she pulled on her robe, scuffed into the kitchen to start a fresh pot of coffee, then paced the floor. Was he still asleep? What did he look like at rest? Was he really dead to the world in the morning? She grimaced as she pictured a corpse lying in her spare bedroom and quickly thrust that disquieting image aside. She knew he could be awake during the day. She had seen him in the afternoon. But all the books and movies said vampires slept like the dead.

Goaded by a growing sense of curiosity, she tiptoed down the hall to the guestroom, then paused with one hand on the door. He was naked in there, but surely he had pulled the covers over him. Hadn't he?

She worried her lower lip between her teeth. Took a deep breath. Opened the door just a crack and peeked inside. Declan lay on his back, his chest bare. The sheet covered him from the waist down. He didn't look dead. Just asleep.

With a sigh of relief, she closed the door.

Angie was amazed at how distracting it was to know there was a vampire sleeping in her guestroom. No matter what task she started, she found herself constantly stopping to tiptoe down the hall and take a peek at Declan. As near as she could tell, he hadn't turned over, hadn't moved a muscle since he'd gone to bed. She couldn't tell if he was breathing and that troubled her, yet she didn't have the nerve to approach him to check. What if he wasn't just resting? What if he had actually died during the night? Was that even possible?

It was near dusk when not knowing if he was alive or dead sent Angie tiptoeing into the guestroom yet again.

She practically jumped out of her skin when, without moving or opening his eyes, he said, "I'm fine, love. Stop worrying."

Feeling like an intruder, she mumbled, "Sorry. I didn't mean to disturb you," as her cheeks warmed with embarrassment.

"You didn't."

"Are you feeling better?" He looked better, she thought. The burn on his cheek had faded to a dull pink. What she could see of the bite on his neck still looked red and angry.

"Yeah, thanks." He sat up slowly. "Angie."

She knew what he wanted before he asked.

"Can I impose on you one more time?"

After a slight hesitation, she moved toward the bed and sat on the edge of the mattress. She shivered as his arm slid around her waist.

"I just need a little," he assured her. "But if you're not up to it, I can go out."

"Not like that, you can't," she said, gesturing at the sheet that had fallen dangerously low.

"Relax, darlin'."

Easy for you to say, she thought, and closed her eyes. Last night he drank from her wrist. Tonight he brushed the hair away from her neck. Last night he had been desperate and she had been frightened. But now, his bite was gentle. A slow sensual warmth enfolded her as he drank, filling her with a sense of euphoria and well-being. It never occurred to her to ask him to stop and she murmured a wordless cry of disappointment when he lifted his head. "What did you do?" she asked, her voice filled with wonder.

"What do you mean?" he asked, although he knew very well what she meant.

"It didn't feel the same today as it did last night. Why?"

"Last night I was in a lot of pain and not quite in control, as you know. Today…" He shrugged one shoulder. "Today I'm more myself and I wanted to give you pleasure in return for your generosity."

Brow furrowed, she stared at him. "So, when you … feed on other women …?" She bit down on her lower lip, uncertain how to phrase her question, or squelch the sudden wave of jealousy that caught her by surprise.

"I try to make it pleasant for them, though I try a little harder for you."

She blinked at him and then she laughed. "You old sweet-talker, you."

"I don't want you to be jealous of anyone else, Angie. I haven't cared deeply for another woman since my wife died."

"I don't believe you."

"It's true, nonetheless."

"So, you've lived like a monk for hundreds of years?"

Now it was his turn to laugh. "Not quite. A man—even a vampire—has certain physical and emotional needs."

She could believe that. She had seen his desire for her in his eyes, heard it in his voice, felt it when he held her in his arms. A shiver went through her when his gaze caressed her. She suddenly realized she was in a very vulnerable position, sitting on the bed beside a naked, fully aroused vampire wearing clad in nothing but a sheet.

Rising with alacrity, she said, "I think I'd better go out and buy you something to wear."

Knowing exactly what she was thinking, he grinned at her. "Don't worry about the cost. I'll pay you back."

"I know." She grabbed a piece of paper and a pen from the bedside table and jotted down the things he wanted and his sizes.

"I'll leave the colors up to you."

"I assumed you'd just want basic black," she said with a wink and a grin as she left the room and closed the door behind her.

Declan debated the wisdom of letting her go out alone, but he'd given as good as he'd gotten last night. No doubt Conor was also holed up somewhere, licking his wounds. Then too, his brother usually shunned the daylight. With that in mind, and knowing he could be at Angie's side in the blink of an eye, Declan reached for his phone.

There were times when being a vampire came in handy, he mused. Now was one of them. A few calls, a little mind control, and he soon had a small army of architects and contractors lined up to start rebuilding the second floor of the Nightmare and repair whatever other damage had been done to the nightclub. With two crews, each working twelve-hour shifts, seven days a week, along with the promise of a hefty bonus, the job would be completed in a matter of weeks instead of months.

Throwing the sheet aside, he gained his feet, gauging his strength as he paced the floor. In a day or two, he would be fully recovered. There was just one thing that bothered him. Conor had bitten him, hard and deep, and in so doing had consumed Declan's blood, which meant that his brother would have no trouble at all finding him in the future.

It was a thought that weighed heavily on his mind as he waited for Angie to return.

Angie wandered through the men's department, considering every item carefully. She bypassed the brightly-colored shirts that were all the rage. Somehow, she couldn't visualize Declan wearing hot pink or bright yellow. Or anything but black. However, she picked out several shirts, all dark colors—navy blue, brown, gray, and black, of course. Trousers and jeans. A black slip-over sweater. A black leather jacket. Shoes and boots and socks.

She felt a little thrill of excitement as she looked at underwear. She had never shopped for a man before, had no idea whether Declan liked boxers or briefs or boxer briefs. Or bikinis. She mulled it over for a moment. If he preferred bikinis, he'd have to buy his own, she thought, as she selected three pairs each of boxer briefs and regular boxers. And then there were tee shirts. V-neck or round? Again, she bought three of each.

Angie had spent a small fortune by the time she walked out of the mall. Was this what it was like to be a wife, she wondered as she loaded everything into the trunk. Buying his clothes and undies, taking care of him when he was sick, worrying when he was hurt, missing him when they were apart even for a short time?

She shook the thought aside. She was falling in love with her vampire, there was no doubt about that. If she was honest, she was already in love with him. But as much as she cared for Declan, as much as she enjoyed being with him, she couldn't see herself marrying a vampire.

But neither could she imagine the rest of her life without him.

Declan grabbed the sheet and wrapped it around his waist when Angie knocked on the bedroom door. "Come on in."

She hesitated a moment before slowly opening the door and peering inside, breathed a sigh of relief when she saw the sheet wrapped around him.

Arms full of bags and boxes, she stepped inside and dumped the packages on the bed. "I bought everything I could think of," she said with a grin. "No wild colors, no plaid, though I was tempted to buy you a hot pink Armani shirt."

"I admire your restraint," he said dryly.

"Well, I'll leave you to it."

"How much do I owe you?"

"The receipt is in there somewhere," she said with a negligent wave of her hand as she headed for the door.

Declan stared after Angie, his thoughts chaotic. He had never meant to care for her, never meant to entangle her in his life. Now, he didn't know how he would ever let her go. And after brushing her mind with his, he knew she was having similar thoughts about staying with him.

Unfortunately, there was no easy answer for either of them.

# CHAPTER TWENTY-ONE

D eclan pulled on a pair of black jeans and a long-sleeved gray tee shirt as listened to Angie moving around in the kitchen. She had obviously paid attention to the colors and fabrics he liked, he thought as he tugged on a pair of black boots, slipped on a black leather jacket, and willed himself to the Nightmare.

The safe behind the bar had survived the fire. He had worked a little vampire magic on it when he bought it so that it was invisible to mortals. Punching in the combination, he withdrew a wad of cash and shoved it in his pants' pocket.

A quick glance around showed the damage to the downstairs wasn't as bad as he'd expected. The windows and most of the glassware was broken, the walls and part of the floor scorched. Vandals had helped themselves to the liquor that had survived the flames, but that was easily replaced. The contractor was scheduled to begin rebuilding the upstairs tomorrow. Until then... he swore under his breath. Damn Conor. The Nightmare hadn't been just his source of income but his primary lair, as well.

Going out the back door, he headed for the garage located behind the Nightmare. A wave of his hand raised the heavy metal door. To his relief, both cars were safe inside.

Leaving the nightclub behind, Declan prowled the night in search of prey. He needed blood too desperately to be picky. The first human he found was a middle-aged drug addict passed out in an alley. He didn't know which smelled worse, the guy's clothing or his breath. He wrinkled his nose with distaste as he knelt beside the man and sank his fangs into his throat.

He drank quickly, eager to get away from the man's stink and return to Angie. He had just sealed the wounds in his prey's neck when he heard amused laughter behind him.

Conor!

Rising quickly to his feet, Declan turned to face his nemesis.

"What happened?" his brother asked with a smug grin. "Did that pretty lady throw you out?"

"Why the hell did you burn down my place?"

Conor lifted one shoulder in a negligent shrug. "Because I could? Because I hate you? Because I intend to destroy you and make that pretty female my own? I don't know. Pick one."

"Keep your filthy hands off her."

"Careful, brother. You're no match for me in your weakened state."

"You think not? I'm warning you, *brother*, get the hell out of my territory or I swear on all I hold dear that I will destroy you or die trying."

Conor hesitated, momentarily taken aback by the fierceness of his brother's tone. They both knew Declan had been turned by a master vampire and because of that, no matter how long they both lived, he would always be stronger, faster, more powerful. It would be a mistake to underestimate him, even now.

"You always were a coward," Declan said with sneer. "Always sneaking around to do your dirty work instead of facing your enemies head on." He paused as Conor tensed, his eyes going red. "Bring it on, little brother. Do your worst."

Conor snarled as he flashed his fangs.

Declan squared his shoulders then shoved his hands in his pants' pockets. "I'm waiting."

Cursing in Romanian, Conor vanished from sight.

Damn, that had been a close call, Declan thought, because his brother was right. He was in no shape to fight it out with Conor.

Drawing upon his preternatural power, he transported himself to Angie's place.

Angie stood in front of the refrigerator, trying to decide if she wanted to scramble some eggs for dinner or order in. And even while thinking about dinner, a part of her mind was wondering what Declan was doing. She had expected to see him by now, looking tall, dark and gorgeous in the clothes she had picked out for him.

Curious as to what was taking him so long, she closed the refrigerator door and headed for the guestroom.

The door was ajar. The boxes and bags had been opened. But there was no sign of Declan.

Frowning, she returned to the kitchen. He could have at least told her he was leaving, she thought as she cracked a couple of eggs in a frying pan. Didn't he realize she would worry about him?

"Looking for me?"

Startled, Angie whirled around, one hand pressed to her heart as he materialized in the doorway. "Declan. Don't do that," she exclaimed. And then she frowned. "How *do* you do that?"

He jerked a thumb toward his chest. "Vampire, remember?"

"I'm not likely to forget," she muttered. "Where did you go?"

"To the Nightmare. My brother torched it last night."

That explained the burns. "I'm so sorry."

"Yeah, me, too."

"It's all gone?"

"Not quite. The first floor is in pretty good shape except for some broken glassware and smoke damage. But all my clothes and personal belongings were upstairs." He tamped down a renewed wave of anger as he thought of the things that had been lost—his wife's portrait. A lock of his daughter's hair. A crucifix that had belonged to his mother. His father's pipe. A few toys that had belonged to his sons. "It wouldn't be so bad, except it was also my...where I took my rest."

"Are you going to rebuild?"

"Yeah. I've already called a contractor. I told the owner I'd double his fee if his men would work overtime and weekends until it was done."

"You can always stay here while they're working on it."

He was about to refuse, but remembering Conor's threat, he decided it wouldn't be wise for Angie to stay home alone. "Thanks, love. Your eggs are burning."

"What? Oh!" Grabbing a dish towel, she lifted the pan from the stove and turned off the burner.

"Dinner?" he asked.

"It was," she said as she scraped burnt eggs into the garbage disposal and filled the pan with soapy water.

"Let me take you out," Declan offered. "It's the least I can do."

"I accept."

"You'll have to drive. Both of my cars are at the club."

Because Angie had been in the mood for breakfast, they went to the local pancake house. She ordered a blueberry waffle. He opted for bacon and eggs, preferring protein to carbs.

"Is something wrong?" Angie asked after they ordered. "I mean, other than your problem with your brother?"

"Why do you ask?"

"You keep checking the door. Are you expecting someone?"

*Shit.* Conor's threat against Angie had unnerved him more than he thought if she could sense his apprehension. "I hope not."

"What does that mean?"

"I need to tell you something that you're not going to want to hear."

"Oh?"

"I ran into my brother tonight."

Feeling suddenly apprehensive, Angie frowned. "And?"

"Conor's always been a little jealous of me. Although we were turned at the same time, my sire was ancient while his was just a fledgling, which means no matter how long he lives, I'll always be stronger and more powerful. Even when we were kids, he always wanted what I had."

An icy shiver of unease skated down Angie's spine as she waited for Declan to go on.

"And now he wants you."

"Me?" A sudden image of Declan's brother rose in her mind—a tall, handsome man with compelling brown eyes.

"I'm afraid so." He fell silent as the waitress delivered their order.

Angie stared at the waffle and then pushed her plate away, her appetite gone. "Am I in danger?"

"I doubt it." Declan stacked his plate on top of hers. "I don't think he means to hurt you."

She knew a moment of relief. And then she shivered again. "He wants to turn me, doesn't he? Doesn't he?"

"I wouldn't be surprised. But it's me he really wants to hurt. Unfortunately, he intends to use you to do it. Come on, let's get out of here." Angie was quiet on the drive home. He couldn't blame her. Knowing a vampire had his sights on her had to be disconcerting, to say the least.

At home, she kicked off her shoes, dropped her handbag on the floor and sank onto the sofa.

Declan paced the floor a moment, his mind in turmoil.

"So, what are we going to do about your brother?"

"If it was just me he wanted, I'd leave town and hope he'd follow me. But leaving you alone now would be a really bad idea." Not that he was sure staying with Angie was a good idea, either, not when Conor could easily track his whereabouts.

"You're not afraid of him, are you?"

"No. But he's almost as powerful as I am." Declan dropped down on the chair across from the sofa. "I vowed to destroy him centuries ago, but I could never bring myself to do it. He's my blood. My only surviving kin. We've battled each other countless times over the years, but..." He shrugged. "I think deep down he's reluctant to destroy me for the same reason. I'm all he's got left."

"Why did you vow to kill him?"

"He killed our mother."

Her eyes widened in horror. "Why?"

"She was sick with a fever. Conor was afraid she might die. He thought he could heal her if he turned her." Declan shook his head with the memory of holding his mother in his arms, watching the life go out of her eyes. "He didn't know what the hell he was doing, so instead of saving her, he killed her."

"Oh, Declan, I'm so sorry."

Remembering that night renewed his anger, his hatred. But then he thought of Conor trying to turn Angie—and failing—and his anger was swallowed up in fear for her life.

One look at Angie's face and he knew she was thinking the same thing. Conor had failed when he tried to bestow the dark gift on their mother. What if he tried and failed again?

Declan stalked the dark streets of the city. He had stayed with Angie until she started to nod off. He had kissed her good night and after warding the house against vampires and humans alike, he had gone in search of his brother. He couldn't track Conor, but if his brother was anywhere in the area, Declan's preternatural senses would catch his scent— or the scent of fresh blood. Now that Conor had tasted his blood, he could find him anywhere, which meant that as far as planning any sort of attack, Conor had the upper hand in deciding where and when they finished this.

Declan roamed the streets for an hour, block by block, and saw no one except a couple of cops in a patrol car. They eyed him suspiciously until he spoke to their minds and sent them on their way.

He was on his way back to Angie's when he caught the scent of vampire. For a moment, he hoped it was his brother, come to end it here and now, but it was only one of the frequent visitors at the Nightmare.

Declan paused to let Jack Reynard catch up with him. Reynard had been turned some forty years ago. He had been one of the first vampires to visit the nightclub when Declan opened for business.

"Hey, what the hell happened to the Nightmare?" Reynard asked, falling into step beside him.

"My brother tried to burn it down."

"Well, he damn near succeeded."

"And damn near sent me up in flames."

"That's rough."

"Tell me about it," Declan said, grinning. "Not only that, but he's running rampant in the city. All those recent deaths among the wealthy? It's Conor's doing."

"Damn. I figured it was one of us, but your brother..." Reynard shook his head ruefully. "I guess that's why we're seeing so many hunters in town."

"Yeah. I've run into a couple of them."

"Me, too. So, are you going to rebuild, or relocate?"

"Rebuild. They're supposed to start tomorrow morning. If you see any of the others, let them know what happened. I'm pretty sure Max at The Pit will make you feel welcome until the Nightmare reopens."

"I guess, although I've never felt comfortable there. And they're a little stingy with the blood in the wine."

"I know, but it'll only be for six weeks or so."

"Good to see you, man. Watch out for that brother of yours."

"Give me a holler if you see him."

"Will do." With a wave of his hand, Reynard disappeared into the night.

Hands shoved in his pants' pockets, Declan strolled down the street, his thoughts tormented. Damn Conor! The man was nothing but trouble, and likely to get worse, a fear that was confirmed when he saw the headline in bold, black type in the early morning paper declaring the serial killer had struck again. The latest victims had been a well-known doctor and his wife, bringing the total deaths to eight.

He stopped at his secondary lair on his way to Angie's. He couldn't be with her every minute of every day. To that end, he threw several sharp wooden stakes—taken from deceased vampire hunters—into a burlap bag, along with a razor-sharp silver dagger taken from the same source, as well as a small bottle of holy water, filched from the local Catholic church.

If worse came to worse, at least she'd be armed.

# CHAPTER TWENTY-TWO

Ian frowned as he watched Samantha feed. She liked it even more than he did and that scared the crap out of him. Time and again, he'd had to interfere before she took too much. He was afraid to let her out of his sight, afraid she'd cross the line and take a life and Declan would destroy her. And he couldn't let that happen, couldn't lose Sam. She was his whole life. He hated to think about what his future would be like if he lost her. He understood what she was going through. He knew the high that came from the chase, from holding a life in your hands, the urge to drink and drink until there was nothing left. His own control wasn't that strong. Sometimes he was tempted to throw caution to the wind and join her. But always, in the back of his mind, was the memory of the look in Declan's eyes when he threatened to destroy him if he took a life. There wasn't a doubt in his mind that the master vampire would enforce that threat without a qualm.

Taking a step forward, Ian grabbed Samantha's arm. "That's enough. You've got to stop. Now."

She lifted her head, eyes red and angry. "He's mine. Let me go."

"Dammit, Sam, he's almost past the point of no return."

"I don't care! He tastes so good."

"Declan will destroy you. And maybe me, too, for not stopping you."

The red faded from her eyes at the mention of Declan's name. Releasing her hold on the man, she wiped what had happened from his mind and sent him on his way and then scowled at Ian.

Ian breathed a sigh of relief. They were safe. For now. Or so he thought, until Samantha laid her hand on his arm.

"Ian."

The way she said his name put him instantly on guard. "What?"

"Declan said we can't kill anyone in his territory, right?"

He nodded, afraid he knew where this line of questioning was headed.

"It's a big country. He only rules a small part of it. We could hunt somewhere else tomorrow night."

"Samantha..."

"Please, Ian. Just once I'd like to see what it's like to let myself go and drink and drink and..."

"Sam, stop it! Once you've killed someone, you'll want to do it again. And again. It's a high like no other, addictive."

"So you've done it?"

"Yeah. And I've regretted it every day since."

"That's so unfair!"

"Then think about this. If Declan finds out you've taken a life, he won't let us stay here. We'll have to find a new place to live, new jobs. Right now, we're under the protection of a master vampire." His gaze bored into hers. "We have a good thing going here, Sam. I don't want to lose it. Promise me you won't do anything foolish."

"I promise," she said, her expression sullen.

"I meant what I said. If you take a life, I'll kill you myself."

# Chapter Twenty-Three

Angie grinned as she settled in front of her computer a week later. Having Declan living under her roof was like being married with none of the perks. They ate dinner together. Went dancing, played cards, watched TV. Shared kisses and caresses on the sofa. But it ended there. She knew he was just as frustrated as she was. It was getting harder and harder to draw the line, to keep from inviting him to her bed. Time and again, she had to remind herself that he was a vampire.

Never was that brought home more forcefully than when Declan went out late at night. He was never gone long. He never said where he was headed. But she knew he was going in search of... prey. Just thinking of the word—and applying it to people—made her stomach turn. She had given him her blood, but only out of necessity, and then only as much as he needed. How much did he take when he was feeding? The wounds and burns inflicted on him by his brother and the fire had completely healed now, leaving no scars. He was a virile, healthy, handsome male and more sexy than any man had a right to be. But he wasn't really a man in the usual sense of the word. She had to remember that.

Though she didn't know how she would ever forget, not when there was a small burlap bag filled with instruments of destruction in the hall closet. She hadn't wanted to take it, but Declan had insisted. Inside were wooden stakes, a bottle of holy water and a silver dagger. "Just in case," he had said when she tried to refuse. Neither had mentioned his brother, but there had been no need.

Putting vampires out of her mind, she pulled up her Christmas monsters column and quickly perused what she'd written before starting a new paragraph.

*The story of Perchta is native to Austria. Today, she is viewed as one who rewards the virtuous and punishes the bad, most especially children. She's said to wander through the Hohensalzburg Castle in the dark of night. She is still featured in festivals and holiday gatherings.*

*Perchta is particularly active during the Christmas season and is said to roam the homes in Austria and Bavaria during the twelve days of Christmas and Epiphany. Discerning which children and which servants had been good all year and who had not, she would reward them accordingly—a silver coin for those she deemed acceptable—and slicing open the bellies of those she considered unworthy.*

*Perchta's name has been translated as "The Bright One" or "The Shining One." She has also been compared to pagan moon goddesses like Diana. She is also believed to be capable of flight and is said to lead the Wild Hunt. If you're not familiar with this ancient myth, it has been recorded since the beginning of history. The Wild Hunt is composed of a spectral, nocturnal horde said to sweep through the forests in mid-winter when the nights are darkest and the winds are the coldest. Heaven help you if they catch you outside. Those unfortunate enough to be caught by the ghostly huntsmen mounted on black horses were likely to be carried off and left miles from home—if they were lucky.*

*While Perchta is not a particularly endearing character, I found her to be quite fascinating, both cruel and kind, a bit comical, a bit tragic.*

*And so, I wish you all a very Merry Christmas, and, just in case Perchta is watching, I remind you to keep your houses clean and tidy this holiday season.*

She read through the column again, from the beginning, then closed the file. In the morning, she would do one last edit before sending it off to Jennifer.

Leaning back, Angie stretched her arms and shoulders. And then frowned as a quiver unlike anything she had ever felt before told her Declan was awake. She examined the feeling closely. Where had it come from? Why now? And what did it mean?

Declan frowned when he realized Angie had somehow sensed that he had awakened from the dark sleep. How the devil was that even possible? They didn't share a blood link. True, he had tasted her before, and had taken her blood to heal his injuries after Conor's attack. But a blood link went both ways—and Angie had not yet consumed his blood—something he intended to fix as soon as possible. Should the worst happen and she fell into Conor's hands, he wouldn't be able to find her without that link. He would be able to read her mind, as long as she was conscious, but he wouldn't be able to pinpoint her whereabouts unless she could tell him where she was.

Throwing the covers aside, he took a quick shower, pulled on a pair of jeans and a tee shirt, and padded barefooted into her office.

Angie glanced over her shoulder. She tried to smile but it fell short.

For a moment, they simply stared at each other across the room.

Declan leaned one shoulder against the door jamb. "You go first."

She didn't pretend she didn't know what he meant. "How did I know you were awake before you even got out of bed?"

"I don't know."

Her brows shot up in surprise. "I thought you knew everything."

"Apparently not. How did *you* know?"

She made a vague gesture with her hand. "I felt some kind of weird sensation and I knew... *knew*... you weren't asleep anymore."

"Have you felt it before?"

She shook her head. "No, never."

He dragged a hand across his jaw. It just didn't make sense.

Looking worried, she asked, "Is there something wrong with me?"

"No. At least, I don't think so. It has to have something to do with my drinking from you, but I've never heard of anything like it before. If you'd tasted me, it would make sense."

A look of revulsion flickered in her eyes.

"Actually, I think that's a good idea."

"Drink from you? No way!" She paused a moment, brow furrowed. "Why do you think I should?"

"It would form a bond between us. I would always be able to find you."

She worried her lower lip a moment and then shook her head. "I don't think I like that idea at all." And then she stared at him, her eyes wide. "This has to do with your brother, doesn't it?"

"Right the first time. It would also allow you to contact me telepathically, if necessary."

"You mean we'd be able to read each other's thoughts?"

He nodded. It was true, but only if he wished it.

"How much of your ... your blood would I have to drink?"

"Only a little. It would also warn any other vampires in the area that you belong to me."

Hot color rose in her cheeks. "I do *not* belong to you, Declan Nicolae, or anyone else. And if this is just some way to make me your ... your slave, you can darn well forget it."

"Calm down, darlin'. That's not what I meant at all. It's simply a warning for others to back off."

"Others? How many vampires are there in the city?"

"Besides Ian and Samantha, there's Raj and Reynard, who frequent the Nightmare, and Max Portman, who owns The Pit, and the two who own Drac's Den and Mel's Hell, plus three others who live in the city. All told, there are ten, counting Sam and Ian. There are others who come and go, but they're not allowed to stay in my territory."

"*Your* territory?"

"Exactly. I say who stays and who goes."

"Really? And who made you the boss?"

"I did. I'm what is known as a Master Vampire. There are only a few of us in the world."

"So, how did you get to be one?"

"By existing for so long. Not many vampires survive more than three or four hundred years."

"Why not?"

"A lot of fledglings are destroyed by older vampires. We tend to be very territorial creatures, jealous of any land we've claimed. Some grow weary of surviving for so long. They grow bored with life. Some can't handle the inevitable changes in the world. They miss their old customs, the old ways. Vampire hunters account for a good number of deaths."

Leaning back in her chair, Angie took a deep breath and let it out in a long, slow sigh. Who would have guessed that a vampire's life was so complicated?

"So, what do you say?"

She stared at him, momentarily confused. What did he mean? And then she remembered. He wanted her to drink his blood.

Declan watched one emotion after another chase itself across Angie's face—fear, curiosity, doubt, an innate sense of revulsion.

"Are you sure this is really necessary?"

He knew what she was really asking. "If you decide you don't want to be involved with a vampire anymore, or you meet someone else and decide to get married, I can block the link between us." But he would always be able to find her.

Her gaze slid away from his. "I didn't mean that."

"Sure you did. I know you have doubts about being with me."

For a moment, Angie wondered how he knew what she was thinking and then she remembered that he could read her mind.

"Do you want to think about it?"

Angie shook her head, her curiosity stronger than her revulsion. "Let's get it over with."

"Come on." Taking her by the hand, he pulled Angie to her feet and led her into the living room. Sitting on the sofa, he tugged her down beside him. He could hear the sound of her heart beat accelerating. "Relax. It's not as bad as you think."

She swallowed hard. "I don't think I can bite you hard enough to draw blood."

"You won't have to." Lifting his arm, he turned his left arm over and bit into his wrist. Several drops of dark red blood oozed from a pair of small punctures.

Angie grimaced when she saw it.

"You only need to drink a very little," he assured her. "Close your eyes if it will help."

With hands that trembled, she took hold of his arm, closed her eyes, and lapped the blood from his wrist. It was warm and thick and pulsed through her like liquid fire. She gasped as sensual pleasure washed over her, filling her with euphoria and a sense of well-being.

Declan let out a sigh as she drank. He'd forgotten how pleasant it was to share his blood with someone he cared about. "That's enough, Angie," he murmured, reluctant for her to stop.

"Do I have to?"

He laughed softly. "Too much at once isn't good for you."

She huffed a sigh of disappointment as she lifted her head. "You didn't tell me it would be so … so …" Her cheeks warmed with embarrassment.

"So pleasant?"

"Yes," she agreed, her blush deepening. "Pleasant." More than pleasant. She was already wondering if he would let her drink from him again.

"For me, as well."

"So, we have a bond now?"

"Can you feel it?"

She tilted her head to the side, eyes narrowing, then widening. "I can! It's like … I don't know what it's like. And now you can find me wherever I am?"

"Pretty much."

"And I can find you?"

"Not physically, but mentally you'll always be able to contact me."

"Vampire GPS?"

"In a way." He debated whether or not to tell her that blocking the link didn't mean it no longer existed. A blood bond could only be broken if he died—or if she did. In the end, he decided against revealing this bit of information, at least for the time being.

Angie stood and paced the floor. She felt amazing, better than she ever had in her whole life—as if she could run a marathon or two, climb Everest, swim the English channel, and start all over again.

Declan grinned at the wonder in her eyes. He knew just how she felt. He had experienced that same sense of supernatural power and strength when he'd been turned, only a thousand times stronger.

"Come on," he said. "Let's go for a walk so you can burn off some of that energy."

They had only gone a few blocks when Declan swore under his breath.

"What's wrong?" Angie glanced around, her gaze searching the darkness. Had Conor found them?

"Nothing." Declan blew out a sigh of resignation as they rounded a corner. Short of grabbing Angie and transporting them elsewhere, there was no way to avoid the couple in front of them.

"Then what's…?" The words died in Angie's throat when she saw Samantha and Ian standing in the shadows, their heads bent over the man and woman in their respective embrace.

Ian's head snapped up at the sound of their footsteps. "Sam, we have company."

Samantha looked up, her eyes widening when she saw Angie. Her gaze darted to Ian as she pushed the man in her arms away and licked the blood from her lips.

A taut silence stretched between them.

Angie blinked back her tears as she stared at Samantha, her heart aching for the loss of her best friend. Try as she might, she could find no trace of the bubbly, carefree woman she had once known. There was only this stranger who resembled Sam standing in her place.

Samantha looked away and then, in the blink of an eye, she was gone.

Ian looked at Declan and shrugged, and then he, too, vanished from sight.

Declan laid a gentle hand on Angie's shoulder. "Are you all right?"

She shook her head, thinking how foolish she had been to ever think she and Sam could be friends again. "Is that how you look when you...you hunt? All wild-eyed and...and...?"

"I might have, in the beginning."

"She's gone, isn't she? The Samantha I knew is gone?"

"I'm afraid so. Wait here a minute."

Angie watched as he approached the man and the woman standing like zombies on the sidewalk, heard him whisper something to each one of them. At his words, they seemed to shake off whatever compulsion had held them, and then the man took the woman's hand and they hurried down the street. "Will they be okay?"

"Yes. Are we okay?"

"What do you mean?"

"I can feel you judging me, wondering if I'm really so different than Sam."

"I know you are. It was just…shocking, I guess, to see her like that."

Declan grunted softly. Ian should never have turned Samantha. He was never going to be able to leave her alone, never be able to trust her. Samantha was a born hunter. Declan knew without a doubt that given the choice, she would have killed her prey without guilt or regret. Sooner or later, she would cross the line and when that happened, there would be no going back. Ian would have to destroy her.

If Sam didn't destroy him first.

Angie was quiet on the walk back to her house. She had been convinced that her decision to stay with Declan was the right one, that, somehow, they could make it work. But seeing Samantha tonight had shaken her faith. Did all new vampires look like that—eyes crazy wild and red? Had Ian? Had Declan and his brother?

Although Declan had never suggested it, Angie knew, deep down inside where she refused to look, that if she stayed with Declan, sooner or later she would have to decide whether to leave him or become what he was. She knew now that she would never willingly choose to become a vampire. Sure, Declan seemed normal, almost human, but it had taken over eight hundred years to achieve that level of control. What kind of hell had he endured as a new vampire? How many people had he killed before he learned to control himself and his actions? He had admitted to killing in the beginning. But he hadn't said how many lives he'd taken.

Declan was fully aware of Angie's troubled thoughts, not that he could blame her for what she was feeling, thinking. He stood behind her on the porch while she unlocked the door.

"I think you need some time alone," he said quietly. "I'm going over to the Nightmare to see how the repairs are going. I'll probably spend the night there."

She didn't argue, merely nodded.

Leaning forward, he brushed a kiss across the top of her head. "I love you, Angie." When she started to speak, he pressed a finger to her lips. "Don't forget to lock the door," he murmured.

And then he was gone.

Troubled by what had happened that night, Declan decided to walk to the Nightmare. He was nearing the place where they had run into Ian and Samantha when he caught the rich, coppery scent of freshly-spilled blood.

Vampire blood.

Dreading what he might find, he followed the scent. He found the body lying in the mouth of an alley near Ian's lair.

For a moment, Declan could only stare at the carnage before him. Ian lay sprawled on his back, arms outstretched. His head had been ripped from his body. A large pool of dark red blood glistened wetly in the moonlight.

He stared at the grisly remains for several minutes, grief and regret rising within him. This was all his fault. Had he destroyed Conor years ago, the boy would still be alive.

Lifting his head, Declan opened his senses.

Samantha was nowhere in sight, but his brother's scent lingered in the air.

# CHAPTER TWENTY-FOUR

Still reeling from the shock of Ian's brutal murder, Samantha stared helplessly at the vampire who had destroyed the love of her life, whisked her away, and now stood staring at her through narrowed eyes. He refused to tell her his name or why he had destroyed Ian and kidnapped her. He looked vaguely familiar, even though she was certain she had never seen him before.

As soon as he had released his hold on her, she had tried to run away, only to find she was incapable of movement. She could feel his preternatural power, an invisible grip that held her immobile. She could only stand there, more scared than she had ever been in her life. Ian had been sweet and patient. Declan was scary in his own way. But this man was hard and cruel. Malevolence rolled off him in palpable waves, though, thankfully, it wasn't aimed at her.

"What do you want with me?" she asked, hating the quiver of terror in her voice. Showing fear in front of a predator could be fatal.

His gaze moved over her, mentally stripping away her clothing and her self-respect. "I can't have the woman I want, at least not at the moment, so I've decided you'll take her place."

Horrified, Samantha closed her eyes, felt the sting of tears as the image of this frightening creature killing Ian flashed across her mind. She choked back a sob, afraid to reveal any sign of weakness.

His hands curled like claws over her shoulders. "Your bond to your sire died with him. From now on, you will be mine."

Samantha stared up at him, let out a gasp of pain as he sank his fangs into her throat. She could feel him drinking from her. Drinking deeply. Did he intend to destroy her, too? Dark spots swam before her eyes. Her legs turned to rubber and she knew she would have fallen if he hadn't been holding her. Just when she thought she was going to die for the second time, he bit into his wrist and held it to her mouth. She wanted to resist, but the hunger was upon her. Hating her need, her weakness, she grasped his arm in both hands and drank greedily.

When he jerked his arm away, she was bound to him until death.

Declan sat in the dark at the bar in the Nightmare, a glass of wine in his hand. He had taken a quick glance around when he first arrived. The construction crew had been hard at work. They had cleared away the debris from the fire and framed the upstairs. He figured a dozen men working around the clock should have the job done in record time.

But it wasn't re-opening the Nightmare that was uppermost in his mind. Why in hell had his crazy brother killed Ian? And what had he done with Samantha? Had Conor carried her away from the scene and destroyed her elsewhere? And if she was yet alive, what did Conor plan to do with her? Nothing good, he was certain of that.

Declan slammed his free hand on the bar. Dammit! He would miss having Ian around. Vampires made few friends, even among their own kind. He had grown fond of the boy, enjoyed his company. He muttered a vile oath. Just one more reason to destroy his brother, something he should have done long ago. Why the hell hadn't be? It was a question he'd asked himself countless times.

Cursing his weakness, he finished his drink and poured another.

What was he going to do about Angie?

He was still searching for an answer when he made his way to the cellar. It was his emergency lair—a small, square room made of cement with an iron door three-feet thick and a stout cross-bar on the inside. A double bed was the room's only furnishing.

Stretching out on the mattress, he closed his eyes and called Angie's image to mind.

Unable to sleep, Angie stared up at the ceiling. What was Declan doing now? Was he still at the Nightmare? Why had he decided to spend the night there? He hadn't said anything about calling her tomorrow, or seeing her again. Had that last kiss goodnight really been goodbye?

In a way, it would be a relief. She wouldn't have to decide, at some future date, whether she wanted to be a vampire. But surely she had years to make that decision. Years she could spend with him. She had never known anyone like him and it wasn't just that Declan was an incredibly gorgeous, sexy, male—although that was a part of it. But it was more than that. And more than his being a vampire. He made her feel cherished, cared for. Loved. He listened to her, really listened. And frequently knew what she was thinking, she mused with a wry grin. But only because he could read her thoughts...

She slapped her hand on the mattress. Of course, he'd read her troubled thoughts tonight and taken the decision out of her hands. No wonder he had decided to take his rest elsewhere.

And yet, her doubts and fears were not without merit. He was a supernatural creature, with incredible powers and abilities that made Superman look like a wimp.

Sighing, she turned onto her side and closed her eyes.

And he was there, inside her dreams, a tall, dark, sexy being with mesmerizing green eyes and a voice that could make angels weep.

He murmured her name as he drew her into his arms. "Angie."

"This isn't real."

His knuckles caressed her cheek. "It's as real as you want it to be."

"I love you," she whispered.

"I know." He ran his fingertips over her lower lip, then kissed her deeply, his tongue teasing hers as his hand skimmed up and down her thigh. "And I love you."

Breathless from his kisses, her whole body burning with need, she murmured, "Tell me what to do."

"I can't," he said, with a sad smile. "This is a decision you have to make on your own."

Angie woke abruptly, her whole body quivering, her lips still tingling from his kisses. She glanced around the room, half-expecting to find him there even though she knew she had been dreaming. But it had been so real. His scent clung to her skin.

Sighing with disappointment, she snuggled under the covers. She wanted him desperately, craved his touch, his kisses. He was like a drug and she was like an addict who knew her drug of choice could kill her, but didn't care. As he had said, staying with him was a decision only she could make, but was she willing to risk the inevitable consequences?

Beset by doubts, she tumbled into a restless sleep.

Declan materialized out of the shadows in the corner of Angie's room. He had told her the choice was hers, but, ultimately, it was his. He had the power to make her forget what he was, to forget everything that had happened between them except that she loved him. Had he loved her a little less, been a little more selfish, it was exactly what he would have done.

Or he could turn her while she slept...

He quickly thrust that thought aside. Having been turned against his will, he had sworn on his mother's life that he would never do such a thing to anyone else.

Or he could do the right thing and let her make the decision on her own.

Even if she decided she wanted to be with him, the final decision whether to stay or go was still his to make.

Leaving her house, he opened his senses as he stalked the dark streets. Where had Conor taken Samantha, and why? What were his intentions? As far as he knew, since being turned, his brother had never loved a woman, never viewed them as anything but prey, whether for food or to satisfy his sexual appetite. His whole personality had changed drastically once he became a vampire. While growing up, his little brother had been sweet-natured, gifted with a fine sense of humor. He had been well-liked by the people in the village, loved by his family.

Declan knew he, too, had changed in many ways. Like it or not, once turned, change had been inevitable, a matter of survival. Yet he had managed to hold on to some semblance of humanity. He had never taken a life once he learned to control his hunger except to save his own. Conor had reveled in killing, growing more brutal and hardened with each mortal he preyed on, feeding not only to satisfy his thirst but to torment those he fed on. He preyed on their horror, their fright, as much as their blood.

And Declan feared that Samantha was just like Conor. Together, they would make a formidable killing machine.

And it was up to him to stop them.

With that thought in mind, he returned to the Nightmare and summoned all the vampires who currently resided in his territory—Raj and Jack Reynard, frequent patrons of the club; Mel Smithfield, who owned Mel's Hell; Max Hayes, who managed The Pit; and Devin Milosch, who ran Drac's Den. There were three other vampires who made their lairs within the city—Saul Gibson, Randy Fontaine, and Delia Montez, who had been the city's sole female vampire until Ian turned Samantha. He was the Master of the City and as such, they were all indebted to him for allowing them to stay in the territory he had claimed and defended as his own.

"What's going on?" Milosch asked.

"My brother is the one behind the recent killings."

Several audible gasps ran through the group.

"Most of you know Ian. He used to work for me. He recently turned his girlfriend, Samantha. The other night,

Conor destroyed Ian and made off with Sam. I have no idea where they are. I don't even know if she's still alive."

"You want us to take his head?"

"No. But I want you to contact me immediately if you see him, or the girl." He quickly gave them descriptions of Conor and Sam.

"What are you gonna do?" Max asked.

"What I should have done centuries ago."

Raj stared at him, eyes wide. "But...you said he's your brother."

"That's right. But he's killed nine people that I know of. His rash behavior has brought half a dozen hunters into the city, putting our kind in danger. And now he's kidnapped someone I considered under my protection. You all need to keep a sharp eye out for hunters. Trust no one. And watch your backs."

"Thanks for the warning," Mel said, clapping him on the shoulder. "Be sure to take your own advice."

# CHAPTER TWENTY-FIVE

The house seemed unusually empty without Declan's presence. Not that Angie was surprised. He was such a virile, powerful man, there was no ignoring him when he was there, even when he was at rest.

Although she had little appetite, she forced herself to eat a bowl of cereal for breakfast. Later, she sat at her computer, but her Muse had abandoned her. All she could think about was Declan. She heard his voice over and over again in her mind—*This is a decision only you can make.* But how could she? The thought of never seeing him again was heart-wrenching. Even though she had known him only a short time, she couldn't imagine living the rest of her life without him. So, he was a vampire, she thought with morbid humor. No relationship was perfect.

She clapped her hand over her mouth as she felt a burst of hysterical laughter bubble up inside. She wished suddenly that Samantha was here. They had always shared everything, talked over their problems, discussed solutions, found humor in heartbreak and hope in despair. Samantha had been the sister she'd never had.

It was bad enough to face the future without her best friend. How could she give up Declan, too? She knew it was the right thing, the smart thing to do, but it wasn't fair.

The words, *no one ever said life was fair,* whispered through the back of her mind.

Was that Declan's thought? Or her own?

Pushing away from her desk, she wandered aimlessly through the house. Where was Declan? What would she say if he came by for her decision?

For the first time in years, she wished she had a better relationship with her mother. It would be so nice to call home and pour out her doubts and fears to someone who loved her unconditionally. But she didn't have that kind of rapport with her mother. Or her father. She couldn't remember the last time either one of them had called her. But the blame wasn't all theirs. She hadn't called either of them in over a year. She had hoped, with the passage of time, that she and her mom could forge some kind of bond, but her mother's whole life was tied up in her new family, with no time left over for her firstborn child.

Feeling lost and alone, she wandered out to the back-yard. It was small by most standards. Rose bushes in shades of pink, red, and yellow bordered the white vinyl fence that enclosed the yard. She made herself comfortable on the small, padded swing that stood under the spreading branches of a willow tree. She couldn't remember ever feeling so lost or so alone in her whole life. Maybe she should get a dog. Or a cat. It would be nice to have another living thing in the house, she thought with a wry grin, and wondered morbidly if Declan qualified as a living thing. Were vampires really alive? Or truly Undead, kind of like zombies?

*Does it matter?* She frowned as that little voice of doubt whispered in her mind again.

"I don't know," she muttered irritably. "How can I make a decision like this when I can't even think straight?"

*Call me when you make up your mind.*

This time, the voice was definitely his.

Three days passed with no word from Declan. Apparently he had decided to stay away while she pondered her decision. Was he afraid his presence would influence her? She grunted softly, thinking it definitely would. Or maybe he had decided on his own that she would be better off without him. She wondered again if that last good night kiss had really been goodbye.

In the morning, she worked listlessly on her December column and after one last edit, she sent it off to Jennifer.

Instead of eating lunch, she drowned her sorrows in a huge bowl of chocolate ice cream smothered in hot fudge and whipped crème and then spent the rest of the afternoon feeling sorry for herself.

In the days that followed, her indecision turned to apathy and then anger. She had given him refuge. Offered him her blood. Taken him in when he was hurt. Confessed her love for him. And what did she have to show for it? Not a damn thing!

Well, enough was enough. She was tired of sitting around pining for a man who didn't even care enough to call and see how she was doing.

That night, Angie decided to go out on the town. She showered, shaved her legs, put on the sexiest outfit she owned, spritzed herself with perfume, and left the house. She treated herself to a spaghetti dinner at Moretti's and then headed for a well-known nightclub that catered to singles.

She wasn't looking for a date, she told herself as she found a place at the bar. She wasn't looking for anything other than the company of regular people having a good time. She ordered a glass of white wine, then sat back, her foot tapping to the music provided by a three-piece band.

She sighed as the band began to play "Some Enchanted Evening." Watching several couples take to the dance floor filled her with a sudden emptiness as she recalled dancing with Declan, being in his arms, feeling as if she belonged there.

"May I have this dance?"

A thrill of excitement raced down her spine when she glanced over her shoulder and saw him standing there.

He held out his hand, one brow arched as he waited for her response.

Sliding off the stool, Angie placed her hand in his. felt a sense of coming home when he drew her into his arms. She wanted to shout at him, demand an explanation for his absence, but she was too happy to see him.

He nuzzled her ear as he whispered, "I missed you, love."

"Did you?"

"I know you're angry with me, and I don't blame you." His lips brushed her hair. "I decided the best thing I could do was leave you alone for a while. I've brought you nothing but trouble, turned your life upside down. I thought a little distance between us would be good for me, too."

"Oh?" She felt her heart sink. Had he come here to tell her goodbye?

"The thing is, I don't want to let you go. My life is empty and not worth living without you. So I'm asking you, begging you, to let me see you again, if not every night, at least once in a while." His gaze searched hers when she didn't answer right away. Angie?"

"I missed you, too," she said, her voice thick with unshed tears. "Let's go home."

Declan had transported himself to the nightclub, so Angie drove them to her house. A million butterflies danced in the pit of her stomach as she unlocked the door and crossed the threshold. She knew Declan was right behind her by the familiar tremor in the air as he followed her inside.

He waited until she dropped her handbag and keys on the table inside the door before sweeping her into his arms.

Angie sighed as she lifted her face for his kiss, her eyelids fluttering down as his mouth found hers. Warmth and peace flowed through her as he pulled her closer, molding her body to his as he rained kisses on her brow, her cheeks, the curve of her throat, before returning to her lips. His mouth was warm, his tongue a flame as it teased and tormented hers, making her think of sweat-sheened bodies bound together in the throes of passion.

Walking backward, their mouths still fused together, he moved toward the sofa and drew her down beside him.

When, at last, he lifted his head, she was breathless. For a time they simply sat there, content to hold each other close.

"Where have you been these last few weeks?" Angie asked when her breathing returned to normal.

He shrugged one shoulder. "Mostly, lurking around your house."

"What? Why?"

"I told you, I missed you." It was the main reason, but not the only one. He hadn't forgotten Conor's revelation that he wanted Angie. The thought of her being at his brother's mercy scared him as nothing else ever had.

Angie shook her head, touched by his words. "So, what else have you been doing? Is the renovation of the Nightmare finished?"

"Just about. I'll probably open next week." As it turned out, the repairs hadn't been as extensive as he'd feared. Even so, he figured the construction crew had set some kind of record. They had certainly earned the bonus he'd promised.

"Well, that's good."

He nodded, his expression implacable.

"What's wrong? Declan?"

"Ian is dead."

"Dead?" She stared at him, eyes wide with shock. "What happened?"

"My brother killed him."

"Oh, no." She hadn't known Ian well, but she'd liked him. "Where's Samantha? Is she okay?"

"I don't know," he said, his voice flat. "Conor's taken her. I've looked everywhere I can think of, but so far, I haven't had any luck."

Feeling numb, Angie sank back on the sofa cushions. Poor Sam, at the mercy of Declan's crazy brother. There seemed to be no end to Conor's killing spree. A new body turned up every three or four days—all drained of blood. Every cop and detective in the city were searching for him. People were afraid to leave their homes after dark unless it was necessary. Everywhere you looked there were patrol cars, some parked in residential areas, other patrolling the business district. People who could afford it were hiring private security guards, installing outdoor cameras and security systems. There was a sudden increase of people at animal shelters looking for large dogs. Gun stores were doing a landslide business as people armed themselves with everything from pistols to AK-47s. She doubted any of those measures would be effective against Conor.

She looked up at Declan. "Do you think she's still alive?"

"I honestly have no idea."

Brow furrowed, Angie let his words sink in. Ian was dead and Samantha was missing. She tried to absorb the news, to make sense of it. Ian was gone. And even if she knew how or where to find Samantha, there was nothing she could do to help her old friend. She had no supernatural powers. She wasn't a hunter.

And then a new thought occurred to her. "You haven't been hanging around my house just because you missed me, have you? You're worried about me, aren't you? That's why you were keeping watch, to protect me in case your brother showed up."

"Okay, I admit that was part of the reason. But I would have been nearby anyway, Conor or no Conor. I meant it when I said I missed you. And speaking of Conor, what were you thinking, going out alone tonight?"

"I know it was foolish, but I angry with you and lonely and tired of being alone."

"Promise me," he said, his gaze holding hers. "Promise me you won't go out alone after dark. I couldn't live with myself if anything happened to you." He kissed the tip of her nose. "Promise me, Angie."

"I promise." The concern in his silky-smooth voice, the look of affection in his deep green eyes, made her heart melt. "You asked me to make a decision," she reminded him. "But you've never asked for my answer."

"I was afraid to find out," he admitted with a sheepish grin. "Afraid the answer would be no. Is it?"

Cupping his face in her hands, she murmured, "Read my mind." And then she kissed him.

His arms slid around her, drawing her body up against his, his mouth hot and hungry against hers, his desire evident in the tension radiating through him as he pulled her down beside him, then covered her body with his.

For a moment, she was drowning in a sea of sensual pleasure, overcome with the fire of his kisses, the thrill of his touch as he caressed her, even as warning bells sounded in the back of her mind, telling her that she needed to put the brakes on now or it would be too late.

"Declan." She pressed her hands against his chest and pushed, but it was like trying to move a small mountain. "Declan, stop!"

For a moment, she thought she had waited too long. But then he lifted his head. Angie went still, not even daring to breathe, when she saw the faint red glow in his eyes.

He bolted upright and turned his back to her.

Angie sat up slowly and straightened her clothing.

"I'm sorry." His voice was strained, his back rigid.

She watched the tension ease from his shoulders as he regained control.

"Angie?"

"I guess you really did miss me," she said, hoping to add a little humor to the situation.

He glanced at her over his shoulder. "I frightened you, didn't I?"

"No." She took a deep breath. "No. I frightened myself because I... I want you so much."

He grunted softly. Her desire for him, strong as it was, cooled whenever she let herself remember that he was a vampire. It was an abyss she wasn't ready to cross.

Perhaps she never would be.

Angie stayed awake long after Declan had taken his leave. They couldn't go on this way forever. He wanted her. She wanted him. And yet she was reluctant—maybe afraid—to let him make love to her. She had never been promiscuous. She'd had numerous dates in high school and college but never met anyone she wanted to go out with more than once or twice. She had dated so rarely in the past couple of years she'd started to think there was something wrong with her. Maybe she was frigid. Or lacked some elemental dating gene. She was twenty-four and still a virgin, something unheard of in this day and age. Many of her old girlfriends from high school and college had married and moved on with their lives. Most had kids. She envied them, in a way, and yet she had been perfectly content with her life.

Until she met Declan. He had turned her world upside down in more ways than one, made her realize there was nothing wrong with her. She wasn't frigid. She wasn't uptight about sex or afraid to commit to a relationship. She had just never met a man she wanted to go to bed with before. Just her luck that when she finally fell head-over-heels in love with a man, he wasn't really a man at all.

Did she love him enough to take him to her bed? She knew he loved her and she was crazy about him, but was that enough? Had he been an ordinary man, she would have said yes without hesitation. But there was nothing ordinary about Declan Nicolae. He drank blood to survive. He could read her mind. He was a hunted man, not just by vampire hunters but by a vindictive brother, as well. He had killed people. She had been miserable when they were apart. It hadn't been so long ago that she had vowed she would never let him go again.

Angie closed her eyes, remembering how unhappy she had been without him, how empty the house had seemed while he was gone. Did she want to feel like that again, maybe for the rest of her life?

The answer was a resounding no. She was about to call him when the doorbell rang.

Angie frowned, and then smiled, thinking Declan had come back. After all, who else would come calling at this late hour?

Her smile quickly faded when she opened the door. "Samantha!" Merciful heavens, what was she doing here?

"Ange, you've got to help me."

Angie stared at her friend. Sam looked awful. Her hair was unkempt, her clothing torn, and she was barefooted. "What's happened?"

"I ran away from Conor. Please, for old time's sake, you've got to hide me. I don't have anywhere else to go."

Angie shook her head. "I wish I could, but..." She took a step back, guilt at refusing warring with the memory of their former friendship.

"Please, Angie, he'll kill me! Just let me stay for an hour or so. I won't hurt you, I swear it. I already fed."

"Sam, I..."

"There you are!"

Angie recoiled as Conor appeared on the sidewalk. Eyes filled with menace, fangs bared, he stalked toward the porch.

"Angie, please!" Samantha wailed.

"All right, Sam, come in."

Samantha hurried across the threshold. Murmuring, "I'm sorry," she sprang forward in a blur of movement, grabbed Angie by the arm and yanked her out onto the porch.

Angie stared at her friend, unable to believe the betrayal.

"I'm sorry," Samantha said again. "He really did say he'd kill me if I didn't get you outside."

Terror rose up within Angie when Conor stepped out of the shadows and pulled her away from Samantha. She stared at Declan's brother. How could two men look so much alike, been raised together, and be so different? Looking into Conor's soulless eyes was like looking into the depths of hell. She had no doubt he would have killed Samantha without a qualm. But that didn't ease the sense of hurt or betrayal. But those emotions paled as fear spiked within her.

She cried out when he grabbed a handful of her hair and jerked her head back, flinched when he forced her to look into his eyes—unforgiving eyes filled with hatred. She tried to look away as blackness descended on her, clouding her mind as she spiraled down a dark tunnel into nothingness.

Declan lifted his head, the prey in his arms forgotten, as his blood-link to Angie went silent. Dread settled over him. Only two things could quell that link—either she was unconscious.

Or she was dead.

He sealed the twin punctures in his prey's throat, then transported himself to Angie's house. The front door was ajar, the lights on, the house empty.

A single deep breath told him everything he needed to know. For some reason he couldn't fathom, Angie had invited Samantha into the house.

And Conor had been outside, waiting for Sam to bring Angie out so he could spirit her away.

Hands clenched, Declan stared into the distance. Conor had Angie and it was all his fault. He never should have left her alone. Guilt seared his soul. He knew all too well the pain and terror his brother was capable of inflicting.

Guilt turned to rage as he transported himself to the Nightmare. Next time he saw Conor, only one of them would walk away.

# CHAPTER TWENTY-SIX

Conor made his lair in the cellar of an abandoned ware-house that had been divided into two large rooms. One held a dilapidated sofa and a big screen TV, though where the electricity came from, Samantha had no idea. The second room held a king-sized mattress, which Conor forced her to share with him, a small dresser, an overstuffed chair, and an iron cot. Not exactly the lap of luxury, Samantha had thought the night he first brought her here, and wondered why on earth he had chosen to live this way when he could easily have stayed in a four-star hotel. A little vampire mind control and he could have lived in the penthouse, rent free, for as long as he liked. She had never asked his reasons, of course. Never spoke a word until spoken to.

But tonight, Samantha summoned her courage. Kneeling on the floor at his feet, her head bowed, she whispered, "What are you going to do with her?"

"Whatever the hell I want."

Samantha risked a sidelong glance at Angie. She didn't know what sort of spell Conor had worked on Angie, but she lay on her back on the cot, unmoving, her body unusually stiff, her breathing shallow but regular.

Samantha bit down on her lower lip, afraid to question Conor further. He terrified her. In the days she had been his prisoner, she had discovered no trace of mercy or compassion or kindness in him. He killed without compunction—men, women, and children, young and old, healthy or infirm—it mattered not. Anyone was fair game.

He had stopped hunting in the city when the number of vampire hunters rose from a few to a dozen. Since then, Conor had dragged her from one town to another. He didn't care if she killed her prey or not. At first she had done so thoughtlessly, the hunger and the freedom to do as she pleased too strong to resist. It was exhilarating to surrender to the urge to take it all until the night she accidentally killed a young woman that reminded her of Angie.

Revulsion for what she'd done had risen up inside her as she imagined her one-time best friend standing at her shoulder, judging her.

Fearful of becoming like Conor, Samantha had vowed then and there never to take another life. It hadn't been easy. The temptation to drink it all was always there, but, so far, she had resisted, taking only what she needed, even though Conor mocked her for it constantly.

"You're a vampire," he taunted with a sneer. "Act like one!"

When she continued to refuse, he had chained her to the wall in his lair until she was out of her mind with hunger, until she dropped down on her hands and knees and begged him for nourishment. With a wicked grin, he had brought her a young boy, perhaps twelve years old. And to her ever-lasting shame and regret, she had drained the frightened child dry. If she lived to be a hundred, she would never forgive herself—or Conor—for what she'd done.

Not that he cared. He thrived on her hatred. He was her sire now, her master, and she was helpless to resist him. It was like being a slave, forced to obey his every whim, his every command—his to do with as he pleased. He humiliated her every chance he got. He belittled her when she mourned for Ian, tortured her when she dared mention his name. Filled with despair, she often prayed for death even though she was certain heaven no longer listened to her pleas.

And now, at his command, she had betrayed her best friend into the hands of a monster.

# CHAPTER TWENTY-SEVEN

Declan scowled into the darkness. It had been almost a week since Conor had abducted Angie. He had no idea if Angie was still alive, or if Conor was still in the city. He had searched for her every waking moment, contacted every vampire in his territory again in hopes one of them had some news of Conor or Samantha, but to no avail. It only added to his frustration and an ever-growing fear that Conor had killed her.

His rage fueled his hunger, rousing the beast he had fought so long to control. Hunting became dangerous for those he preyed upon and it took every shred of self-control he possessed not to succumb to the anger that surged within him. What had Conor done to Angie? Where had he taken her?

Declan hadn't prayed in years, certain Heaven had stopped listening centuries ago, but he prayed now, prayed fervently that Angie was still alive and that he would find her before it was eternally too late. Was she still alive, or had Conor killed her out of hand? It was all he could think about. If she was alive, his brother would have to release her from whatever spell that was keeping her unconscious and allow her at least a few minutes to eat and drink. It might be his only chance to find her.

Hands shoved into the pockets of his jeans, he wandered the dark streets, his heart aching and afraid. The thought of losing Angie, of never again seeing her smile, never hearing her laugh, never holding her in his arms again ... it was too painful to bear.

He howled his pain and frustration into the night where it was picked up and sent back to him by every dog within hearing distance.

Angie woke slowly and wondered why she couldn't move, couldn't speak. Her head ached and when she tried to remember where she was, her mind refused to work. Try as she might, she couldn't form a coherent thought. Most frightening of all, she couldn't see anything but darkness.

"Angie? Are you awake? I brought you something to eat."

She frowned and turned her head toward the sound of Samantha's voice, even though she couldn't make sense of the words. As if she were an infant, Sam fed her a sandwich, held up her head while she drank a bottle of water.

Footsteps moving away from the bed told her that Sam—if indeed it had been Sam—had left the room—or wherever she was.

She let out a shriek when unseen hands gripped her shoulders, gasped with pain as fangs bit deep into the side of her throat.

And then darkness engulfed her once again.

A vile oath escaped Declan's lips as the bond that had lain dormant flared to life and then died away before he could home in on it. Angie was alive! But he'd had no sense of where she was and when he'd tried to probe her thoughts, it was as though someone had wiped her memory clean. Conor! Where had his brother learned to do that?

His hands clenched as he imagined ripping his brother's heart from his chest and burning the remains. Somehow, some way, he would make Conor pay for his treachery.

Trapped in darkness, her mind not her own, Angie had no sense of time passing. Had she died and gone to hell? Was she in a coma? Trapped in some kind of perverted Neverland?

On rare occasions, she felt Declan was near but before she could be sure or call his name, darkness enveloped her again.

And then, one night, she woke clear-headed. Although it was dark in the room, she could make out vague outlines of furniture—a small dresser, a chair. She knew a moment of hope when Samantha stepped into view, a tray in her hands.

"Sam! Thank the Lord! Get me out of here!"

"I can't."

Angie glared at her. "It's your fault I'm here."

Guilt flitted across Samantha's face. "I'm sorry, really I am. But he'll destroy me if I let you go. He … he has plans for you."

Fear turned Angie's insides to ice. "What kind of plans?"

"He's going to bring you across tonight."

Angie's stomach recoiled in horror at the thought of becoming like Sam. "Please get me out of here. We used to be friends. If you help me, Declan will protect you."

Samantha snorted. "Fat chance. He'll kill me for what I've done."

"No, he won't. He'll forgive you if you take me home. I know he will."

"You swear it?"

"Yes."

Muttering, "Oh, shit!" Samantha cloaked her intentions from Conor as best she could before slashing through the ropes that bound Angie to the bed. After jerking Angie to her feet, Sam wrapped her arms around her friend's waist and transported the two of them to Angie's front porch.

Before Angie could ask what had just happened, Declan appeared beside them. "Get inside, quick!" His gaze searched the darkness and then he followed the women inside and slammed the door.

With eyes only for Angie, he drew her into his arms.

She clung to him like a cocklebur, her whole body cold and trembling, her tears wetting his shirt front.

Declan's gaze met Samantha's over Angie's head. "What the hell happened?"

Samantha took a wary step backward. "Conor forced me to get her out of the house. He said he would destroy me if I refused. And I believed him."

"And yet you let her go."

"She's...was...my friend. The best friend I ever had. I couldn't let Conor do to her what Ian did to me."

"I thought you loved being a vampire."

"I did, when Ian was with me. Without him..." Samantha shrugged. "I really don't care if I live or die."

"I'd be happy to end your existence here and now for what you did."

"No," Angie said. "I promised you'd protect her."

"Fine," Declan said. "She can stay in my secondary lair." He glanced at Samantha. "It's warded against humans and vampires alike. You should be safe there, as long as you're careful. But I warn you, if you betray Angie again, you'll be sorry you were ever born."

"I believe you." Samantha glanced around the living room, her expression melancholy. "I don't suppose Angie would let me stay here."

"She might," he said, brushing a kiss across the top of Angie's head. "But I won't. I will, however, let you spend the night."

Murmuring her thanks, Samantha headed for the guestroom.

"Angie?"

Sniffing back her tears, she cupped Declan's face in her hands. "Is it really you?"

"Damn right. And I'm not letting you out of my sight again until my brother is dead."

Declan ran a hot bath for Angie, and after assuring himself she was all right, he went into the guestroom. Samantha looked up, eyes wide with fear. "Have you come to destroy me, after all?"

"No, but I am going to mess with your mind."

"What are you going to do?"

"I guess you could say I'm going to hypnotize you so you'll be impervious to Conor's suggestions, and then I'm going to break the link between you."

"Can you do that?"

"I'm a master vampire. I can do almost anything. Sit down and close your eyes."

Samantha perched on the edge of the mattress, her eyes closed, mouth set in a tight line.

Laying his hand on her head, Declan called on his preternatural power to block his brother's influence on Sam's
mind. It was sort of like building a wall between Sam and
her sire. To enforce it, and to break the blood link between
her and his brother, he drank a good bit of her blood and
had her consume some of his.

Looking up at him, she asked, "Is that it?"

"Yeah. How do you feel?"

"Free," she said. And smiled for the first time in days.
"How long will it last?"

"Hopefully, until I break it. Have you fed tonight?"

"Yes."

"All right then. I'll see you tomorrow night." Leaving the
room, he closed the door behind him. And then, because
he didn't trust her, he warded the door and the window so
she couldn't leave.

When he returned to Angie's bedroom, he found her
sitting on the bed wearing a long nightgown and a robe.

"How are you feeling?" he asked.

"Better. What did he do to me? I couldn't think, couldn't
move, couldn't see. It was like being ... like being dead but
not, if that makes any sense."

Declan sat beside her, hesitated a moment, then slipped
his arm around her waist. "It was a spell of some kind."
Similar to the one he'd used on Sam, but not so invasive.

"Did I hear you tell Sam she could stay here?"

"Just for tonight."

"Is it safe? For me, I mean?"

"She can't get out of the guestroom."

Angie looked at him, eyes wide.

"I worked a little vampire magic on the door and the
window, that's all."

"Conor will come for her, won't he?"

"Most likely. But he can't get inside the house."

Angie shivered. Even when she'd been unable to see or think or move, she had sensed Conor's malevolent presence. It had crawled over her skin like the cold hand of evil. Of death itself.

"You're safe now," Declan said, drawing her into his arms. "I'm here."

"How did Sam get us here so fast? One minute we were in that horrible room and the next we were on my front porch."

"She transported you."

"Transported?"

"Vampires have the ability to travel incredibly fast."

"It felt sort of like flying." Something she wasn't crazy about. Must be nice, she thought, being able to just zap yourself from one place to another. Being carried through time and space at warp speed had been terrifying—and yet kind of exhilarating. But she wasn't sure she ever wanted to do it again.

"Get some rest," Declan said, caressing her cheek.

"I don't want to be alone. Stay here tonight."

"I told you, love, I'm not leaving you alone as long he's still a threat."

"I meant stay *here*," she said, patting the mattress. "With me."

"Are you sure?"

"Yes."

"All right."

Rising, she removed her robe and slid under the covers.

After a moment, Declan removed his boots and jeans, peeled off his tee shirt and then stretched out on top of the covers beside her. Every breath carried her scent to him—a mingling of soap and velvety skin and the tantalizing call of her life's blood. And overall, the unique scent of the woman herself, warm and sexy and intoxicating.

He clenched his hands at his sides to keep from reaching for her. It was, he thought, going to be a hell of a long night.

A faint cry pierced the dark sleep. Instantly awake, Declan jackknifed to a sitting position, his gaze sweeping the room. But there was no one there. Just Angie, caught in the throes of a nightmare. After turning on the lamp beside the bed, he leaned over and gently shook her shoulder. "Angie."

She woke with a start, arms flailing as she screamed, "No! Let me go!"

"Angie, calm down, love. You were dreaming."

She stared at him blankly, her eyes wide with terror, and then loosed a breath that seemed to come from the soles of her feet. And then she threw her arms around his neck, sobbing.

"That must have been some hellacious nightmare," he murmured, stroking her back.

"Oh, Declan, it was awful. I was back in that room, unable to move or think or see." She heaved a shuddering sigh. "And then Conor released me from his spell and ordered Sam to bite me. And she buried her fangs in one side of my throat while Conor's fangs dug into the other side. I could feel the blood leaving my body, and..."

"Shh. Don't think about it, love. It was just a bad dream. I won't let anything like that happen to you, I swear it."

She snuggled closer to him, tears streaming down her cheeks onto his bare chest.

He continued to stroke her back, assuring her that she was safe now. Gradually, she relaxed against him, her fingers delving into the hair at his nape, sliding over his shoulders, tracing the line of his spine.

Her touch sizzled through him like lightning and he sucked in a deep breath. "Angie."

She leaned back a little, then touched his cheek as if to make sure he was really there. "Thank you for staying," she murmured, and kissed him.

Declan groaned softly as her mouth covered his, stoking his desire. His body hardened instantly, urging him to take that which he wanted so desperately. When he would have pulled away, she clung to him, her hands kneading his back, her breasts warm and firm against his chest. "Angie," he gasped. "Angie, stop."

Lifting her head, she pressed her fingertips to his lips. "Make love to me."

He closed his eyes. He told himself she didn't mean it. She was just frightened and seeking solace. But her tongue was hot against his as she kissed him again and again, her body clinging to his, begging for his touch.

Capturing her hands in his, he gazed deep into her eyes. "Angie, if we make love tonight, I will never let you go. Never. And I will kill any man who tries to take you from me. Do you understand?"

His words should have frightened her. But they didn't. She knew what he was and she didn't care. He was the man she loved, her knight in shining armor, and she knew, in the deepest part of her heart and soul, that she would never love anyone else. "I understand."

"From this night forward, you will be my woman. My wife in all but name only," he said, his voice caressing her. "Until tomorrow, when I will make you legally mine."

"And you will be mine," she whispered.

And he was lost.

A thought removed her nightgown, baring her body to his gaze. For a moment, he simply looked at her. She was exquisitely made, he thought, every curve perfect, her skin the color of rich cream, the texture like smooth velvet.

She trembled at his touch, her own hands exploring his broad chest and shoulders, his ridged belly. A little gasp escaped her lips, her eyes widening when she saw the evidence of his desire.

Time ceased to exist as they kissed and caressed, their hands lazily exploring each other. His kisses ignited a fire deep inside her that warmed her blood and made her whole body tingle with need, until the spark of passion blazed into an inferno. For this one moment in eternity, there was nothing in all the world but the two of them, his mouth hot on hers, now teasing, now seductive.

She knew a brief moment of fear as he rose over her—a powerful, magnificent creature. There was a fleeting stab of pain as his body melded with hers, and then only pleasure as two bodies became one. Lost in a rhythm as old as time, she cried out as he carried her over the edge to paradise and then, with a long, shuddering sigh, he followed her there.

Sated and content, Angie fell asleep in his arms, smiling.

In the guestroom, Samantha curled onto her side and wept bitter tears of sorrow and regret as the heavy scent of lovemaking seeped into the room. Her heart cried out for Ian, for the love that had so briefly been theirs, for the life she had lost that would never be hers again.

Closing her eyes, she prayed for death to release her from the hell of her existence.

# CHAPTER TWENTY-EIGHT

Angie woke slowly, vaguely aware that she was naked under the covers and not alone. Glancing to her left, she saw Declan lying on his back beside her, sound asleep. In the blink of an eye, the events of the night before came rushing to the forefront of her mind. She had asked Declan to stay the night because she had been afraid to be home alone, afraid that Conor would somehow come for her again. She'd had a horrible nightmare and Declan had been there to hold her close, to comfort her with his presence.

She had asked him to make love to her.

And he had agreed—with the stipulation that they would be married. Tonight.

A hundred thoughts tumbled through Angie's mind as she considered what marriage to a vampire might entail. But not once did she regret what had happened. No marriage license could bind them together more closely than the love they had shared last night. He was hers now, and she was his. Forever.

Slipping out of bed, Angie headed for the bathroom, where she showered, then pulled on her robe and padded into the kitchen in search of coffee. She smiled as she waited for it to perk, thinking that she hurt in places that had never hurt before. But it was a wonderful kind of ache,

a reminder of the ecstasy she had found in Declan's arms—
and couldn't wait to experience again.

When the coffee was ready, she poured a cup and carried it into the living room. She sat on the sofa, lost in
thoughts of Declan, of the sweet words he had whispered in
her ear, his voice low and seductive. He had been so gentle
with her, so tender, it was a night she would never forget.

She glanced at the clock, wondering how long Declan
needed to rest, glad that he didn't have to wait for the sun
to set before he could rise. The thought reminded her that
there was another vampire sleeping in her house, in the
guestroom.

Samantha. Was it safe for her to be here? Was it even
safe to be around her? And what if Declan's brother came
looking for Sam? Angie shuddered at the thought. She
never wanted to see Conor again. The man was pure evil
and more frightening than anything she had ever seen or
imagined. Next to him, Samantha looked like an angel, she
thought with a wry grin, even though there was nothing
funny about it.

Samantha. Angie sighed. She couldn't help worrying
about her best friend's future. What if Conor's threat was
real? What if he really intended to kill Sam?

Feeling a headache coming on, Angie headed for the
bathroom to find some aspirin, but she never made it past
the bed when she saw that Declan was awake. She felt herself
blush from head to foot when she recalled the night before
and knew, from the look in his eyes, that he was remembering, too.

When he patted the mattress, it seemed like the most
natural thing in the world to shed her robe and slip under
the covers beside him.

His hand caressed her hip, her thigh, as his gaze searched hers. "No regrets?" he asked, his voice a low rumble.

Straddling his hips, she purred, "What do you think?"

"I think I'm going to have to start waking up earlier in the day," he growled, and in one fluid move, he tucked her beneath him and claimed her lips with his.

And just like that, her headache was gone.

It was hours later when Angie woke again. A quick glance at the clock showed it was after three in the afternoon. For the second time that day, she slipped out of bed, grabbed her robe, and padded into the kitchen. While fixing a very late lunch, she wondered if Declan had been serious when he said they were getting married tonight. She had never planned a wedding and had no idea where to start. Did they need a license? A blood test? She grinned at the image of a vampire giving blood. And what about a church? Could vampires even enter a church? The only thing she did know was that she didn't have a thing to wear!

She thought, briefly, of going shopping for a new dress or a modest gown, but the thought of leaving the safety of her house soon squashed that idea. Conor was out there somewhere and the mere thought of running into him was enough to keep her behind locked doors.

After clearing her dishes, she booted up her computer and quickly checked her email. Most of it was spam. The only other new mail was from her editor.

*Angie, love the Christmas column. Do you have any similar ideas for January or February? Best, Jennifer.*

Going to her old friend, Google, Angie spent an hour searching for New Year's myths and legends, but the site she liked the best was about New Year's superstitions. After doing some research, she began to write.

*How superstitious are you? I was surprised to learn there are many superstitions associated with the New Year. For instance, have you ever wondered why you kiss your spouse or other loved one at midnight? It's believed that kissing your loved one will insure that love and affection will be yours in the coming year. If you fail to do so, you may find yourself sorely lacking.*

*Other superstitions abound. If your cupboard is bare, you may find yourself in need of the basic necessities in the coming year.*

*You should beware of starting the new year with unpaid debts.*

*If you open all your doors and windows at midnight, the remains of the old year, and, hopefully, all its ills, will drift away.*

*It's believed that babies born on New Year's Day will be blessed with good fortune all their lives.*

*Eating anything that is round on New Year's Eve—a donut, for instance, perhaps a pizza or a bagel, will supposedly bring you good luck in the new year. Likewise, in some Latin countries, eating twelve grapes, one for each stroke of midnight—is believed to bring good fortune for the next twelve months.*

Angie was re-reading what she'd written when Declan came up behind her and kissed her cheek.

"Hello, love."

"Hi." She smiled as his breath tickled her skin.

"Any chance I can lure you away from whatever you're doing?"

"I don't know. Maybe. What did you have in mind?"

"We're getting married tonight." His tongue laved the sensitive place beneath her ear. "Did you forget?"

"Hardly. But how? And where? And who will marry us?"

"Leave that to me." Taking her by the hand, he tugged her gently to her feet and into his arms. "Be ready when I get back."

"But... I need a dress."

His gaze skimmed over her. "I'll see what I can do." He kissed her lightly. "Whatever you do, don't leave the house. Don't open the door for anyone, friend or stranger. And don't, under any circumstances, open the guestroom door."

"Do I need to be afraid of her?"

"Not while she's locked up. Or when I'm here." He kissed her again, long and slow and deep. "I won't be gone long," he promised.

A faint stirring in the air and he was gone from her sight.

Angie shook her head. How on earth did vampires do that? But she had other things to think about.

Going into the bathroom, she showered again, shaved her legs, washed her hair. Wrapped in a towel, she blow-dried her hair and then used her curling iron, so that her hair fell in soft waves around her shoulders. She applied her make-up and a bit of perfume, and with each task, excitement fluttered anew in the pit of her stomach.

She was getting married.

To Declan.

Tonight.

She pulled on her sexiest underwear, then donned her robe again. She was about to return to the living room to wait for Declan when she heard a pounding on the guestroom door.

The sun had set.

Samantha was awake.

Sam glared at the closed door. The lingering signature of vampire magic hung in the room. Not only had Declan messed with her mind, she thought angrily, he had warded the door and the window to keep her trapped inside.

He didn't trust her one damn bit.

Or maybe Angie had suggested it. Hah! Some best friend.

A low growl rose in her throat at the mere idea and kicked her outrage up a notch. To hell with both of them. What right did they have to keep her here? She wasn't some wild animal to be locked in a cage!

Muttering every curse word she'd ever heard, she paced the floor, back and forth, back and forth, her sense of betrayal growing with every footstep.

Damn Declan! He had locked her up! And what was he doing while she prowled the confines of her prison like a caged tiger? No doubt having sex with her former best friend!

Frustrated beyond enduring, she threw back her head and screamed, "Let me out of here!"

Angie stopped dead in her tracks, chills slithering down her spine at the sound of Samantha's fury. Any and all hope she'd had of remaining friends with Sam were obliterated by the hatred in that beastly-ferocious roar. There had been nothing human about it.

Absolutely nothing.

She clapped her hands over her ears when it came again and yet again.

Declan grabbed the dress and veil he had purchased for Angie, threw a handful of bills on the counter, and ran out of the store. Outside, he took a quick look around and when he was sure no one was looking, he transported himself back to her house.

He materialized in the living room, dropped the gown and veil on the sofa, and hurried toward the guestroom. "Samantha! Be quiet!" When the screaming stopped, he slipped inside.

She glared at him. "Let me out of here!"

"No way. You're half out of your mind."

"Can you blame me? How would you feel if someone locked you up in a cage?"

"You think I don't know how it feels?"

The rage faded from her eyes. "Somebody locked *you* up? I don't believe it."

He shrugged. "It was centuries ago." And not something he was likely to forget. "I was still a fledgling at the time. I don't remember where Conor was. Two hunters trapped me. They were young, full of piss and vinegar, and thought it would be fun to torture me before they killed me."

"Yeah?" she asked skeptically. "Where did this happen?"

"In Hungary. They bound my hands and feet with silver chains and locked me in a dungeon in the bowels of a deserted castle. The cell reeked of old death and pain and bloodshed. There were numerous instruments of torture in that hell hole. They used them all on me, one by one, day by day. The pain of the silver chains against my skin was not only constant torture, but it drained my powers, leaving me weak and helpless. I don't know how long it went on. They denied me any nourishment, so I fed on the rats.

"One night one of the men came in alone. He was bragging about what he had in store for me when he made the mistake of getting too close to the cage." He paused, remembering. "I grabbed him and buried my fangs in his throat and drank him dry. When he was dead, I found the keys in his pocket and unlocked my chains, then hid in the dark, waiting for the other one."

"What happened next?" Eyes wide, Sam leaned forward, spellbound by the tale.

"Just what you think. I killed him, too. So, yes, I know what it's like to be locked up. Now, if you promise to behave yourself, I'll take you hunting."

"I promise."

"I'll go tell Angie we're leaving and then we'll go."

Angie stared at him. "Do you think taking her out is a good idea?"

"She has to feed."

"But Conor could be out there, just waiting."

"It's a chance I've got to take. Why don't you try on that dress while we're gone, see how it fits?"

"All right."

His gaze searched hers. "You were listening at the door, weren't you?"

The rush of color in her cheeks told him everything he needed to know. "We won't be gone long."

The dress Declan had picked for her was like something made of stardust for a fairy-tale princess and easily the most beautiful thing she had ever seen. She gasped when she saw the price tag. Nine hundred dollars. Where on earth had he found it? She was pretty sure none of the shops in town sold anything that costly.

Almost afraid to touch it, she tried it on, set the matching veil in place, then stood staring at her reflection. The sleeves were long and sheer, the neck square, the skirt long and full. Tiny brilliants that were sewn across the bodice and sprinkled across the skirt sparkled like diamonds. And it fit perfectly, making her think he must have peeked into her closet to check her dress size.

She was so caught up in the exquisite beauty of the gown that, for a moment, she forgot all about Declan and Samantha.

"Him," Samantha said, pointing at a tall, blond young man clad in the uniform of a Marine. "I want him."

"You know what to do," Declan said. "Just don't get carried away."

"I'm fine!" she exclaimed angrily. Proving that she wasn't fine at all, as far as he was concerned.

She approached her prey stealthily, like a hungry cat stalking a mouse.

Declan watched her every move, knew the exact moment when her power took hold of the Marine's mind. She drank quickly, and he watched her like a hawk. She wanted to drink it all, but, to her credit, she stopped just short of too late.

He breathed a sigh of relief when she released her prey. "Cutting it a little close, weren't you?"

"I didn't kill him, did I?" she snapped.

"Not for lack of trying," he muttered, taking hold of her arm. "Come on, let's go."

"What's the hurry? It's early and I'm still hungry."

"It can wait. I'm getting married tonight. We need to stop and find you something to wear."

❧   ❧   ❧

Angie choked back a startled cry when Declan and Samantha appeared in the living room. She stared wide-eyed at Samantha. The last time she had seen Sam, she'd been wearing jeans and a tee shirt. Now she wore a lavender, tea-length dress with a scooped neck and a flared skirt, as well as a pair of beige heels.

Angie looked at Declan askance.

"I don't want to leave her here alone," he explained with a shrug. "She's going to be your bridesmaid."

"Believe me, it wasn't my idea," Samantha said sullenly.

*Nor mine*, Angie thought, but there was no graceful way to say so. In any case, Declan was right. If they left Sam at the house, she'd likely start screaming again, which might cause one of her neighbors to call the police. And they definitely didn't want that. Forcing a smile she was far from feeling, she said, "You look beautiful, Sam."

"Thanks," she muttered. "So do you."

Angie noted that Declan had also found time to change clothes. He looked dashing in a black Hugo Boss suit that looked like it had been made for him, though surely that was impossible in such a short time.

"Are you ready, bride?" he asked.

"I guess so, groom," she said as she stepped into a pair of white satin heels.

With a nod, he slipped one arm around Angie's waist and the other around Samantha's.

Angie gasped as the world fell away. It took her a moment to realize what was happening—Declan was transporting them. She wondered if she would ever get used to the sensation of hurtling through time and space.

A breathless moment later, they were standing on the steps of a white stone church set in the midst of a swath of green lawn. Declan took Angie's hand in his and then Sam's and they entered the church.

A rather plump, gray-haired woman wearing a gown the same color as her hair was seated at the organ.

A minister, perhaps thirty years old and clad in a black cassock entered the chapel from a side door. He glanced at the three of them. "Are we ready to proceed?"

Declan's gaze locked with Samantha's. "Don't move," he warned, his voice pitched low so only she could hear. When she nodded, he smiled at the reverend. "We're ready."

"Please, join hands," the minister said.

Declan took Angie's hand in his and gave it a squeeze as his mind brushed hers. When he sensed no hesitation, no last-minute doubts, he smiled at her.

Angie gazed into his eyes as they exchanged their vows. The ceremony was brief, and yet the words sank deep into her heart and soul as he promised to love and cherish her as long as they lived.

*As long as you both shall live.* The words seemed to echo in her mind as she repeated her own vows. *As long as you both shall live.* Never had her own mortality seemed so real. It was possible that Declan, and even Sam, might live another eight centuries. She would not be so lucky.

Turning to Declan, the minister asked, "I believe you have a ring?"

Angie bit down on her lower lip. A ring! She had never even thought about that. But Declan had. Reaching into his pocket, he withdrew a wide silver band crusted with diamonds that sparkled like sunlight even in the dim light inside the church.

"Repeat after me, With this ring, I thee wed."

Angie's eyes welled with tears of joy as Declan murmured the words and slipped the ring on her finger.

"I now pronounce you man and wife," the minister declared. "You may kiss your bride."

Angie's heart pounded with excitement as Declan lifted her veil and took her in his arms. He kissed her as if they were the only two people on earth and had all the time in the world.

A polite cough from the minister reminded them they weren't alone.

Looking up, Declan pulled a crisp one-hundred dollar bill from his pocket and handed it to the reverend.

The minister's eyes widened as he tucked it out of sight. "God bless you, my children," he said fervently, and followed the organist out the side door of the chapel.

"I can't believe I forgot to buy you a ring," Angie said. "But I'm going to remedy that as soon as possible. I want every other woman in the world to know you're taken."

Before Declan could reply, Samantha cut in. "Ian should have been here," she said, her voice quiet and laced with bitterness.

"It's not Angie's fault," Declan said, "and I won't have you ruin this day for her."

"It's all right," Angie murmured, noting the tears welling in her friend's eyes. It had been a mistake for Declan to bring Sam here. Surely he must have realized it would stir painful memories and remind her of all she had lost.

Declan lifted his head, nostrils flaring. "We need to go."

Before Angie could ask what was wrong, the three of them were back in her living room.

"What the hell?" Samantha exclaimed.

"Conor was outside the church, waiting for us," Declan said curtly.

"Why didn't he come inside?" Sam asked.

"He's not as strong as I am. He hasn't quite recovered from our last encounter."

"Sounds like the perfect time to go after him," Sam said.

"I'm not as strong as I'd like to be, either," he admitted. "And now it's time for you to go."

Angie laid her hand on his arm. "Declan, I don't think..."

"I'll be all right," Samantha said, her voice cool. "I know you don't want me here anymore than I want to be here. Declan has offered to let me stay in his secondary lair."

Angie glanced from one vampire to the other. The tension between the two of them was palpable.

"I know this has been hard for you," Angie said. "But I'm glad, for the sake of the friendship we once shared, that you were with us tonight. Please be careful."

Samantha nodded curtly. And then she was gone.

Angie turned an accusatory stare on her new husband. "You should have made her stay here."

"I don't think that would have been a good idea. It isn't safe. Not for her. Not for you. I can't watch Sam every minute, and I can't keep her locked up all the time."

He was right, of course. She knew that. And yet Samantha wasn't in control, Angie thought. Even she could see that. What if Conor had followed them here? What if he was lurking out there in the dark, just biding his time as he waited for the perfect moment to strike?

"Angie."

Every other thought fled her mind as he drew her into his arms. "I'm sorry, wife," he murmured. "But there are some things even I can't fix."

*Wife.* Her eyelids fluttered down as her husband claimed her lips with his.

This was her wedding night, she thought as he deepened the kiss. She would worry about Sam and Conor and everything else tomorrow.

But tonight was hers.

A million butterflies took wing in the pit of Angie's stomach as, hand-in-hand, they made their way to her room where they took turns undressing each other. She didn't know why she was so nervous. They had made love before. But, somehow, this was different. This was for always.

She blushed from head to toe as Declan's heated gaze moved slowly over her, followed by a sigh as he caressed her, then swung her into his arms and lowered her onto the bed. Feeling suddenly bold, she began a slow exploration of her husband's hard-muscled body, measuring the width of his biceps with her hands, marveling at the way his muscles bunched and flexed at her touch. He was beautiful, so beautiful, his skin cool beneath her fingertips, his hair like silk against her skin.

With a low growl, he rose over her, the desire in his eyes burning like a flame as his body melded with hers.

She was lost in a world of pleasure when he bit her, ever so gently. She let out a startled gasp as every emotion, every touch, was suddenly intensified ten-fold and she felt as if she was floating in a crimson sea, drifting from one indescribably erotic sensation to another until, at last, she tumbled over the edge crying his name.

# CHAPTER TWENTY-NINE

Conor strolled down a back alley, his thoughts as black as the night. So, Declan had taken a bride. But then, his brother had never had any trouble with women. As far back as he could remember, women had fallen all over themselves to be with him. Even when Declan was a gangly youth, girls had flocked around him, begging for his attention. Mihaela had been no different. He had loved her beyond reason, but she had chosen Declan.

And now his brother had married again. Another beautiful woman had practically fallen at Declan's feet. Jealousy coursed through Conor as he slammed his fist against a block wall, the force hard enough to topple a section to the ground.

And then there was Samantha. Declan had snatched her from his grasp as if he had every right to do so. Dammit, how many women did his brother need?

He swore a vile oath as his anger grew and multiplied. It boiled up inside him like acid, eating at his insides, until he thought he'd go mad.

As always, whenever his rage overcame him, he struck out against humanity. He hated them all.

Fangs bared, he attacked the first woman he saw, drank her dry and tossed the husk aside. To hell with the hunters, he thought, as he caught the scent of fresh prey around the corner. Let them come! One or a hundred, he'd take them all on and glut himself with their life's blood!

He grinned as he imagined the headlines in the morning paper.

Serial killer strikes again!

# CHAPTER THIRTY

Angie refused to open her eyes, content to lie in bed with Declan beside her, and relive the unbelievable pleasure she had enjoyed in his arms only hours ago. The first time they made love had been wonderful, but last night— she sighed with the memory. There were no words in the English language—and likely not in any other—to describe it. Sensation after sensation had flooded her being, filling her with ecstasy, fulfilling every dream, every fantasy she'd ever had—and some she hadn't.

Smiling with the memory, she glanced at her sleeping husband. Had it been that wonderful for him, as well? And then she shook her head. How could it have been, when he wasn't on the receiving end?

Eventually, nature called. Slipping out of bed as quietly as she could, Angie tiptoed into the bath room. After a long, hot shower, she pulled on a pair of lived-in jeans and a tee shirt and padded, smiling, into the kitchen. Her body ached in places she'd never known she had, but it was a wonderful reminder of a wonderful night, one she couldn't wait to repeat as soon as possible.

She made tea and toast, fired up her phone, and scanned the morning headlines.

And wished she hadn't as the real world came crashing down.

*SERIAL KILLER STRIKES AGAIN! Local police woke to a nightmare this morning when two officers on routine patrol discovered the grisly remains of six bodies—four women and two men –stacked one on top of the other in the middle of the city park. No further details were disclosed pending notification of the deceased. Chief of Police, Paul Michaels, advises residents to stay inside their homes after dark, if possible. Police have no leads as to the identity of the killer. Or killers.*

Conor, Angie thought bleakly. It had to be Conor. She felt a momentary twinge of guilt. Last night, while she was reveling in her husband's caresses, his brother had been roaming the city slaughtering innocent people.

She didn't know how long she'd been sitting there, staring at nothing, when she felt a hand on her shoulder. Lost in thought, she almost jumped out of her chair until she heard Declan's voice.

"Are you all right?" he asked, a note of worry in his tone.

"No."

Frowning, he took the seat across the table from her. "What's wrong? Is this about last night?"

"What?"

"Last night. Did I ..."

"No, no, it's nothing to do with you." She picked up her phone and handed it to him.

The muscles in his jaw clenched as he read the story, muttering in a foreign language as he did so. Angie had no idea what he was saying but curses sounded pretty much the same in any language.

He read the story a second time, his face tight with rage, eyes blazing red.

She had never seen him look like that. It was a fearsome sight. The very air around him vibrated with his anger and frustration. She reacted instinctively, going very still, hardly daring to breathe, even as she told herself she had nothing to fear. Declan loved her. He would never hurt her.

He set the phone on the table very carefully, as if afraid he might crush it, then stood and began to pace the floor. Back and forth, back and forth, as restless as a tiger in a cage. She didn't know what he was thinking, what he was planning, but she felt her blood run cold with the very real fear that the next time the Nicolae brothers met, only one of them would walk away.

To Angie's dismay, things only got worse from there. That evening, as soon as the sun slid behind the horizon, Declan received a frantic phone call from Samantha.

Angie watched the play of emotions over his face as he listened to what Sam had to say. He grunted once, then put his phone down.

"What is it?" Angie asked anxiously. "What's wrong?"

"Conor texted Sam with a message for me."

"What did it say?"

"It said if I don't turn Sam over to him by the end of the week, he's going on a killing spree that will make everything else look tame. First two, then four, and so on, until I agree."

Angie went cold all over. She had no doubt his brother would do exactly as he threatened, and take great pleasure in doing so. And then she frowned. "I thought you said it was me he wanted?"

"I'm sure that's still true. But he's angry because Samantha helped you, and because I took her away from him. He wants revenge. I told you before, vampires are very territorial. They don't like to lose what they've claimed as their own."

"What are we going to do?"

"We?" He shook his head. "In this case, there is no 'we'."

"You can't give Sam to that monster!"

"If you've got a better idea, I'm listening."

"I don't, but…" Angie stared at him. Was this the same man who had made love to her so tenderly, so exquisitely, just last night? Did he truly intend to hand Sam over to Conor? "You can't! You know what he'll do, what he's capable of. She is…was…my best friend! Even if she was my worst enemy, I wouldn't let you do it."

"The only way to catch him is to bait the trap."

"And Sam's the bait?"

"I'm afraid so." He wrapped his arm around her. "Are you ready?"

"Ready for what?"

"I need to see Sam and I'm going to get us there the quickest way I know how."

"Oh." Angie closed her eyes. She gasped as she was overcome by a sudden, familiar sense of weightlessness, of speeding through a dark tunnel. This was getting to be a habit, she thought. It wasn't as frightening this time. Perhaps because she was expecting it. Or maybe she was just getting used to it. Without the fear, it was kind of fun, like some wild, carnival roller coaster ride.

When the world righted itself, they were standing in front of a small stone house. It stood alone in the middle of a grassy field. Stomach still roiling, she asked, "Where are we?"

"My secondary lair. Are you okay?" She looked a little disoriented, but that was normal.

"I guess so." Angie followed him up a narrow dirt path to the house. A wave of his hand unlocked the door. More vampire magic, she thought.

Samantha let out a squeak of surprise when the door opened and Declan and Angie stepped into the room. She stared at Declan, arms crossed over her chest, eyes wide with fear.

"Calm down," Declan said. "I'm not going to hand you over to my brother."

"What *are* you going to do?"

"I'm not sure. Where is he holed up?"

"I don't have any idea, but I don't think it's in town. When we went hunting, he always blindfolded me before we left his lair, and he always transported us to our destination, usually small towns."

"He wasn't taking any chances, that's for sure. Dammit! We need to come up with a plan, and we need to do it damn quick."

Samantha paced the floor, then sat on the edge of the sofa, hands clenched in her lap. "Do you think he meant what he said about killing all those people?"

"You've spent time with him," Declan remarked. "What do you think?"

"Maybe I should just go with him," Sam murmured.

"No!" Angie exclaimed.

"Have you got a better idea? It's me he wants."

"But…" Angie glanced at Declan for help.

"Actually, that might be the best way to do it. Sam can pretend to escape. Sooner or later, he'll find her and when he does, she can contact me and let us know where he is."

Angie glared at Declan. "It's too dangerous. What if he kills her on sight?"

"It's a chance I'm willing to take," Samantha exclaimed. "I can't go on living like this. It's not fair to Declan, expecting him to babysit me all the time. You're a new bride. Declan shouldn't be thinking about anything but you. And it's not fair to me, either, being locked up all night, afraid to go out."

Angie frowned as Samantha's gaze locked with Declan's. Something passed between the two of them, something intangible. Declan nodded, then reached for Angie's hand.

"Let's go," he said.

"What?" Angie stared at him. "Go where? We haven't solved anything."

"Yes, we did." Samantha hugged Angie. "Goodbye, Ange."

Before Angie could ask what was going on, Declan transported them back to her house.

As soon as the world stopped spinning, she turned on him. "That's it? You're just going to let her sacrifice herself to that monster?"

"She wants to die, Angie."

"What? I don't believe you."

"She's miserable without Ian."

"But... that's no reason to..." She frowned. "What went on between the two of you back there?"

"Some people take to being a vampire like a duck to water." Sitting on the sofa, he took Angie's hand and tugged her down beside him. "Some don't. Sam hates what she is, but she loves the excitement of the hunt, the indescribable high, the blood, and it makes her feel guilty. She's constantly fighting the urge to kill her prey, and that scares her, because I threatened to destroy her if she killed anyone in my territory."

Angie swallowed her revulsion and then said, "She could leave town. Go somewhere else where..." She couldn't say the words, couldn't make it sound like it would be all right for Sam to kill as long as it was outside Declan's territory.

"There has to be something else we can do to help her. Some other way. There just has to be!"

"This whole thing is my fault," he said quietly. "I should have destroyed Conor years ago, but every time I had the chance, I backed off." He scrubbed a hand over his jaw. "I just couldn't bring myself to do it. But the stakes are higher now and it's got to be done. Anyway, she thought the idea of pretending to run away from me was a good one, and so do I. It's risky, sure, but if she plays the part well and convinces Conor she thinks her life is in danger if she stays with me, it might work."

"He'll never believe it! Conor killed Ian. He must know she'd never forgive him for that."

"All we really need is for her to be with him long enough to let me know where he is. Hopefully, between the two of us, we can put an end to my brother's killing spree."

"And what if you can't?"

He shrugged. "I have to try." He felt guilty as hell for the lives Conor had taken. Those people would still be alive if he had fulfilled his vow centuries ago. And so would Ian.

"Wait a minute! How's Conor going to know that Sam ran away?"

"All she has to do is spend a few nights wandering the city streets. Chances are he'll find her. Or she'll find him."

Sighing, Angie rested her head on his shoulder. There had to be something else they could do, some way to protect Sam, destroy Conor, and live happily-ever-after, but no solution came to mind. Out of the four vampires she knew, Ian had seemed relatively well-adjusted, all things considered. Conor could be the poster boy for movie monsters—a vicious, mindless killer. Sam was miserable. Only Declan seemed to have made peace with what he was.

"Angie."

His breath was warm against her ear, his voice husky, intimate. She shivered as his tongue laved her neck.

"I'll do my best to keep Samantha safe," he murmured. "I promise. But if she's determined to end it, a dozen master vampires wouldn't be able to stop her."

"I can't believe this is happening. It's like some horrible nightmare."

Declan went still, his arm suddenly rigid.

Feeling the change in him, she lifted her head. "What's wrong?"

"You tell me."

She frowned a moment, then cupped his cheek in her hand. "I'm not blaming you. And I'm not sorry we met. Sam started dating Ian months before I went to the Nightmare. If you and I had never met, things might still have turned out this way." She smiled faintly as his body relaxed. "I love you, Declan. No matter what."

Declan groaned her name as he buried his face in the wealth of her hair, his arms tightening around her. For a moment, he had been afraid he'd lost her, that she blamed him for everything that had happened to Samantha, that she would look at him differently, or, worse, decide she wanted nothing more to do with him.

Angie murmured his name as she stroked his hair. When he looked up, she cupped his cheek in her palm and kissed him. "I'll never leave you, Declan. Don't you know that?"

"Angie, I love you more than my life."

"I know." She tugged his shirt from the waistband of his jeans, her hand delving underneath to caress his chest. "But why don't you show me?"

His gaze searched hers, as if unable to believe she wanted him.

She lifted the tee shirt over his head, unfastened his belt buckle, unzipped his fly, then tilted her head to the side. "Do I have to do everything?"

A wry grin played over his lips as he toed off his boots, stood and removed his jeans, then tugged her to her feet. His eyes were hot as he lifted her sweater over her head and tossed it on the chair, then slid her jeans over her hips and thighs, his hands pausing along the way to cup her breasts, stroke the curve of her calf.

Her body tingled wherever he touched.

They never made it to the bedroom.

# CHAPTER THIRTY-ONE

Samantha wandered aimlessly through the night. How quickly life could change, she thought glumly. Not long ago, she'd had a promising future, a great apartment, a job she loved. She had met a man—the first man she had ever met that she wanted to spend the rest of her life with, only to learn that he was a vampire. Oddly enough, that hadn't really bothered her. He'd been so sweet, kind and funny, everything she had ever dreamed of. She would have been content to spend the rest of her life with him. And then he'd turned her and everything had gone to hell. She lost her job, her apartment, and her best friend. And then Conor had destroyed Ian in the most brutal way she could imagine. Never, in a million years, would she be able to erase that gruesome image from her mind—the shock, the horror, the look of stunned surprise and disbelief on Ian's face moments before he died.

Right or wrong, she blamed Declan for Ian's death. True, Declan hadn't been Ian's sire, but he had taken him in. He should have protected him. What was worse, he didn't even seem to give a damn about what had happened. Oh, sure, he wanted Conor dead, but not because of what his brother had done to Ian, but because of some stupid vow he'd made centuries ago.

In a way, she blamed Declan for what had happened to her, too. He should have warned her that Ian was a vampire, given her the chance to decide whether she wanted to continue their relationship. Knowing what she knew now, she would have put an end to it right quick. The few months of happiness she had known with Ian didn't make up for the misery and sorrow she felt now.

She thought about Angie and hated her. Hated her because Angie had everything Sam had ever wanted—a lovely home and a husband who adored her. Once, she had hoped for those things, too, but such dreams had died with Ian.

Ian. Without him, she hated what she'd become—the constant lust for blood, the sense of living in someone else's body. She had killed innocent people—complete strangers—just for the thrill of it. She tried to feel guilty for the lives she had taken, but the truth was, she didn't. Except for the young boy. And she blamed Conor for that.

She yearned to take another life, to experience the excitement of the hunt, savor the first sweet taste of fresh, hot blood on her tongue, the exhilaration of knowing she held a life in her hands, the rush of power that flowed through her as she drank and drank...

Conor would let her do whatever she wanted.

She thrust the thought away. But it quickly returned. Angie didn't want to be her friend anymore. Declan didn't care what happened to her. If she wanted to kill, all she had to do was leave his territory. She was a vampire. Why not live like one? She didn't have to stay here, where no one gave a damn about her. She could transport herself anywhere she wanted to go.

But first she wanted revenge against those responsible for destroying the man she loved.

❧ ❧ ❧

Conor lifted his head as a familiar scent tickled his nostrils. Tossing the empty husk of his prey aside, he raced down the sidewalk, only to come to an abrupt halt when the scent vanished.

Samantha. He growled low in his throat. She had been here only moments ago.

Frowning, he stared into the distance. She had been alone. Why? Declan had been protecting her. What had changed?

She must have run away, he thought, as he licked a bit of blood from the corner of his mouth. His perfect brother wouldn't have let her go, not when innocent lives hung in the balance. Because Declan knew all too well that Conor didn't make empty threats. Declan was nothing if not a realist. He would have weighed his options—protect Sam and be responsible for more lives lost, or turn Sam over and save the innocent?

So, Sam had run away to save her own skin, he thought, grinning. Exactly what he would have done.

If she was smart, she would come to him. He knew her longing to kill. Only with him could she fully embrace her vampire nature. Together, they could destroy Declan and take over the nightclub and the city.

Whistling softly, he strolled down the street. Sooner or later, he would find her again.

# CHAPTER THIRTY-TWO

A ngie woke smiling, her head pillowed on her husband's shoulder. She was a married lady now. Mrs. Declan Nicolae. Mrs. Angie Nicolae. If she had her high school notebook, she'd be writing their initials inside a red heart.

Grinning, she slipped out of bed, donned her robe, and tiptoed into the kitchen. Angie Nicolae. It sounded perfect. She hummed softly as she made a pot of coffee, poured a cup, and carried it to the table.

With the warm mug cupped between her palms, she wondered how their day-to-day life would unfold. She wouldn't have to fix breakfast or lunch for Declan, but what about dinner? He didn't need food to survive. No big deal. She was used to eating alone. But maybe he would wouldn't mind sharing a meal with her on Sundays. She thought of all the meals he'd eaten while they were dating. She knew now he'd probably consumed them just so she wouldn't ask why he *didn't* eat.

He would probably be gone most nights, working at the Nightmare. Funny, she hadn't considered that before. Then again, maybe he wouldn't spend too much time there as long as Conor was a threat.

Conor brought thoughts of Samantha to mind. Declan had said Conor and Sam would find each other. Would they? And what if they did? What if Samantha decided to stay with

Conor? Angie couldn't imagine why Sam would do such a thing, seeing as how Conor had killed Ian. Still…even though Angie hated to admit it, Sam and Conor seemed to be two of a kind. What if they teamed up? Angie shivered. They would make a formidable pair. The Bonnie and Clyde of vampires. She assured herself that Declan was stronger than both of them together and prayed she was right.

After breakfast, she padded into her office and called up her New Year's document. She read it through, made a few minor changes, and sent if off to Jennifer. So, Halloween, Christmas, and New Year were in the bag. Were there similar myths and monsters for Valentine's Day?

With that thought in mind, she opened Google.

After an hour of research, she began to write:

*A lot of people believe Valentine's Day was invented by greeting card companies. Of course, this isn't true. The day—and cards—existed long before Hallmark. In the Victorian era, people sent cards and love notes on February 14th, just as we do today. Companies were quick to jump on the band wagon. Cadbury was the first company to pack their chocolates in heart-shaped boxes way back in 1868. Esther Howland of Worcester, Massachusetts, published the first Valentine made in America in 1849. Hallmark first offered Valentine's Day cards in 1913 and began mass producing them in 1916.*

*Valentine's Day is celebrated in Mexico, France, Australis, Denmark, Italy, Canada, the United Kingdom, and the U.S.A.*

*Saint Valentine is believed to be the inspiration for the day: however, there were several saints named Valentine and no one really knows which one is credited with the holiday. However, according to legend, there was a theologian and teacher named Valentinus back in 269 A.D. Valentinus was sent to prison for his Christian beliefs and sentenced to death. While imprisoned, legend has it that he restored the sight of his jailer's daughter. On the night before he was sentenced to die, he wrote a note of farewell to the girl and signed it, "From your Valentine." He died on February 14th.*

*Of course, everyone links Cupid with Valentine's Day, but he isn't the pink-cheeked cherub we know today. In mythology, Cupid is the god of love, desire, and erotic affection. He is often portrayed as the son of Venus and Mars, or of Venus and Mercury. It's believed his arrows inspire love. Depending on the source, Cupid is portrayed as callous and careless, or mischievous.*

*In Greek mythology, he is known as Eros, the God of Love. His quiver was said to be loaded with golden arrows to inspire love and with leaden arrows to evoke an aversion to those stricken.*

*Shakespeare said, "Love looks not with the eyes, but with the mind, And therefore is winged Cupid painted blind."*

*Perhaps that's where the saying, "Love is blind" originated.*

*In poetry, Cupid was portrayed as an amazingly handsome young man who was irresistible to human and immortal alike.*

Grinning, Angie sat back in her chair. Sort of like her vampire, she mused. Irresistible.

No sooner had the thought crossed her mind than Declan was standing behind her, his lips moving in her hair, his hands sliding seductively up and down her arms as he murmured, "Good morning, wife."

"Husband."

"Am I interrupting anything?" he asked, nuzzling her neck.

"Not really. I was just waiting for you to wake up."

"Oh, I'm up, all right," he said, laughter evident in his voice.

"I'll just bet your are." She didn't object when he tugged on her hand, urging her to her feet. "What would you like to do?" she asked with wide-eyed innocence.

"I'll think of something," he promised as he carried her swiftly into their bedroom and closed the door.

Hours later, Angie again woke with a smile on her face, her whole body aching in a most delicious way. "Cupid's got nothing on you, my husband," she muttered.

Propping himself up on one elbow, Declan looked at her and frowned. "Cupid? Do I look like an over-weight baby in a diaper?"

"So you've heard of him."

"Cupid." He growled low in his throat. "I've been called a lot of things in my day, but never that."

Angie shook her head, laughing too hard to speak. Wiping tears from her eyes, she said, "I was in the middle of writing an article about Valentine's Day when you interrupted me."

"Ah, yes. Cupid. Bows and arrows, red hearts and pink roses." Leaning down, he kissed the tip of her nose. "I promise I'll shower you with all the expected gifts when the day arrives."

"See that you do. And I'll shower you with chocolate vampires on Halloween."

Two hours later, they emerged from the bedroom, freshly showered and dressed.

"Does it bother you to be awake during the day?" she asked. "I mean, if you need to rest, I'll understand."

"Not to worry, love."

"What's it like when you're at rest?" She sat on the sofa, her legs curled beneath her. "Is it like being asleep?"

"No." He dropped down beside her, his arm sliding around her shoulders. "I don't know how to describe it. I'm

not really 'asleep' and I don't dream. It's like … hell, I don't
know what it's like. But even when I'm deeply at rest, on
some primal level, I'm aware of what's going on around me.
Any sign of danger awakens me. A lot of hunters try to find
our lairs during the day because it's easier to destroy most
of us while we're at rest." He slid his fingers into the hair
at her nape. "This is rather morbid talk for a honeymoon,
don't you think?"

"Maybe, but I need to know everything there is to know
about my husband."

"Just know that he loves you more than you can imagine."

Declan waited until Angie went to bed before he left the
house. Standing on the porch, he reinforced the wards that
protected the property from vampires and mortals alike.
It was all too easy for vampires to hypnotize humans and
force them to do their bidding, whether it was kidnapping
or breaking and entering.

His first stop was the Nightmare. He noted that the
usual crowd had gathered for the evening. He questioned
each of them about Conor and Samantha. No one had seen
one. They all reported an increase in the number of hunters in the city, though there had been no encounters so
far. Surprisingly, there had been no reports of new human
deaths, either.

Declan pondered that as he left the club, leaving him
to wonder if Conor knew that Sam was no longer under his
protection. If that was true, what did it mean? Had Conor
moved on? Or just decided to take a few nights off?

Declan was searching for prey when he heard a faint cry.
Honing in on the sound, he followed it to a vacant lot on the

outskirts of town where Reynard was valiantly trying to fight off a pair of hunters.

"Let's even things out, shall we?" Declan growled as he grabbed one of the hunters around the neck and pulled him away from Reynard.

The other hunter decided he didn't like fighting one on one. He released his hold on Reynard and high-tailed it for the truck parked a few feet away.

Declan released the man in his grasp, who took off running after his partner. A moment later, the truck sped away.

"You okay, Jack?" Declan asked.

Reynard staggered toward him. "Damn hunters. One of them managed to cut me."

Declan glanced at the blood leaking from a long, narrow gash in Reynard's left arm.

"Weakened me just enough to let them get the upper hand. Glad you came along when you did."

"No charge." Declan paused before asking the question uppermost in his mind. "You haven't seen my brother lately, have you?"

"Can't say as I have. I saw that female Ian turned. Sam, isn't it? Pretty little thing."

"Yeah. How is she?"

"All right, I guess. She was just wandering up one street and down another, like she was looking for someone."

Declan grunted softly. Was Samantha looking for Conor as part of the plan to destroy him? Or thinking of changing sides? Although he wouldn't mention it to Angie, he feared that Sam and his brother were very much alike, which left him to wonder again whether Sam's intent was to bait the trap, or join Conor in his killing spree?

# CHAPTER THIRTY-THREE

Samantha woke soon after the sun slipped below the horizon. She had abandoned Declan's secondary lair because if and when she found Conor, she didn't want him following her there. He had to believe she had turned her back on Declan and Angie. And she had to believe it, too, Sam thought. Declan had blocked the blood link between them, which meant Conor could no longer find her, and that he couldn't use it to find Declan. She wasn't sure how it all worked, but she knew that it did.

Rising, she headed into the bathroom to shower. She had been staying in houses that were empty and for sale, a different house every night. This one was a lovely, two-story home, just the kind of place she had hoped to own one day, before her whole life had been turned upside down.

She dressed in clothes she had stolen from a high-end store in a nearby mall, pulled on a pair of five-hundred dollar boots, and left the house. Her first order of business was to find some sexy hunk to prey upon, the second to find Conor.

Conor's head snapped up, nostrils flaring, eyes narrowing as he caught a familiar scent. Samantha.

He shoved the woman in his arms aside, a faint smile curving his bloody lips as he let her go. Declan would be so proud of him for letting his prey live.

Conor homed in on Samantha's scent, his suspicion growing as he drew closer. He had been hunting her for a week without success. Why had she suddenly left her hidey-hole to wander the streets of town?

He paused to open his preternatural senses, but there was no hint of Declan lurking nearby.

Another block and he came up behind her, then fell into step beside her. "Samantha, my sweet, we meet again."

"I've been looking for you."

"Indeed?" He arched one brow as his hand curled around her wrist. "To what end, I wonder? Surely you haven't forgiven me for killing your lover."

She flinched as his nails dug into her arm, drawing blood.

His nails bit deeper. "Have you?"

"No," she gasped.

"You ran away from me," he said, his voice low and filled with menace. "And took my prize with you."

"I know. I was wrong. I thought Angie and I could still be friends. But she hates me and now she's afraid of me. And Declan... he doesn't trust me, either. He wanted to keep me locked up. A prisoner in a cell." Tears filled her eyes. "He won't let me hunt as I wish. He won't let me kill."

"I thought you'd given up killing?"

"I thought so, too, but I was wrong and you were right. I'm a vampire. I'll always be a vampire, so why fight it?," she said with a shrug. "Killing is what we do."

His gaze bored into hers. She could feel his mind brushing hers. She summoned all her rage, all her hatred for what she was, all the envy she felt for Angie, and then she let him in.

A slow smile spread over his face. "I was going to kill you on sight for betraying me, you know," he said, his voice surprisingly mild as he dragged her into his embrace. "But now I think you might be useful." He ran his tongue along the length of her neck as his hand cupped her breast. "In more ways than one."

Angie stood at the front window, gazing out into the darkness. Overhead, a full moon rode high in the sky. The house across the street was having a party in their backyard. Music blared from a loud speaker. "It's been more than a week since Samantha left. Do you think that means she hasn't found Conor?"

"Either that or she's thrown in with him again."

Angie glanced over her shoulder to where Declan slouched on the sofa. "Would she do that?"

"I'm afraid she might. She's angry and confused and jealous of you."

"Me?"

"You have everything she ever wanted and will never have. Her innate instinct is to kill, something Conor will encourage. And the more often she does it, the harder it will be for her to ever stop."

Angie stared at him, tears blurring her eyes. "We shouldn't have let her go."

Declan stood and drew her into his arms. "I couldn't keep her a prisoner forever," he said quietly. "Sooner or later, I would have had to let her go, or she would have

figured out a way to escape. The decision of how to live her
life has to be up to Sam."

"You're right, I guess."

"I know I am. Angie?"

She looked up at him, her eyes damp with tears.

"Never mind."

"You're going to destroy her, aren't you?"

"I don't want to. But if she becomes a danger to you…"

Angie nodded. Once she would never have believed
Sam capable of hurting her or anyone else, but that was no
longer true. The Samantha she had known had died the
night Ian turned her and there was no going back.

Samantha shuddered in Conor's arms as his body claimed
hers. He was a tireless lover, inventive, sometimes cruel, and
she reveled in it. He was arrogant, domineering, without
mercy or compassion, and yet she felt free for the first time
in her vampire life. There were no restrictions on her, no
one giving her pitying looks. No one judging her when she
killed her prey. No one bossing her around, dictating what
she could and couldn't do. It was freeing, exhilarating.

Conor didn't love her, she knew that. He didn't know
the meaning of the word. And yet, in his own, twisted way,
he cared for her.

And for now, that was enough.

# CHAPTER THIRTY-FOUR

Declan sifted his fingers through Angie's hair. They had made love earlier. Now, she lay beside him, her head pillowed on his shoulder, their bodies still damp. It amazed him that he loved her more every day, but what was even more amazing was that, in spite of everything, she loved him in return. He wanted to believe she was happy, but she couldn't hide the sadness in her eyes or the sorrow she still felt at the loss of her best friend.

He only dropped by The Nightmare once or twice a week to check on things, and because he was afraid to let Angie out of his sight, Declan insisted she go with him. It really wasn't fair, he knew that, and yet what else was he to do? Hire another vampire to protect her when he was away? To do so would put another life in danger. Conor was threat enough, but Conor and Sam together... He shook his head. They were both stone-cold killers.

He didn't know what to make of the fact that there had been no vampire-related deaths in the city for the last three weeks. Either Samantha and Conor had moved on or they were hunting elsewhere. His best guess was that they had left the city, although he found it hard to believe that was true. Still, he wasn't comfortable with leaving Angie home alone. Maybe he should just take Angie and get out of town for a while. The more he thought about it, the better it sounded.

Turning on his side, he rained kisses along the side of her neck. "Angie, we never went on a honeymoon. How would you feel about taking a trip?"

"A trip? Where?"

"Wherever you'd like to go. I think we could both use a change of scene, don't you?"

"Yes," she murmured, a faint look of interest sparking in her eyes.

"So..." He slid his hand up and down her thigh. "Where to?"

"I don't care, as long as it's somewhere you've never gone with anyone else."

He grunted thoughtfully. He had been just about everywhere in the world at one time or another, usually with a woman at his side. Surely there was some place on earth he hadn't been, someplace he could see for the first time, with Angie beside him.

And then he grinned. He had never been to Santa Catalina Island, located off the coast of Southern California. It wasn't Rome or London. It didn't have any ancient cathedrals, but it didn't hold any memories, good or bad, either.

"Sounds great!" Angie exclaimed when he suggested it. "I've never been there, but I've always wanted to go." It wasn't an exotic locale by any means, but she would be sharing the sights and the nights with the man she loved in a place neither of them had ever been before. A place they could begin to make their own memories. And that was enough.

In the morning, while Declan was at rest, Angie logged on to Google and looked up the history of Santa Catalina Island, thinking one day she might write a column about it.

To her surprise, she learned the island had been inhabited by Indians seven thousand years ago before being claimed by Spain in 1542. She leaned back, momentarily stunned by the realization that, incredible as it seemed, the man she loved had been alive back then.

Reading on, she discovered that William Wrigley, the chewing gum tycoon, had purchased the island in 1919 and immediately set about turning it into a soon-to-be famous destination for vacations. In 1921, he built the Catalina Casino, which included the world's largest circular ballroom and the first theater that was built to show talking pictures. In the 30s, 40s, and 50s, it was a favorite destination for stars like Charlie Chaplain, John Wayne, Errol Flynn, Humphrey Bogart, and Johnny Weissmuller of "Tarzan" fame. More than five hundred movies had been filmed on or around the island.

The more she read, the more excited she was about going.

She pounced on Declan as soon as he woke up. "I need a new wardrobe for our vacation," she said, her voice filled with excitement. "At least a new bathing suit."

"I think I can afford that," he said with a grin. "Just let me shower and get dressed."

Declan sighed as he followed Angie through the women's section of the clothing store. A new bathing suit apparently included new sandals, shorts, shirts, a floppy-brimmed white hat, a colorful beach towel, a long, flowing, multi-colored skirt and gauzy white blouse, a sundress for dinner, a cocktail dress for dining and dancing, and three pairs of sunglasses.

They made a brief stop in the men's department so Declan could pick up a pair of swim trunks before heading for home.

They left the following evening just before sundown. Angie gasped as Declan transported them across land and water to the island. Vampire Air, she mused as she glanced around. It was the only way to fly.

"What if someone saw us?" she asked. "How would you explain it?"

"No one did. I veiled our arrival."

"But what if they had?"

He shrugged. "I'd just erase the memory from their minds."

Angie shook her head, wondering if there was anything her husband couldn't do.

Declan had rented a condo with a view of Hamilton Cove Bay. Her eyes widened as he carried her across the threshold. It was the most luxurious place she had ever seen, with beautiful mahogany hardwood floors. A large floral sofa and matching chair were arranged in front of a limestone fireplace. A small kitchen held everything anyone could need, the bathroom contained a shower and a large, free-standing oval tub with a Jacuzzi. The bedroom featured a king-sized bed, a mahogany chest of drawers, and a small, walk-in closet. A thick carpet the color of white sand covered the floor, the walls were a pale sea-foam green.

"Well?" Declan asked, coming up behind her. "How do you like it?"

"I love it!"

He glanced at her and then the bed. "So, what do you want to do first?"

Smiling, Angie wrapped her arms around him. "What do you think?"

Two hours later, their hair still damp from an extended stay in the shower, they went out to dinner at the Bluewater of Avalon restaurant, located on the waterfront. They chose to sit outside on the patio, which gave them a gorgeous view of the bay.

"Happy?" Declan asked.

"More than happy." Lifting her glass, Angie sipped her champagne. "I feel like my fairy godmother waved her magic wand and gave me everything I ever wanted and then some."

After dinner, they strolled along the beach. It was a beautiful night, the air warm, the sky clear, studded with a million stars that were reflected in the water. Declan slipped his arm around Angie's waist and she leaned into him, wanting to be as close as she could.

They walked until the lights of the harbor were behind them and only darkness lay ahead.

A few minutes later, Declan stopped, drew her into his arms, and held her tight.

Angie frowned as he blew out a long, shuddering sigh. "Is something wrong?"

"No, love. I just can't believe you're mine." He brushed a kiss across her brow, her cheeks, before settling on her lips.

Angie pressed herself against him as he deepened the kiss, then sank down on the sand, drawing her down beside him, his lips never leaving hers.

"Declan ... not here," she murmured.

"No one will see us."

"But ..."

"Angie."

The need in his voice melted her resistance, replaced by a sense of daring as he unfastened his belt. Ravished on a beach, Angie thought as he lifted her skirt. Another first.

And then there was no time for thought. He bit her, ever so gently, increasing her sensitivity, making her as aware of his pleasure as she was of her own. It was an amazing experience and she writhed beneath him as he whispered love words in her ear—some in Romanian—but she understood them just the same.

She let out a muffled cry as he carried her over the edge, sighed as she felt him convulse a moment later.

For a time, they lay locked in each other's arms, the only sounds their ragged breathing and the gentle lapping of the waves just a few feet away.

With a contented sigh, Angie fell asleep in his arms.

Late the next morning, after a breakfast of coffee and a chocolate croissant at the Catalina Island Brew House, Angie went for a walk along the beach. The view was like a picture postcard, the ocean a clear blue, scattered, puffy white clouds overhead, colorful sails in the distance. She passed teenagers tanning on the sand and a handful of mothers splashing in the shallows with their toddlers. She felt a momentary sadness at the thought of never having a child of her own, but it faded from memory when Declan came up behind her and slipped his arms around her waist.

"You're up early," she murmured as she turned in his embrace and lifted her face for his kiss.

"I missed you beside me." He kissed her again, longer, deeper. "What would you like to do today?"

"Take a ride in a glass-bottom boat? Go shopping?"

"I think we can do both," he said, taking her by the hand. "Come on."

After a full day of adventure, Angie relaxed in a hot bubble bath. The glass-bottom boat had been amazing. She had seen a wide variety of fish and let out a startled shriek when a flying fish landed inside the boat. She felt a little less embarrassed when another lady did the same a few minutes later. They had enjoyed a leisurely lunch on the beach, wandered through boutiques and souvenir shops, and gone dancing after dinner—always one of Angie's favorite ways to be in her husband's arms. Truly, a wonderful day. Everywhere they went, women had paused to look at Declan. Not that she could blame them. In jeans, a black tee shirt and sunglasses, he looked like a movie star. One brave, elderly lady had even asked if she could have her photo taken with him, and Declan had good-naturedly agreed.

"Will the picture come out?" Angie had asked. "I seem to remember reading somewhere that vampires couldn't be photographed."

"Those days are gone," he'd replied, "thanks to the discovery of digital technology."

But the best part of the day had been later that night, cocooned in Declan's arms, feeling his love pour over her, sweeter than honey, warmer than the sun at noon day.

❧ ❧ ❧

Declan transported himself to the Nightmare later than night after Angie had fallen asleep. He had taken the precaution of warding all the doors and windows before he left. Now, he sat at the bar, a glass of the house wine in his hand as he glanced around the room. The crowd was light. Finishing his drink, he skirted the dance floor, nodding at Randy Fontaine and a few of the other regular patrons. One of them, a middle-aged woman named Maria Calderon, caught him by the arm.

"Declan," she purred, "long time, no see."

"How've you been, Maria?"

"Missing you." She tilted her head to the side, giving him easy access to her throat. An unspoken invitation. When he hesitated, she placed her hand behind his head and drew him down toward her. "Please," she whispered.

An easy meal was not to be refused. Nevertheless, Declan felt a twinge of guilt as he considered her offer, though he wasn't sure why. He was a vampire, doing what vampires did. Still, drinking from someone he knew seemed like cheating on Angie, while feeding from his prey didn't. It made no sense, but there it was.

Maria looked up at him, obviously confused by his hesitation.

"Sorry, not tonight," Declan said, and sent her on her way.

He was about to return to Catalina when Jack Reynard appeared beside him. "Where have you been?" Reynard asked.

"Enjoying a few days with my bride, why?"

"Your brother's back in town."

Declan grunted softly. "What's the body count so far?"

"Six in the last two days."

"Is there a female vampire with him? Brown hair, brown eyes?"

"Yeah. They've been in here a couple of times looking for you."

*Shit!* "Thanks for letting me know."

With a nod, Reynard drifted toward a pretty young woman sitting alone at a table in the far corner of the room.

Brow furrowed, Declan resumed his place at the bar. He knew Conor was looking for him, but why the hell was his brother going around making it known?

He tried to think of a reason but no good answer came to mind.

Angie sighed as she packed her bags. She hated to leave Catalina, but they'd done all there was to do on the island, seen all the sights from the flying fish to the buffalo, dined at all the best restaurants. Last night, they had gone for a midnight swim and made love on the beach. It had been the perfect end to a perfect honeymoon. Still, she hated to leave. For these few days, Conor and Samantha had seemed far away, a distant threat.

She glanced at Declan, who was checking to make sure they hadn't forgotten anything. He had been preoccupied all morning. She knew something was bothering him, but he hadn't seen fit to share it with her. She told herself she was imagining trouble where there wasn't any, but she couldn't shake the feeling that something terrible was about to happen.

# CHAPTER THIRTY-FIVE

Samantha strolled down the street, Conor at her side. She had grown tired of killing. She hadn't been able to quit completely, but it was rare for her now. Maybe because there was no one telling her she couldn't. Surprisingly, Conor hadn't chided her about it, for which she was grateful. He seemed content to spend his whole existence hunting and killing, but she wasn't. She might live for centuries and in the last few weeks, she had come to realize that she wanted more out of life than blood and death. There were times when she wondered if it were possible to find a nice mortal man to fall in love with. After all, Angie was happy with Declan. Maybe there was hope for her, too. And if she couldn't find a human to love, maybe another vampire?

She glanced at Conor. The more time she spent with him, the less she understood him. He hunted with a single-minded ruthlessness that frightened her, and yet, to her surprise, she thought she had discovered a crack in his armor earlier that very night, albeit a tiny one, when they found a baby bird on the sidewalk. She had expected him to step on it. Instead, to her astonishment, he had picked up the helpless creature, then floated upwards and replaced the bird in its nest. Of course, just as she had decided that maybe he wasn't as evil as she'd thought, he had extinguished that hope by callously killing a teenage boy who had the misfortune to cross their path a few minutes later.

"You're awfully quiet tonight," Conor remarked as they headed for home. "What's wrong?"

"Nothing."

"Don't lie to me."

"Don't you ever get tired of killing?"

He looked at her as if she had lost her mind. "What else is there?"

"Lots of things. Home and family. Love…"

"Love!" He spat the word as if it had scorched his tongue. "What the hell good is it?"

Samantha stared at him. "Don't tell me you've never been in love!"

"What's it to you?"

She shook her head as an unexpected wave of pity washed through her. "Never?" she persisted. "Not once?"

"What the hell do you want from me?"

The tone of his voice told her he'd been in love, at least once, and it had not ended well. "What happened, Conor? Tell me."

He shoved his hands in his pockets, his jaw rigid, making her think she had gone too far.

"It was in Romania," he said, his voice flat. "A few years after we were turned. Declan and I had parted ways by then. Her name was Catina and she was the prettiest thing I'd ever seen. I ran into her several times in the village where she lived. One night I walked her home and after that, we saw each other almost every night for several months. Everything was fine until she started asking me to come to her house for dinner or to go walking in the afternoon, or accompany her to church." A muscle twitched in his jaw. "I couldn't do any of those things. Finally, she accused me of seeing someone else. I swore that I wasn't but she didn't believe me. She accused me once too often and I blurted the truth of what I'd become. She didn't believe me, of course, until..."

"Until you bit her."

"Yeah. It was just a little taste, but it freaked her out. I went to see her a few days later to try to apologize." He snorted. "Imagine my surprise when two hunters answered her door. They attacked me in the yard, right in front of her. Catina just stood there and watched. I killed them both. She stared at me for a long time, her face pale and filled with loathing, and then she slammed the door in my face."

"I'm sorry, Conor."

"Don't be. It was a lesson I never forgot. I haven't trusted a woman since." He stared into the darkness. It wasn't Catina who had embittered him, but losing Mihaela to Declan. She had been his one true love, and she had chosen Declan over him.

Samantha thought about what Conor had said later that night. Little wonder that he was bitter and hated everyone, and that he was jealous of Declan. Was it too late for Conor to change? If she could just make him see there was much more to life than just killing, maybe he would make peace with Declan. Maybe she and Angie could be friends again.

"Conor, why don't we find a nicer place to live? I have some money in the bank. We could rent an apartment. Or maybe a house."

"There's nothing wrong with this place."

"Seriously? This place is a dump. It's damp and moldy and dark."

"It's perfect for vampires."

"Maybe for Dracula."

"Forget it. The only thing I want is my brother's head."

"Is that right? You know how to find him, so why don't you confront him and get it over with?"

An odd expression flitted across his face and was gone.

"It's the only thing you have to live for, isn't it? Revenge? Once you kill him, your life won't have any meaning."

"Shut the hell up!"

"It's true, isn't it?"

Eyes narrowed, he slapped her across the face, once, twice, then vanished from her sight.

Samantha lifted a hand to her throbbing cheek. He didn't want to destroy Declan. And she had a feeling that Declan had no real desire to destroy Conor.

But with so much bad blood between them, there seemed no way to bring the brothers together.

The next evening, she told Conor she needed some time alone, and after he left the lair, she went house hunting. She found just what she was looking for in one of the poorer sections of town—an old farm house that had been vacant for the last three years. It wasn't large or very modern—a mid-sized living room, two bedrooms, a bathroom, kitchen, and a small dining room. But it had a nice-sized attic and a cellar that could easily be turned into a comfortable lair. It was the kind of place she had hoped to share with Ian.

For a moment, her hatred for Conor overcame every other feeling. But there was no point in dwelling on the past, or on what might have been. No point in hating Conor for behaving like a vampire. It was an exercise in futility. Ian was gone and by some cruel twist of fate, she was living with the man who had destroyed him. It sounded like a really bad soap opera.

She withdrew funds from her bank account and paid the first and last month's rent. The landlord was happy to let her move in as soon as she wished.

Now came the hard part, she thought as she returned to Conor's lair. Convincing him to move out of this dreary place.

"I thought I told you no," Conor said brusquely when she mentioned it later that night. "I'm perfectly happy here."

"Well, I'm not."

"What the hell do you want, anyway?"

"I want what Angie has, a home, a man who loves me."

It was the wrong thing to say.

Conor snorted disdainfully. "Honey, you're looking in the wrong place. Now, get the hell out of here before I make you wish you'd never been born."

"You're too late," Samantha retorted bitterly, and vanished from the house.

Conor stared at the place where she'd stood only seconds before, unable to believe what had just happened.

Unwilling to admit that he might miss her.

That he might need her.

# CHAPTER THIRTY-SIX

Declan strolled into the Nightmare an hour after Angie had gone to bed. In the last week, the body count had risen steadily—not just in his territory, but in several nearby cities. He had tried his darndest to locate Conor, but his brother had managed to avoid him at every turn. And yet Declan knew he was nearby. He caught his brother's scent from time to time, making him wonder if Conor was lurking in the shadows, just waiting to spring. It was damned disconcerting. Conor had consumed his blood. He could find him easily enough. Why hadn't he? What was he waiting for?

And what about Samantha? Declan wondered absently. Had she made peace with his brother? Or gone off on her own? He had tasted her blood. He should have been able to track her, but he couldn't. His best guess was that Conor had done the same thing he had done—taken some of Sam's blood and given her some of his own in order to break the link between Declan and Sam.

Declan bit out a curse. Conor had drank from Sam, and because Sam had tasted Declan's blood, Sam's blood would now strengthen his brother's preternatural power.

He blew out a sigh, hoping Conor had grown as sick and tired of this game of cat and mouse as he had. But only time would tell. Time. He swore again. How many more centuries would they waste hunting each other?

Forty minutes before closing time, Samantha suddenly appeared beside Declan.

"Dammit, Sam," Declan exclaimed, glancing around. "What the hell do you think you're doing? Not everyone who comes to the club knows that vampires are real."

"I'm sorry. I felt the need to see a friendly face."

"And you came here?"

"I don't blame you for being angry."

"Have you been with my brother all this time?"

"Yes. We were getting along pretty well, in spite of everything. I thought... I'd hoped I could change him, you know, make him think of something besides killing and revenge. I found a nice place for us to live. I thought maybe if he stopped living in that horrible lair... if I could convince him there was so much more to life than just killing." She blew out a sigh. "I should have known he wouldn't go for it. He threw me out."

"So what do you want from me? We had a deal before and you broke it."

"I'm scared he'll come after me."

"And?"

"I can't hide from him and I'm afraid to be alone."

"So, I'll ask you again," he said, his voice cool. "What do you want from me?"

"Your protection."

He cocked one brow. "What do I get in return?"

"My gratitude?"

"I'll want more than that."

"You want to know where he keeps his lair?"

"Damn right."

"Can I think it over for a night or two?"

Declan regarded her, eyes narrowed thoughtfully. "I trust you'll make the right decision. You remember there's to be no killing in my territory?"

"I remember. I … I don't do that anymore."

"Or any less?"

A faint smile curved her lips. "Not as often as I used to. I swear it. The longer I spent with Conor, the less appealing it was. I don't want to be like him."

"All right. You can rest in my lair here in the club's basement. It's warded and well-fortified. I'm about to close up for the night. Think hard about your decision."

"I will. I really appreciate your letting me stay here."

He grunted softly. "If you leave the club after I've gone, you won't be able to get back in."

Samantha nodded that she understood.

"One more thing." Folding his hands over her shoulders, Declan bit her.

"What did you do that for?" she exclaimed when he released her.

"So I can keep track of you."

"You don't trust me, do you?"

"Not one damn bit. Why should I?"

She had no answer for that.

Declan watched her go out the side door that led down to the basement, wondering if he was making yet another error in judgement.

He lingered in the club, waiting until the vampires—always the last to leave—drifted out into the night.

After locking up, he transported himself home. Angie was in bed, asleep. He undressed in the dark, then slid under the covers beside her. Her scent tickled his nostrils, the nearness of her body warmed his. He sighed as a sense of peace, of belonging, followed him into oblivion.

Angie had just finished wrapping up her Valentine's Day column when Declan stepped into her office, his hair still damp from a shower.

"I'm not catching you in the middle of anything, am I?" he asked.

"No, I was just about to send this off to Jennifer."

"Congratulations." He brushed a kiss across her cheek. "What's next?"

"I have no idea. I've done Halloween, Christmas, New Year's, and now Valentine's Day. Can you think of any other holidays with spooky myths?"

"April Fool's Day? Mother's Day?"

"Mother's Day!"

"Maybe stepmothers. Lots of stories about evil stepmothers, you know? Cinderella. Snow White. Hansel and Gretel."

"Hmm. A column about wicked stepmothers might be fun," Angie mused, adding Tangled to the list.

Declan kissed the top of her head. "I'm sure whatever you come up with will be brilliant," he said as he lightly massaged her neck and shoulders.

"That feels so good." She closed the file, attached it to her email and hit Send. A moment later her stomach let out a very unladylike rumble.

"Sounds like it's time for lunch," Declan remarked as she pushed away from her desk and turned her chair around.

"A ham and cheese sandwich for me," she said. "Can I get you anything?"

"Depends on what you're offering." He flashed a wolfish grin as he took her in his arms.

Batting her eyelashes at him, she murmured, "Depends on what you want."

"Maybe a quick bite? Or two?" he said with a seductive smile.

"Be my guest." She tilted her head to the side, sighed with pleasure as he bit her gently. How was it possible for anything that should have been gross to feel so wonderful, so arousing? It was like being drenched from head to foot in sexual heat.

"Angie." He growled her name as desire and hunger warred within him.

She shivered as he bit her again, a little harder, a little deeper. "Declan..."

Cursing softly, he knelt in front of her. "Dammit, Angie, do you have any idea how much I want you?"

"I think so," she said dryly. "I can see it in your eyes."

He looked away until the red faded. It still surprised him that she wasn't afraid of him, even when his vampire nature was evident. If he turned her, his desire for her blood would no longer be a problem. Vampires rarely drank from each other, and never for pleasure. They had never really discussed it...

Rising to his feet, he thrust the thought aside. "Come on," he said gruffly. "Let's get you something to eat."

He followed her into the kitchen and sat at the table while she fixed a quick sandwich before taking the seat across from him.

"Is something wrong?" she asked. "You seem... troubled."

He didn't want to tell her what he'd been thinking. They had never really discussed the possibility of her becoming a vampire, although he knew she had considered it. Rather than bring that up, he said, "It's Samantha. It seems she's tired of living the way Conor does," Declan explained. "She wants a home. I gather she gave my brother an ultimatum and he threw her out. I could have told her she was wasting her breath. He doesn't want to live anything like a normal life. He loves the hunt, the blood. He despises what he is, and he hates mortals because he envies them. The last thing he wants is a home." He blew out a sigh "Anyway, Sam's afraid he'll come after her, so I let her stay at my lair in the Nightmare."

Angie stared at him in disbelief. "You're letting her stay there? Do you think that's a good idea?"

"Probably not. But I'm hoping she'll tell me where to find Conor."

"Do you really think she will?"

"I don't know."

"Even if she told you, would you believe her?" Angie felt a twinge of guilt for not trusting her former best friend, but she couldn't help it. Sam had changed, and not for the better. Angie worried her lower lip between her teeth and then sighed. "I just don't see how you can believe anything she says. How do you know Conor didn't send Sam to spy on you? Or burn the place down again?" She had no right to judge Sam, Angie thought. She had no idea how she would react if she had been suddenly transformed into a vampire.

"I don't trust her," he admitted. "And I'm well aware that having her at the Nightmare is a risk, but I think she's genuinely worried and afraid of him. Anyway, I'd rather have her where I can keep an eye on her."

"I guess that makes sense," she agreed dubiously. "Do you really think she'll tell you where your brother is?"

"I guess we'll find out. She asked for a day or two to think about it."

Angie frowned. "There's something I don't understand. You said Conor bit you and then drank from you and that he can find you whenever he wants. If that's true, why hasn't he?"

"I don't know, but this has to end, one way or another."

He was right, Angie thought, but try as she might, she couldn't imagine an outcome that didn't involve bloodshed and the death of one of the brothers—or perhaps both.

Conor stalked the deserted streets, his hatred rising with every step. He had lost Samantha, though, in truth, she had never been his. Still, he had lusted for her and though he was loathe to admit it, he missed her.

He knew where she was—hiding out in the basement at the Nightmare.

All he had to do was go and get her.

And while he was there, he would confront his brother and put an end to the conflict between them.

A glance at the sky told him dawn was fast approaching.

"Tomorrow night," he muttered darkly. "One way or another, it ends tomorrow night."

Samantha paced the floor of Declan's basement lair. It was roomy. It was clean. It had a TV and books. The bed was comfortable, but it was still a prison. Was she going to spend the rest of her existence locked up in one prison or another? She was sick of it, sick of others telling her what to do. And yet she lacked the courage to stand up to Conor or his brother. Both were far more powerful than she was.

Both could destroy her with little more than a thought. It was time to pick a side and stick to it. She couldn't keep going back and forth from one to the other. So...did she want to go back to Conor, who didn't care a fig about what she did, or cast her lot with Declan, who put limits on what she could and couldn't do and threatened to destroy her if she killed in his territory?

Did she want to side with the one who had killed Ian? Or remain under Declan's control and be constantly reminded of the friend she had lost and the kind of life she would never have?

Did she want to be a vampire forced to live by Declan's iron-clad rules? Or one who made her own decisions? If she were stronger and more powerful, if she had more experience, she would leave Declan's territory without a second thought and strike out on her own. But she was still weak, still adjusting to being a vampire, still testing her powers and abilities. On her own, she would be an easy mark for hunters. Not only that, but Conor had warned her that vampires were territorial creatures, and that not all master vampires were willing to share their territory with others of their kind.

What to do, what to do? The sun would be rising soon and time was running out. She had to make a decision, had to decide whether or not to tell Declan where to find Conor's lair.

She paced back and forth like a caged animal until her skin began to tingle, warning her that the sun's rising was only moments away. She fought off the dark sleep as long as she could, but she wasn't old enough or strong enough to resist.

As the blackness closed in around her, Samantha fell back on the bed, dragged into the nothingness of oblivion, still not knowing what to do.

# Chapter Thirty-Seven

Angie woke with an overpowering sense of impending doom, made worse when she glanced out the window and saw the angry gray clouds scudding across the sky, accompanied by the distant rumble of thunder.

She glanced at Declan, resting beside her. As always, she was amazed that out of all the women he had known, all the women in the world, he had fallen in love with her. Yet even as the thought warmed her heart and soul, that feeling of imminent disaster chilled her to the bone.

After kissing his cheek ever so lightly, she slid out of bed and shuffled into the kitchen. Thinking how lucky she was to have found him, she made a cup of hot chocolate and carried it into the living room. Opening the drapes, she stood at the window and stared at the sky. Clouds hung low overhead, dark and ominous.

Angie shivered. Something bad was going to happen today. She knew it as well as she knew that her troubled thoughts had roused Declan.

A moment later he came up behind her, his arms sliding around her waist. "What's wrong, love?"

"I don't know." She set her cup on the table beside the window, then leaned back against him, sighing as he cupped her breasts.

"Is it that you don't know, or you don't want to talk about it?"

She shrugged. "It's probably just my imagination, but I can't shake the feeling that something terrible is going to happen today, something that will change everything."

Placing his hands on her shoulders, he turned her to face him, his arms again drawing her close, his gaze holding hers. "I won't let anything happen to you, love, I swear it on my life."

"It's not me I'm worried about."

One corner of his mouth lifted in a half-smile. "You're worrying about me?"

"I can't help it."

"There's no need, Angie. I've survived this long, I think I can make it through one more day."

"It isn't funny!"

"What do you think is going to happen?"

"I don't know! I've never felt like this before, but I know something awful is coming."

She jumped as a blinding flash of lightning lit up the room, following by a deep-throated rumble of thunder that shook the windows.

Declan's arms tightened around her as his mind brushed hers. He didn't know what had her so upset, but he could feel her fear. It was a palpable thing.

She clung to him, her whole body trembling.

"It's still early," he murmured. "Come back to bed. Try to get some sleep."

With a nod, she followed him to their room and stretched out beside him. His arm curled around her shoulders as she rested her head on his chest. She needed to be close to him, to touch him, feel his breath in her hair, inhale the intoxicating masculine scent that was his alone. She told herself she was worrying for nothing. He was a powerful being. He had survived for centuries. But she couldn't shake off the terrible premonition that disaster waited just around the corner.

Angie sighed as Declan drew her closer. His hand slid under the tee shirt she wore to bed, his fingers making lazy circles on her breast, her belly. She closed her eyes as warmth spread through her. She felt her body relax as he whispered in her ear, telling her he loved her, would always love her. She turned onto her side, her mouth seeking his as her hands began a slow exploration of their own, measuring the width of his biceps, tiptoeing across his flat belly, teasing the waistband of the sweat pants he'd worn to bed. She needed him, she thought, as she tugged them off and tossed them aside. Needed him more than her next breath.

He groaned deep in his throat, a groan that became a growl as he bared her body to his gaze and rose over her, his mouth covering hers as he possessed her, driving every thought, every fear from her mind but her desire for this man above all others.

His bite, when it came, carried her over the edge, multiplying her pleasure until she was swept away to a place where only he could take her.

Conor woke an hour before the setting of the sun. It had stormed earlier in the day. The lingering scent of rain hung in the air. Although he could be awake during the day, he shunned the light. He was a creature of the night. He reveled in the darkness, where sins were hidden and evil rode the wings of the night. Mortals who hid their true natures by day came out after dark—all those who pretended to be moral and righteous on the outside. Hypocrites, all, he thought disdainfully. Like Declan, who liked to pretend he was one of the good guys.

He pulled on a pair of jeans, tugged on his boots, and slipped a black tee shirt over his head. He glanced up as he left his lair. The sky was clear, the air still warm from the setting of the sun. He cringed as the lingering heat enflamed his skin. Once, soon after he'd been turned, he had ventured out before dark. It had been centuries before he tried it again. Even now, he remembered the agony as the sun's light seared his flesh, pieces of his skin turning black, some of it blistering in the heat.

He transported himself to the Nightmare and walked around the building. Samantha was still at rest inside, her heartbeat slow, barely audible even to his preternatural hearing. She wouldn't rise for another hour or so.

He paused near the vacant lot adjacent to the club, his senses picking up the lingering scent of violence and death. Several bodies had been buried here, one recently. Conor grinned inwardly. So, his brother had his own cemetery. Handy. But then, Declan had always managed to make the best of things, always come out on top no matter the circumstances.

The woman, Angie, had been at the club not long ago. Perhaps Declan would bring her with him tonight. He grunted softly. Perhaps there was another way to draw him out.

Pleased at the thought, he transported himself to his favorite hunting grounds in the wealthy part of town. There was an hour or two until the club opened.

And he was hungry.

He grinned, thinking it was his lucky night, when he heard the raucous sounds of music and laughter coming from one the estates. Young adults, having a party, he thought. Lots of beautiful men and women in their early twenties who smelled good and tasted better. A veritable smorgasbord of scents and tastes.

No one noticed when he strolled into the backyard and helped himself to a bottle of wine. A little something to whet his appetite, he mused, as a buxom young woman sashayed up to him.

"I've never seen you at one of Jim's parties before," she remarked. "I know I would have remembered you."

Conor tossed the bottle aside, then grabbed her arm and pulled her up against him. He took a deep breath, drawing in the scent of her blood. "Honey," he purred, "you're never going to forget me."

Declan bolted upright as the scent of freshly-spilled blood tickled his nostrils.

A lot of blood.

"What is it?" Angie asked. "What's wrong?"

"You were right," he said, throwing back the covers and reaching for his pants. "Something bad just happened."

"Before she could ask what was going on, he vanished from her sight.

There was blood everywhere—on the cement around the pool, in the pool, on the chairs and tables, the grass. Seven bodies lay sprawled in the yard, grotesque in the pale light of the moon.

A deep breath confirmed his suspicions. Conor had been here.

❧ ❧ ❧

Angie stared at Declan, a look of horror on her face as he told her what he'd found.

"You have to stop him," she said, her voice thick with unshed tears for the lives lost.

"I intend to. Get dressed." Leaving the bedroom, he opened his link to Samantha. *Get the hell over to my house right now.* He closed the link as Angie stepped out of the bedroom.

She started to ask what he was going to do about Conor, but he silenced her with a look.

❧ ❧ ❧

Samantha arrived a few minutes later. "You're going to kill him for what he's done tonight, aren't you?"

"Damn right. Where can I find him?"

Samantha glanced at Angie, who was tucked into a corner of the sofa, her face pale. "Isn't there some other option?" Sam asked.

"Like what?"

"I don't know."

"You don't approve of what he's done, do you?" Angie asked.

Samantha shook her head. "No. No, of course not, but…"

"But what?" Angie exclaimed. "He's butchering inno-cent people."

"He's had a rough life," Sam said. "Maybe there's a way…"

"There's only one way to stop him," Declan said, his voice laced with steel. "Either tell me where to find him, or get out of here."

Sam sent a pleading glance in Angie's direction.

"I don't know how you can defend him," Angie said. "He's a monster. Surely you can see that."

"There's good in him. I know there is," Samantha insisted. "There has to be."

"You're a damn fool," Declan declared. "You know as well as I do—maybe better—what he's capable of."

"You're right," Sam admitted in a small voice. "I know you are."

"You're in love with him," Angie said, her voice thick with disbelief.

A pair of tears tinged with red slid down Samantha's cheeks. "I can't help myself. We could have had a good life together if he'd just been willing to try."

"I told you before, that's not what he wants," Declan said. "He's had hundreds of years to change."

"You're right," Sam said again. "He takes his rest in the basement of an abandoned warehouse about twenty miles east of here. He ..." Her words trailed off and she let out a strangled cry, one hand clutching her throat.

Angie jumped to her feet as Sam fell to her hands and knees. "What's wrong with her?"

"Dammit! Conor's taken hold of her mind. He's trying to destroy her."

"What?" Angie stared at Samantha, who was writhing on the floor, her face twisted in agony. "Stop him!"

"I'm trying, but his link to her is stronger than mine."

"Can he do that? Can he really kill her from a distance?"

Declan nodded as he concentrated on homing in on his link to Samantha. He could feel his brother's power growing stronger. Not knowing what else to do, he sank his fangs into Sam's throat. It had the hoped for effect of startling Conor so that he lost his concentration.

With a sob, Samantha curled into a ball, her whole body trembling.

Murmuring, "Oh, Sam," Angie sat on the floor beside her, blinking back her tears as she lightly stroked Samantha's back.

Declan muttered an oath, every instinct urging him to go after Conor, but there was no way he was leaving Angie home alone with Samantha. Dammit! He paced the floor, weighing his options, which were few, only to come to an abrupt halt when Samantha's eyes went red.

In a blur of movement, he grabbed Angie and thrust her behind him.

Samantha stared up at him, eyes blazing with hunger and a rage that wasn't entirely her own.

Holding her gaze, Declan drew on his preternatural power, his mind searching hers, but it was Conor's thoughts he found.

*Brother.* Conor's voice in his mind, thick with disdain. *Don't bother coming to look for me. I've moved my lair.*

With an oath, Declan closed the link. Conor had learned a new way to manipulate Sam, he thought.

Worse, his brother was even stronger than he had suspected.

What do we do now?" Angie asked after he told her what had happened.

"Beats the hell out of me." He glanced at Samantha, still sitting on the floor, her face expressionless.

"What did he do to Sam?"

"I'm not sure, but he's taken over her mind."

"How is that even possible?"

"I don't know." Suddenly restless, Declan paced the floor. "I can control human minds, but not from a long distance. I've never heard of anything like that. All I know is that she can't stay here."

"What are you going to do with her?"

"I'm not sure." Moving to the window, he stared out into the night. Where the hell was Conor? Maybe if he went to his brother's old lair, he'd be able to track him to the new one, wherever that might be, he thought, and then quickly dismissed the idea. He didn't dare leave Angie alone with Samantha.

"I can't believe this is happening," Angie said, a note of hopelessness in her voice. "It's like a nightmare that won't end." She brushed a lock of hair from Samantha's cheek, pity rising up within her. Poor Samantha, all her hopes and dreams shattered.

Angie smiled faintly when Sam looked up and met her gaze, felt a strange kind of lethargy sweep over her as Samantha leaned forward and buried her fangs in her neck. She drank deeply, quickly.

The scent of blood caught Declan's attention. He turned away from the window, a hoarse cry of denial rising in his throat.

Alarmed, Samantha looked up. Scrambling out of his way, she grabbed the fireplace poker and drove it upward into his chest. Shrieking, "She's mine!" she buried her fangs in Angie's throat again.

Teeth clenched, Declan yanked the poker from his chest. "Dammit, let her go!"

"Never!" Samantha stared at him, her eyes red and wild. "Conor said I can have her."

"Over my dead body!" Declan snarled, and drove the poker through Samantha's heart and out the other side.

Declan knelt beside Angie. Her face was pale. Blood oozed from the savage wounds in her throat, her heart beat was slow and thready. Dammit! How had Samantha taken so much so quickly? But it didn't matter. Angie was teetering on the brink of death. With luck, he could give her a little of his blood and it would revive her. If not… the alternative didn't bear thinking about.

Sitting back on his heels, Declan lifted Angie into his arms. Her skin was cold, so cold, her lips turning blue, her heartbeat now so faint he could scarcely hear it, even with his preternatural hearing. He had to make a decision soon, before she reached the point where nothing he did would save her.

If he turned her, would she thank him? Or hate him? She had asked a lot of questions about what it was like to be a vampire. She had done a lot of studying about his kind on the Internet. She had accepted him readily enough. But she had never expressed any desire to become a creature of the night.

He gazed at her pale face. Centuries ago, he had sworn on his mother's life that he would never turn anyone against their will. But Angie was in no condition to make the decision. He closed his eyes as pain knifed through him. How could he let her go when he could save her?

"Angie," he groaned. "What should I do?"

A long, shuddering sigh wracked her body.

He ran his knuckles over her cheek. She was his life, the light in the darkness of his existence. Without her, he had no reason to go on, nothing to look forward to. He had waited for her for centuries. How could he let her go when there was so much he wanted to show her, to share with her? He couldn't. It was as simple—and as complicated—as that.

Hating himself for what he was about to do, he brushed the hair away from the side of her neck. Then, murmuring, "Forgive me, love," he sank his fangs into her soft, tender flesh.

# CHAPTER THIRTY-EIGHT

"What the hell?" Conor's head snapped up as an image of Samantha flitted across his mind, followed by a startled shriek of terror. And then nothing as the blood link between them was severed.

He murmured her name, surprised by the sudden sense of loss he felt at her death. A slow rage burned within him. Samantha had been the only woman he'd cared about in centuries and his brother had destroyed her. And for that, Declan's woman would pay. It would be a far more satisfying form of revenge than destroying his brother. Killing Declan would be too easy, to quick, but his brother would grieve for the woman as long as he lived.

# CHAPTER THIRTY-NINE

Angie woke abruptly. For a moment, she felt so strange, she wondered if she was sick She lifted a hand to her forehead. She didn't have a fever. If anything, her skin was cooler than usual. Glancing out the window, she was surprised to see that it was dark outside. It was dark inside, too, yet she saw everything clearly.

Frowning, she sat up. Something was wrong. Where was Declan? Where was Sam?

Swinging her legs over the edge of the bed, Angie padded into the living room. Relief flooded through her when she saw Declan standing there, and then, noting his solemn expression, she frowned again. "Is something wrong?"

"How do you feel?"

"Sort of weird. I don't know how to explain it. Where's Sam? Did you send her back to the Nightmare?" A sudden image of Samantha lunging at her, fangs bared, quickly reminded her of the events of the previous night. "She bit me!"

Declan nodded, tension thrumming through him as he wondered what her reaction would be when she realized what had happened. "What else do you remember?"

"Nothing." Angie lifted a hand to her neck. "Sam bit me," she said again, as if she couldn't quite believe it. Feeling suddenly cold, she wrapped her arms around her middle. "Where is she now?"

"She's gone." He had done what was necessary to insure that Samantha wouldn't rise again and then buried her in the lot behind the Nightmare.

"Gone?" Angie looked up at him, brow furrowed. "Gone where?"

He didn't answer, merely stood there, watching her, his eyes filled with sadness.

Angie stared back at him and she knew why she felt so strange, why she had been able to see so clearly in the dark. She lifted her hand to her throat as the memory of Samantha's attack unfolded in her mind—the fear, the pain of Samantha's fangs savaging her throat, the horror of knowing Sam was drinking her blood. "Sam turned me, didn't she?"

Declan took a deep breath and released it in a long, shuddering sigh. "No."

"No?"

He cringed at the flicker of hope in her eyes. "I did."

"You...why...how could you? How could you?" Angie screamed the words as fear and outrage exploded within her. She darted forward, pounding her fists against his chest. "How. Could. You?"

He made no move to defend himself, didn't say a word, just stood there while she pounded her fists against his chest as hard as she could, again and again. As her anger intensified, she raked her nails down his face, leaving long, bloody furrows behind.

Angie stared at the dark-red blood dripping down his cheeks as though mesmerized. The sight of it! The tantalizing scent of it! Her stomach knotted as pain knifed through her. Hardly aware of what she was doing, she went up on her tiptoes and licked the blood from his cheeks. It was warm, so warm. It chased the cold from her body and filled her with a sudden sense of euphoria.

Gripping his shoulders in her hands, she licked some more, lapped it up like a kitten with a bowl of fresh cream until it was all gone. Horrified by what she'd done, she took a step back. She waited for him to berate her, to do something, say something, but he just stood there, watching her. "Tell me why!" she demanded. "Why did you do it?"

"I couldn't let you go," he said quietly. "Not when I could save you."

"You didn't save me! You turned me into a vampire! A monster!"

"Is that how you see me now?"

"No." She frowned, confused and angry. And then she doubled over as pain ripped through her again.

"You need to feed," he said, his voice flat. "It's the only thing that will make the pain go away."

*Feed. Prey on human blood.* "I don't want to."

"Yes, you do."

"I don't know how."

"It's my duty to teach you."

She shook her head in denial.

"Angie, I'm your husband, and now I'm your sire. You will do as I say."

Hands knotted into fists, she screamed, "I hate you!"

The words cut into his soul like a knife. "I know. But you can't go hunting alone. Even if you wanted to, I wouldn't let you. Have you forgotten Conor is still out there?"

*Conor.* Oh, Lord, he really *was* a monster, Angie thought dully. And now, so was she.

Declan flinched as he read her thoughts. He didn't blame her for hating him. Right now, he hated himself. But he could live with her hatred. Better that than to live without her. "Go get dressed."

Angie stormed into the bedroom, tore off her nightgown, pulled on a pair of black jeans and a black tee shirt. Stomped into a pair of black boots. She paused in front of the mirror on the back of her door. The books she'd read said vampires cast no reflection, but they were obviously mistaken, as she saw herself quite clearly. She looked the same as always, she thought, and then frowned. Not quite the same. Her hair seemed thicker, more lustrous. Her skin looked a trifle paler, her eyes a deeper shade of blue.

*Vampire.* She felt it again, that sense of horror, of living in someone else's skin. She flinched when Declan knocked at the door.

"Let's go, Angie."

She wanted to argue, to refuse, to scream that she never wanted to see him again, but the pain in her gut was agonizing, like nothing she had ever known, and he was the only one who could help her.

Jaw clenched, she opened the door and followed Declan into the night.

Angie stared at the world around her, feeling as though she were seeing it for the first time. She gazed at the heavens. The stars looked so big and bright, so close, she felt like she could reach up and pluck one from the sky. Even though it was dark, she saw everything clearly—trees and flowers that had once looked faded at night appeared just as colorful now as they did during the day. She covered her ears as a cacophony of sounds assaulted her—screeching tires, sirens, blaring TVs, the cry of a baby, the wail of a siren. Every breath carried myriad scents—grass and foliage, oil and gas.

"You'll learn to tune it all out, in time," Declan said.

He should know, she thought bitterly. He'd been a vampire forever.

"In the meantime, let's go to the Nightmare."

She looked at him askance as he slid his arm around her waist.

"You won't have to hunt there. A few of my customers enjoy being bitten."

She was still trying to imagine that when they reached the club's back door.

"Not all my customers believe in vampires," he explained as he led her down a narrow hall that ended where the bar began. "So it's not a good idea to just suddenly appear."

Angie sat on a stool, her gaze sweeping the room. It was early and the crowd was light. To her amazement, she could easily detect the other vampires in the room. The *other* vampires, she thought dully. She was one of them now.

Sitting beside her, Declan gestured for a muscular young man with short blond hair to join them. "Thad, this is Angie. She's new and she's hungry. Are you game?"

Thad looked her up and down and then smiled. "Sure. Come on, pretty lady, let's dance."

"Dance?" Angie shot a glance at Declan.

He nodded.

"But…"

"Just do what comes naturally," Declan said, his voice cool. "Thad will tell you when to stop. He's an old pro at this."

Feeling like she was in some bizarre alternate universe, Angie followed Thad onto the dance floor.

"First time, huh?" he remarked as he took her in his arms.

"Yes."

"Don't be nervous, sweetheart. Just don't bite down too hard. Like the boss said, I'll tell you when to stop."

"I…" Angie shook her head. This couldn't be happening. And then she remembered the times when she had danced with Declan. The music was slow and sensual. The scent of the man's blood—her prey—enticed her. Was this what Declan felt when he held her in his arms, this overwhelming desire? Resisting the urge to bury her fangs—oh, Lord, she had fangs!—in his throat, she bit him as gently as she could, and all the while she waited for a sense of revulsion, of horror at what she was doing. But it never came.

"That's it," Thad murmured. "Slow and easy."

*You're doing fine, love. Take your time. There's no hurry.* Declan's voice in her mind, low and reassuring.

"That wasn't so bad, now was it?" Thad asked as he walked her back to her seat.

"No, not at all," she admitted, with some surprise. "Thank you for making it easy."

"My pleasure." Nodding at Declan, Thad strolled away, whistling softly.

"Why did he let me do that?" she asked, staring after him.

"I told you, some people like it." His impassive gaze met hers. "You did."

"I hate you."

"I know. Have you had enough? Or do you need more?"

"No," she said, surprised by her answer. She hadn't taken very much, she thought, frowning. Weren't new vampires supposed to be ravenous, driven by an uncontrollable urge to hunt, to kill?

"Most of them are," Declan said. "But you were turned by a master vampire, and you've tasted my blood a few times when you were mortal. It's made you stronger, more in control. I know you hate me for what I've done, Angie, but, would you have been happier if I had let you die?"

She refused to answer. He'd had no right to do it without her consent, none at all, and she would hate him for it for as long as she lived.

Or so she told herself as he transported them back home.

Declan paced the floor in the living room. As soon as they had reached home, Angie had gone to their room and slammed the door. He could hear her now, crying softly. Dammit. He didn't know how to breach the wall she had erected between them. Not that he blamed her. And yet he'd do it again. Love and hate were two sides of the same coin. Perhaps, in a hundred years or so, she would forgive him.

Angie sat on the edge of the bed, the word *vampire* repeating in her mind over and over again while silent tears—tears with a slight red tinge—dripped down her cheeks. How could Declan have done this to her? Sure, she'd thought she might ask him to turn her in ten or twelve years, but to do it now, without even asking her… how could he?

*Would you have been happier if I had let you die?*

His words echoed in the back of her mind. Was she sorry he'd saved her? Would she rather be dead? Hah! She was dead. Or Undead.

Pushing off the bed, she paced the floor. She didn't feel dead. She felt... wonderful. Lighter than air. As if, simply by thinking it, she could float above the ground...

She let out a squeal of surprise when she realized she *was* floating above the floor. Was it really that easy, she wondered, as she felt the carpet beneath her feet again. If she thought herself out in the backyard, would she be there?

She closed her eyes and pictured the backyard, felt a giggle rise in her throat when a wayward gust of wind stirred her hair. She'd done it, she thought as she looked around. She was outside! She fought down a rising sense of excitement. It didn't matter that she could now do supernatural things, she told herself harshly. She had lost the daylight. All the foods she loved to eat. Her best friend. Maybe her job... but no, not that. She could write any time as long as she met her deadlines.

Angie felt a shift in the air and knew without turning around that Declan was standing behind her. "Are you okay?" he asked quietly.

"I'm a vampire," she said, her voice laced with bitterness. "What could be wrong? Vampires don't get sick." She didn't have to see his face to know that she'd hurt him. She felt his pain as if it was her own.

"Angie."

Hearing the love in his voice, the regret, brought tears to her eyes. What would she have done if she had been a vampire and Declan had been dying? Would she have stood by and let him go if there was even the slightest chance she could save him? Would she really rather be dead now, or spend the rest of her life with the man she loved? For love him, she did, in spite of everything.

"Oh, Declan," she cried, throwing her arms around him, "please forgive me for the way I've behaved. I don't hate you. I love you."

"Angie!" He wrapped his arms around her, hugging her so tightly she knew if she'd still been mortal, he would have crushed a rib or two. He covered her face with kisses, whispering that he loved her, apologizing again and again for what he'd done.

She covered his mouth with her hand. "I forgive you," she said, and kissed him.

He sank down on the grass, drawing her down on top of him, his hands caressing her, arousing her, as he showered her with kisses. Somehow, their clothes were gone, but it didn't matter. She didn't feel the cold or the dampness, only Declan's hands caressing her, arousing her, his voice whispering love words in her ear.

Angie gazed into his eyes, eyes blazing with love and desire, laughed softly as he rolled over and tucked her beneath him.

"Tell me," he growled. "Tell me you want me."

"I want you," she said, her voice ragged. "Now, Declan." She writhed beneath him, her fingers tangling in his hair. "Right now!"

"Tell me you love me."

"I love you." Angie gasped the words as he thrust into her. For a moment, the world stopped and there was nothing but the two of them locked together. He was Adam and she was Eve and there was no one else in all the world.

Feeling utterly content, Angie threw her arms out to the side and gazed up at the sky. Millions and millions of twinkling lights, shining down on them like a benediction, but it was nothing compared to the love she saw in her husband's beautiful, deep green eyes.

She frowned as she felt a shift in the air. Before she had time to wonder what it meant, Declan rolled away from her.

Angie sat up, then scrambled to her feet, her arms folding over her naked breasts when she saw Conor stranding a short distance away. The snake had arrived in Eden.

Declan came up beside her, then moved to stand in front of her.

Conor laughed. "Hope I didn't disturb you."

"Hope you enjoyed the show," Declan retorted, his voice laced with sarcasm.

"I only saw the climax," Conor replied with a leer. "Quite impressive,"

"Have you decided to give up killing and become a peeping Tom?"

"You destroyed Samantha."

"I had no choice," Declan retorted. "She was trying to kill Angie."

"You shouldn't have done that," Conor said, and lunged forward, a stake in one hand.

Declan pushed Angie out of the way, then pivoted to the right, so that his brother swept past him.

Conor whirled around and the two came together in a rush.

Angie's heart was in her throat as she watched the struggle. They fought like tigers, fangs and claws ripping and tearing, until both were splattered with blood. She held her breath every time the stake came close to Declan's chest, but time and again he managed to elude it.

A distant part of her mind wondered how long the battle could last. Both were vampires—tireless, nearly indestructible. The fight could last for hours. Perhaps days. Hope soared in her heart as Declan began a brutal assault, seemingly oblivious to Conor's attack.

And then Conor feinted right and went left, the stake in his hand arrowing toward Angie's heart. It happened so fast, he was on her before she knew what he intended. She let out a strangled cry and then, suddenly, Declan materialized in front of her and the stake meant for her heart slammed into Declan's chest.

Conor let out an exultant shout as Declan dropped to the ground, one hand clutching the stake.

Conor looked at Angie triumphantly. "You're mine now."

Angie screamed, "No!" as Conor reached for her. Darting past him, she plucked the stake from Declan's chest and when Conor turned to grab her, she drove it unerringly into his heart. Stunned by what she'd done, she backed away. In a distant part of her mind, she realized that had she not been a vampire, she wouldn't have been able to react so quickly.

Conor stared at her, then at the stake protruding from his chest.

And then, as if in slow motion, he sank to the ground and fell forward.

With a cry, Angie knelt beside Declan and lifted his head onto her lap. "Don't be dead," she wailed, as she bit into her wrist and held it to his lips. "Please don't be dead. I don't want this life without you."

An overwhelming sense of relief swept through her when his hand closed on her wrist. He swallowed once, twice, and then he grinned at her. "Well, done, vampire."

"You're all right! How...?"

"He missed my heart."

"So you just lay there? He could have killed me!"

"I wouldn't have let that happen, love. I knew you could handle it."

Angie shook her head. Even though he was a powerful vampire, he likely needed a few moments to recover from being stabbed so close to his heart. "I'm sorry I stole your revenge, but I'm glad I got to avenge Samantha."

Declan stroked her cheek. "To tell you the truth, I'm glad it was you and not me." He felt no regret that Conor was dead, only relief that his brother hadn't died by his hand.

Angie glanced over her shoulder, and let out a gasp. "He's gone!" She looked back at Declan. "I thought you said I killed him?"

"You did."

"Then where is he?"

"Old vampires tend to turn to ash when they're destroyed."

Rising, she went to stand where the body had been, watched in morbid fascination as a faint breeze stirred a pile of ashes and carried them away.

Sighing, Angie pulled Declan to his feet and into her arms, thinking there was nowhere on earth that she would rather be.

# CHAPTER FORTY

Declan frowned as he watched Angie move around the living room, straightening a pillow here, moving a chair. Three days had passed since Conor's death and she had been uncharacteristically quiet. Was she mourning Samantha's death, trying to come to terms with being a vampire, or regretting that she had taken a life, although how she could regret destroying Conor was a mystery. When asked, she had insisted it was nothing. Knowing it was a lie, he had been tempted to read her mind several times but had always decided against it.

Until now.

Opening his senses, he let his mind brush hers. As he'd suspected, she was grieving the loss of her best friend, for the good times they had once shared. She didn't harbor any remorse over Conor's death, only relief that the killings in the city had stopped and that she and Declan had both survived the battle. Amazingly, she was quickly adjusting to being a vampire. Once or twice, she had surprised him by joking about her new powers, saying she might go to Hollywood and try out for a part in the next Wonder Woman movie. To his relief, the one thing that hadn't changed was her love for him. It burned as bright and hot as ever. And she proved it in his arms every night.

Deciding she needed something to take her mind off the last few days, he slipped his arms around her waist and nuzzled her neck. "What do you say we get out of the house for a few hours?"

"Sure, if you want," Angie said, without much enthusiasm. "Where do you want to go?"

"I was thinking of Disneyland."

"Disneyland?" She stared at him. Vampires in the Magic Kingdom? The very idea seemed ludicrous and yet... she grinned in spite of herself. What better place than Fantasyland for a couple of vampires?

"What do you say?"

"Sounds like fun." Something that had been in short supply in the last few days, she thought.

"Have you ever been there?" Declan asked.

She shook her head. "Have you?"

"No. It'll be another first for both of us."

Twenty minutes after sunset, they were passing through the turnstile to the Happiest Place on Earth. Thanks to a little vampire magic, they had bypassed the long lines waiting to get in. Angie's bag had been checked, their hands were stamped, and they were walking down Main Street toward Sleeping Beauty's castle. Angie couldn't help noticing how the crowd just sort of parted to let them through.

She looked up at Declan. "Are you working your magic on all these people?"

"Not intentionally. It's just their innate reaction to predators. So, where would you like to go first? Fantasyland? Tomorrowland? Frontierland? Adventureland? Galaxy's Edge?"

"Fantasyland, of course," she said with a grin as they neared the drawbridge to Sleeping Beauty's castle. "I mean, what could be more fantastic than vampires in Disneyland?" She paused on the bridge to admire the white swans swimming in the moat below.

There were so many fun adventures—Mr. Toad's Wild Ride, The Matterhorn, the tea cups, Angie loved them all, but her favorite was It's a Small World, probably because Declan kissed her every time they sailed to a new country.

From Fantasyland they went to Adventureland. Here, her favorite ride was The Jungle Cruise, with its elephants and rhinos. Declan loved the Indiana Jones ride, which was non-stop adventure from start to finish.

Angie was somewhat surprised to discover that the cotton candy and the churros didn't tempt her in the least, which was strange. She tried to feel some regret, but it didn't seem to matter. Still, she wondered if, like Declan, the day would come when she could again indulge in some of her favorite treats.

She decided the Pirates of the Caribbean ride was the most fun of all, so they went on it twice. The first time they watched the swashbuckling adventure; the second time, they sat in the back row and made out like a couple of horny teenagers.

They were headed for The Haunted Mansion, hand in hand, when Declan's whole demeanor changed. When his hand tightened on hers, she glanced up at him, suddenly concerned His jaw was clenched, his expression as hard as flint.

"What is that?" she asked, as she felt an odd stirring in the atmosphere around them, accompanied by a tightness in the pit of her stomach. "Why do I suddenly feel so...so on edge?"

"It's one of your vampire senses warning you that you're in danger." He jerked a thumb over his shoulder. "There are two seasoned hunters trailing us. A man and woman. They're wearing matching Star Wars tee shirts."

"Did they follow us here?" Alarmed, Angie glanced over her shoulder, her eyes widening when she spotted them. They didn't look like hunters. Just two ordinary people waiting patiently in line on a warm summer night. "How could they know we'd be here?"

"They didn't. It's just bad luck that they came to the park the same day we did."

"You don't think they'll attack us in the middle of New Orleans Square, do you?"

"No," he said dryly.

"So, what are we going to do?"

"Nothing. The mansion is just ahead."

This time they took their place near the back of the line. As the queue snaked back and forth, Declan managed to keep an eye on the hunters without making it obvious. It made Angie nervous to know they were now right behind them. At one point, Declan and the man made eye contact. When the man nodded at him, Declan nodded back.

When they stepped though the mansion's doors, Angie pressed herself against Declan, which wasn't hard, since the crowd was packed together like sardines in a can. She gasped along with everyone else when the hanged man dropped from the ceiling.

She found it hard to enjoy the ride, knowing there were two hunters in the same room—hunters no doubt armed with sharp wooden stakes. Even harder when she glanced over her shoulder and saw that the couple were again right behind them.

She was trembling when she stepped into the car that would carry them to the end of the ride.

The hunters settled into the car behind them.

They were in the darkest part of the ride when it stopped abruptly.

Angie clutched Declan's arm. With a wink, he gently removed her hand. Then, before she could ask what he was doing, he was out of the car. She craned her neck around the side as he leaned into the hunters' car. Moments ticked into eternity before he resumed his place beside her. As soon as he sat down, the ride started again.

"Did you stop the ride?" she asked.

"Indeed."

"What did you do back there?" she asked, as singing ghosts and ghouls popped up all around them.

"I merely planted the suggestion in their minds that they didn't feel well, and they should go home and come back another day."

Murmuring, "My hero," Angie kissed him on the cheek as the ride neared the end. She laughed as three spirits suddenly appeared, looking as if they were riding in the car with them. They exited onto a moving ramp where a ghostly apparition reminded them to hurry back and not to forget their death certificates.

Declan paused when they left the ride. Standing beside him, Angie watched the hunters hurry past without even glancing their way. Amazing, she thought.

Later, they found a place to watch the fireworks.

"Are you ready to go home?" Declan asked as the crowds dispersed.

"Not until we go on Splash Mountain."

"Whatever my lady wishes."

Once again, they magicked their way to the front of the line. Angie screamed as they plunged over the edge.

They wandered through the gift shops on Main Street as they made their way toward the exit. Wanting a souvenir, she bought a stuffed Minnie Mouse, a Disneyland tee shirt, and a pair of Mickey Mouse ears. She tried to buy a pair for Declan, too, but he muttered, "No way."

Outside the gates, Declan found a dark spot and transported them into their living room at home.

Angie kicked off her shoes, then wrapped her arms around Declan. "Thank you for such a wonderful, magical day."

"You're welcome, my love."

She slid her fingertips into the hair at his nape. "Are you tired?"

"Vampires don't get tired," he said with a wry grin.

"They don't?" She yawned behind her hand. "Are you sure? I think I'm ready for bed."

He gazed down at her, one brow arched. "Are you ready for bed?" he asked, "or ready to go to sleep?"

She looked up at him, a seductive smile playing over her lips. "First one," she murmured as she took his hand and led him into the bedroom. "And then the other."

"Perhaps I can show you a fantasy of my own," he said as he fell back on the bed and pulled her down on top of him. "One that even the great Walt Disney never imagined."

"Walt was wrong," she gasped as Declan's clever hands teased her secret places. "Disneyland isn't the happiest place on earth. It's right here, right now, with you. Tonight and every night."

## ~ *finis* ~

# In The Dark of the Night
# By Amanda Ashley

## *Available Now*

In a time of desperation, Lorena Halliday's father sold her into service to wealthy Lord Fairfield. After years of servitude and unwanted sexual advances, Lorena finds the courage to run away, only to be accosted by a man with a knife.

Standing on the roof of his home, Demetri witnesses the attack and goes to the young woman's rescue. After dispatching her assailant, Demetri takes the unconscious woman to an inn and procures a room for her, tucking her into bed. She is young and beautiful and her blood calls to him like no other.

Needing to see her again, Demetri returns to the inn and offers the lovely redhead a position in his home as his housekeeper. Desperate and with nowhere else to go, Lorena accepts. She soon discovers that her mysterious benefactor hides many secrets. Nevertheless, Lorena finds herself falling in love with a man who lives In the Dark of the Night.

# In The Dark of the Night
## Chapter One

D emetri stood atop the roof of the old manor house he called home. Located in the small village of Woodridge Township, it stood at the peak of a high plateau overlooking the small seaside town below. All looked peaceful in the light of the midnight moon, but with his preternatural vision, he could see the footpads haunting the dark streets, the night guards patrolling the wealthier part of town, the drunks huddled in the alleys, bottles clutched like lovers to their chests, the light skirts plying their age-old trade along the wharf.

He frowned when he saw a young woman creeping down one of the back streets. She stopped frequently to glance over her shoulder. Even from a distance, he could see the fear in her eyes. He rarely involved himself in mortal affairs, but he found himself wondering who she was running from, and why.

He leaned forward as a man wearing a black mask stepped out of the shadows and trailed the woman. The stalker caught up with the woman a block later. Catching her around the throat, he slammed her up against the side of a building.

Moonlight glinted off the knife in his hand.

Lorena let out a strangled cry as she tried to fight off her attacker, but to no avail. She couldn't stop staring at the knife in his hand, knew she was moments from death.

And then, from out of nowhere, another man appeared. At first, she feared he was in league with the first, until he jerked the knife from her assailant's hand and drove it deep into his chest.

Lorena stared at the second man, but it was too dark to see him clearly. Nor did it help that he was dressed in black from head to foot. All she saw before she fainted dead away was a pair of glittering red eyes.

Demetri caught the woman before she hit the garbage-littered street. Cradling her in his arms, he carried her swiftly to the nearest decent inn where he procured a room for her. He paid for a week in advance, then carried her up the stairs and put her to bed. She was a pretty thing. Her hair, dark red and curly, fell to her waist. Earlier, he had noticed that her eyes were grey, her lashes long and thick, her skin unblemished. He wondered again what she had been doing skulking through the dead of night.

The scent of her hair, her skin, the whisper of the rich, red blood flowing through her veins stirred his senses. Did she taste as good as he imagined? Bending down, he brushed her hair aside and gently sank his fangs into the slender curve of her throat, satisfying both his thirst and his curiosity.

Lorena came awake with a start, the remnants of last night's nightmare still fresh in her mind. She had been accosted in the street by a stranger wielding a knife, and then another man had appeared, seemingly out of nowhere and killed the first. She must have fainted then, because she didn't remember anything after that.

Sitting up, she glanced around. She was fully dressed, in an unfamiliar bed, in an unfamiliar room with no recollection of how she had gotten there.

Rising, she tiptoed to the door and opened it. A glance left and right showed a carpeted corridor with rooms on either side. An inn, she thought, someone had brought her to an inn. But who? And when? And why?

Brow furrowed, she made her way down the stairs, then stopped at the desk.

"Good morning, miss," the clerk said with a cheerful smile. "I'm glad to see you looking better this morning. How may I help you?"

"This may sound a little strange, but do you know who brought me here?"

"Why, no, miss. The gentleman didn't leave his name. I assumed..." He cleared his throat, his cheeks suddenly flushed. "That is, I, ah, assumed he was your husband."

"No. How much do I owe you for the room? I'm afraid I can't pay you right now but–"

"No need. The gentleman paid for a week's rent."

"He did?" Lorena shook her head. Why would a stranger do that?

"Yes, miss."

Nodding, she turned away from the desk. She had no money to pay for a room or for anything else. Not even a cup of tea, she thought, as her stomach rumbled in a most unladylike way.

Feet dragging, she returned to her room. Better to go hungry than go back to Fairfield Manor, she thought glumly.

307

She was trying to think of a way to earn enough money to pay for transportation out of town when there was a knock at the door. Frowning, she called, "Who is it?"

"Robert Carstairs. I'm the desk clerk."

Wondering what he could want, she opened the door.

"I…uh…thought you might like something to eat," he said, thrusting a cloth-covered tray into her hands.

Lorena stared at him.

"You don't have to pay me back," he said, the words coming out in a rush.

"I don't know what to say."

"No need to say anything. I've got to get back to the desk." And so saying, he turned and practically ran down the hall.

Lorena kicked the door closed with her heel, then carried the tray to the small table in the corner. Sitting down, she lifted the cloth, revealing two poached eggs, a thick slice of ham, toast and marmalade, as well as a cup of tea. Bless the boy!

She hadn't eaten since yesterday and it took all her self-control not to gobble her food like some hungry street urchin.

When she was finished, she sat back, wondering how long she would be able to hide from the monster who owned her body and soul. Lord Fairfield was a powerful man. A wealthy man. Sooner or later, he would find her and drag her back to Fairfield manor.

Blinking back her tears, she crawled into bed and sought forgetfulness in blessed sleep.

Demetri rose with the setting of the sun. He washed quickly, combed his hair, and dressed, strangely eager to see the woman he had rescued last night. She didn't look like a harlot, she hadn't been wearing a wedding ring. Yet it was obvious she wasn't from the gentry, since he had found her creeping along a back alley. A thief, perhaps? Or a runaway?

No matter. He wanted to see her again.

He quickened his steps. If she had left the inn, it would take but little effort to track her down.

Lorena looked up when there was a knock at the door. Hand pressed to her heart, she took a deep breath, wondering who it could be. No one knew she was here, she thought. Perhaps it was Carstairs, kindly bringing her another meal. Her stomach growled as she padded to the door. It had been several hours since breakfast.

She was reaching for the latch when the door swung open. Her heart threatened to leap out of her chest when it wasn't Carstairs standing in the hallway, but a tall, broad-shouldered stranger with hair as black as the devil's breath and eyes as blue and dark as a midnight sky. "Who...who are you?" she squeaked. "What do you want?"

Uninvited, he stepped into the room and closed the door behind him. "I merely wished to see how you were faring this evening."

Taking a wary step backward, she stared at him. His voice was like dark velvet, tinged with an accent she didn't recognize.

"I see you do not remember me. I came to your rescue last night."

"Oh. I...thank you. If you've come to collect for the room, I'm afraid I can't repay you."

Smiling wryly, he shook his head. "I am not in need of your money."

Lorena took another step back, her arms crossing protectively over her breasts. "What do you want?"

"Not what you are thinking."

"What, then?"

Demetri lifted one shoulder and let it fall. "I have not yet decided." He glanced around the room. It was small and clean. The table in the corner held the remains of a morning meal. He wrinkled his nose against the lingering stink of cooked meat and eggs. "What are you running from?"

"I'm not running from anything," she exclaimed with a defiant tilt of her chin.

"You are a poor liar."

She puffed up like a ruffled hen. "How dare you!"

He shook his head. "I can smell a lie at a hundred paces."

She glared at him. Then, shoulders slumped, she sat on the edge of the bed, hands tightly folded in her lap. "I ran away from the man who owns me."

"Owns you?"

"Some years ago, my father lost a great deal of money on several bad investments. When he couldn't pay his debts, he sold me to one of his creditors to pay the mortgage on our home and keep food on the table." Even though she understood her father's reasoning, she had never got over the hurt. Never seen her mother or her sisters since that awful night.

Demetri swore under his breath. Selling a child wasn't an unusual occurrence. He knew it happened all the time. Why it bothered him now was beyond his comprehension. "Shall I kill him for you?"

"What? No! Of course not!"

He shrugged. "How are you called?"

"Lorena."

His assessing gaze moved over her from head to heel. "And your surname?"

"Halliday."

"Come along, Miss Halliday," he said, reaching for her hand. "I have need of a housekeeper."

"But… I don't know anything about you. Not even your name."

"I am Demetri. That is all you need to know."

She stared up at him. He was an austere man. Judging by the cut of his clothes and his imperious manner, he was obviously a man of good breeding and accustomed to giving orders. Some might call him handsome, with his clean-cut features but she found him quite frightening. Still, she shuddered at the thought of going back to Lord Fairfield's estate and fighting off his unwanted advances—advances that had grown more frequent and increasingly more intimate since his wife's passing a few months ago.

"Shall we?"

She stared at Lord Demetri's outstretched hand. Some said better the devil you know, but she didn't agree. Hoping she wasn't making a dangerous, perhaps fatal, mistake, she put her hand in his and let her new employer pull her to her feet. For better or worse, her fate was now in his hands.

# About the Author

Amanda Ashley started writing for the fun of it. Her first book, a historical romance written as Madeline Baker, was published in 1985. Since then, she has published numerous historical and paranormal romances and novellas, many of which have appeared on various bestseller lists, including the *New York Times* Bestseller List and *USA Today*.

Amanda makes her home in Southern California, where she and her husband share their house with a Pomeranian named Lady, a cat named Kitty, and a tortoise named Buddy.

For more information on her books, please visit her websites at:

www.amandaashley.net

and

www.madelinebaker.net

Email: darkwritr@aol.com

# ABOUT THE PUBLISHER

This book is published on behalf of the author by the Ethan Ellenberg Literary Agency.
https://ethanellenberg.com
Email: agent@ethanellenberg.com

Made in the USA
Middletown, DE
29 June 2021

43330643R00186